MEMORIAL

MEMORIAL

BRYAN WASHINGTON

THORNDIKE PRESS
A part of Gale, a Cengage Company

Copyright © 2020 by Bryan Washington.
Thorndike Press, a part of Gale, a Cengage Company.

Thorndike Press® Large Print Basic.
The text of this Large Print edition is unabridged.
Other aspects of the book may vary from the original edition.
Set in 16 pt. Plantin.

LIBRARY OF CONGRESS CIP DATA ON FILE.
CATALOGUING IN PUBLICATION FOR THIS BOOK
IS AVAILABLE FROM THE LIBRARY OF CONGRESS.

ISBN-13: 978-1-4328-8512-0 (hardcover alk. paper)

Published in 2021 by arrangement with Riverhead, an imprint of Penguin Publishing Group, a division of Penguin Random House, LLC

Printed in Mexico
Print Number: 01   Print Year: 2021

For A, D, and L

Everybody everywhere, I think, is always
talking about the same shitty thing

RACHEL KHONG

The world is wonderful, terrible.

ANDRÉS NEUMAN

Does love need a reason?

MASAO WADA

■ ■ ■ ■

BENSON

■ ■ ■ ■

1.

Mike's taking off for Osaka, but his mother's flying into Houston.

Just for a few weeks, he says.

Or maybe a couple of months, he says. But I need to go.

The first thing I think is: fuck.

The second's that we don't have the money for this.

Then it occurs to me that *we* don't have any savings at all. But Mike's always been good about finances, always cool about separating his checks. It's something I'd always taken for granted about him.

Now he's saying that he wants to find his father. The man's gotten sick. Mike wants to catch him before he goes. And I'm on the sofa, half listening, half charging my phone.

You haven't seen your mom in years, I say. She's coming for *you.* I've never *met* her.

11

I say, You don't even fucking like your dad.

True, says Mike. But I already bought the ticket.

And Ma will be here when I'm back, says Mike. You're great company. She'll live.

He's cracking eggs by the stove, slipping yolks into a pair of pans. After they've settled, he salts them, drizzling mayonnaise with a few sprigs of oregano. Mike used to have this thing about sriracha, he'd pull a hernia whenever I reached for it, but now he squeezes a faded bottle over my omelette, rubbing it in with the spatula.

I don't ask where he'll stay in Japan. I don't ask who he'll stay with. I don't ask where his mother will sleep here, in our one-bedroom apartment, or exactly what that arrangement will look like. The thing about a moving train is that, sometimes, you can catch it. Some of the kids I work with, that's how their families make it into this country. If you fall, you're dead. If you're too slow, you're dead. But if you get a running start, it's never entirely gone.

So I don't flip the coffee table. Or one of our chairs. I don't key his car or ram it straight through the living room. After the black eye, we stopped putting our hands on each other — we'd both figured, silently, it was the least we could do.

12

Today, what I do is smile.

I thank Mike for letting me know.

I ask him when he's leaving, and I know that's my mistake. I'm already reaching to toss my charger before he says it, tomorrow.

We've been fine. Thank you for asking.

Our relationship is, what, four years old? But that depends on how you count. We haven't been to a party in months, and when we did go to parties, at first, no one knew we were fucking. Mike just stood to the side while whatever whitegirl talked her way into my space, then he'd reach up over my shoulder to slip a finger into my beer.

Or he'd sneeze, stretch, and wipe his nose with my shirtsleeve.

Or he'd fondle my wallet, slowly, patting it back into place.

Once, at a dinner, right under the table, he held court with a hand in my lap. Running his thumb over the crotch. Every now and again, someone would look, and you could tell when they finally saw. They'd straighten their backs. Smile a little too wide. Then Mike would ask what was wrong, and they'd promise it was nothing, and he'd go right back to cheesing, never once nodding my way.

■ ■ ■

We knew how we looked. And how we didn't look. But one night, a few weeks back, at a bar crawl for Mike's job, all it took was a glance at us. He works at a coffee shop in Montrose. It's this fusion thing where they butcher rice bowls and egg rolls — although, really, it's Mexican food, since unless your name is Mike, that's who's cooking.

They'd been open for a year. This was their anniversary celebration. Mike volunteered us to help for an hour, flipping tortillas on a burner by the DJ.

I felt miserable. Mike felt miserable. Everyone who passed us wore this look that said, Mm. They touched our shoulders. Asked how long we'd been together. Wondered where we'd met, how we'd managed during Harvey, and the music was too fucking loud, so Mike and I just sort of shrugged.

I don't say shit on our way to the airport to pick up his mother, and I don't say shit when Mike parks the car. IAH sits outside of Houston's beltways, but there's always steady traffic lining the highway. When Mike pulls up to Arrivals, he takes out the keys, and a line shimmers behind us, this tiny constellation of travelers.

Mike's got this mustache now. It wavers over his face. He usually clips all of that off, and now I think he looks like a caricature of himself. We sit beside the terminal, and we can't have the most fucked-up situation here, but still. You have to wonder.

I wonder.

I wonder if he wonders.

We haven't been good at apologizing lately. Now would be a nice time.

The airport sees about 111,500 visitors a day, and here we are, two of its most ridiculous.

Hey, says Mike.

He sighs. Hands me the keys. Says he'll be right back with his mother.

If you leave us stranded in the parking lot, says Mike, we'll probably find you.

It took all of two dates for him to bring up Race. We'd gone to an Irish bar tucked behind Hyde Park. Everyone else on the patio was white. I'd gotten a little drunk, and when I told Mike he was slightly shorter than optimal, he clicked his tongue, like, What took you so long.

What if I told you you're too polite, said Mike.

Fine, I said.

Or that you're so well-spoken.

I get it. Sorry.

Don't be sorry, said Mike, and then he boxed my shoulder.

It was the first time we'd touched that night. The bartender glanced our way, blinking.

I just hope you see me as a fully realized human being, said Mike. Beyond the obvious sex appeal.

Shut up, I said.

Seriously, said Mike, no bullshit.

Me Mifune, he said, you Yasuke.

Stop it, I said.

Or maybe we're just fucking Bonnie and Clyde, he said.

Three different cops peek in the car while Mike's in Baggage Claim. I smile at the first two. I frown at the third. The last guy taps the window, like, What the fuck are you waiting for, and when I point toward the airport's entrance, all he does is frown.

Then I spot them on their way out. The first thing I think is that they look like family. Mike's mother is hunched, just a little bit, and he's rolling her suitcase behind her.

16

For a while, they saw each other annually — she'd fly down just to visit — but the past few years have been rocky. The visits stopped once I moved in with Mike.

The least I can do is pop the trunk. I'd like to be the guy who doesn't, but I'm not.

Mike helps his mother adjust the back seat as she gets in, and she doesn't even look at me. Her hair's in a bun. She's got on this bright blue windbreaker, with a sickness mask, and the faintest trace of makeup.

Ma, says Mike, you hungry?

She mumbles something in Japanese. Shrugs.

Ma, says Mike.

He glances at me. Asks again. Then he switches over, too.

She says something, and then he says something, and then another guy directing traffic walks up to my window. He's Latino, husky in his vest. Shaved head like he's in the army. He mouths at us through the glass, and I let down the window, and he asks if anything's wrong.

I tell him we're moving.

Then move, says this man.

The next words leave my mouth before I can taste them. It's a little like gravity. I say, Okay, motherfucker, we're gone.

And the Latino guy just frowns at me.

Before he says anything else, there's a bout of honking behind us. He looks at me again, and then he wanders away, scratching at his chest, wincing back at our car.

When I roll up the window, Mike's staring. His mother is, too. She says something, shaking her head, and I pull the car into traffic.

I turn on the radio, and it's Meek Mill.

I flip the channel, and it's Migos.

I turn the damn thing off. Eventually we're on the highway.

All of a sudden, we're just one more soap opera among way too many, but that's when Mike's mother laughs, shaking her head.

She says something in Japanese.

Mike thumps the glove compartment, says, *Ma*.

My parents pretend I'm not gay. It's easier for them than it sounds. My father lives in Katy, just west of Houston, and my mother stayed in Bellaire, even after she remarried. Before that, we took most of our family dinners downtown. My father was a meteorologist. It was a status thing. He'd pick up my sister and my mother and me from the house, ferrying us along I-45 just to eat with his coworkers, and he always ordered our table the largest dish on the menu — basted pigs spilling from platters, pounds of steamed crab sizzling over bok choy — and he called this Work, because he was always Working.

A question he used to ask us was, How many niggas do you see out here telling the weather?

My mother never debated him or cussed him out or anything like that. She'd repeat exactly what he said. Inflect his voice. That was her thing. She'd make him sound important, like some kind of boss, but my father's a little man, and her tactics did exactly what you'd think they might do.

Big job today, she'd say, in the car, stuck on the 10.

This forecast's impressive, she'd say, moments after my father shattered a wineglass on the kitchen wall.

I swear it's the last one, she'd say, looking him dead in the eyes, as he floundered, drunk, grabbing at her knees, swearing that he'd never touch another single beer.

Eventually, she left. Lydia went with our mother, switching high schools. I stayed in the suburbs, at my old junior high, and my father kept drinking. He lived off his savings once he got fired from the station for being wasted on-air. Sometimes, he'd sub high school science classes, but he mostly stayed on the sofa, booing at the hourly prognoses from KHOU.

Occasionally, in blips of sobriety, I'd come home to him grading papers. Some kid had called precipitation *anticipation.* Another kid, instead of defining cumulus clouds, drew little fluffs all over the page. One time my father laid three tests on an already too-cluttered end table, all with identical handwriting, with only the names changed.

He waved them at me, asked why everything had to be so fucking *hard.*

A few months in, Mike said we could be whatever we wanted to be. Whatever that looked like.

I'm so easy, he said.

I'm not, I told him.

You will be, he said. Just give me a little time.

It's past midnight when we pull onto our block. Most of the lights are out. Some kids are huddled by the curb, smoking pot, fucking around with firecrackers.

When a pop explodes behind us, the kids take off. That's their latest thing. Mike's mother doesn't even flinch.

Ma, says Mike, this is home.

We live in the Third Ward, a historically Black part of Houston. Our apartment's entirely too large. It doesn't make any sense. At one point, the neighborhood had money, but then crack happened and the money took off, and occasionally you'll hear gunshots or fistfights or motherfuckers driving way too fast. But the block has recently been invaded by fraternities from the college up the block. And a scattering of professor types. With pockets of rich kids playing at poverty. The Black folks who've lived here for decades let them do it, happy for the scientific fact that white kids keep the cops away.

Our immediate neighbors are Venezuelan. They've got like nine kids. Our other neighbors are these Black grandparents who've lived on the property forever. Every few weeks, Mike cooks for both families, sopa de pescado and yams and macaroni and rice. He's never made a big deal about it; he just wakes up and does it, and after the first few times I asked Mike if that wasn't patronizing.

But, after a little while, I noticed people let him linger on their porches. He'd poke at their kids, leaning all over the wood.

21

Sometimes the Black folks invited him inside, showed him pictures of their daughter's daughters.

Mike's lived here for years. I left my father's place for his. On my first night in the apartment, I couldn't fall asleep for the noise, and Mike said I'd get used to it, but honestly I didn't want to.

Now Mike's mother drops her shoes by our door. She runs her hand along the wall. She taps at the counter, toeing the wood. When she steps into the foyer, Mike grins my way, the first smile in what feels like months, and that's when we hear it: slow at first, after some hiccups, before Mike's mother begins to cry.

A few years after they split, my parents took me to lunch together in Montrose. We hadn't all sat at the same table in years. Lydia had mostly cut them off; she'd moved out, and moved on, and she'd told me to do the same, but what I did instead was order a Reuben.

The week before, my father had walked in on some guy jerking me off. It wasn't anyone who matters. We'd met on some fucking app. My father opened the door, coughed, and actually said, I'm sorry, as he backed out of the room. The boy beside me made a face like, Should we finish or what.

That night, after he left, I waited for my father to bring it up. But he just sat on the sofa and drank his way through two six-packs. The incident dissolved in the air. Before he drove off, the guy had asked to see me again, and I told him I didn't think so, because we probably weren't actually going anywhere. I still hadn't learned that there is a finite number of people who will ever be interested in you.

When our waiter, a skinny brown guy, asked if we needed anything else, I spoke a little too quickly. He smiled. Then my mother smiled.

You know you can talk to us, she said.

Both of us, she added.

My mother smelled like chocolate. My father wore his nice shirt. You'd have been hard-pressed to think that this was a man who'd thrown his wife against a wall. Or that this lady, immediately afterward, stuck a fork into his elbow.

Awesome, I said. Thank you.

About anything, said my mother, touching my hand.

When I flinched, she took hers back. My father didn't say shit.

That night, my father dropped me off at the house. He said he'd be back in the morning.

Not even an hour later, I texted back the boy from the other day. When I opened the door, he looked a little uncertain, but then I touched his wrist and he got the biggest grin on his face.

I let him fuck me on the sofa. And then again in the kitchen. And then again in my father's bedroom. We didn't use protection.

He left the next morning, but not before we ate some toast. He was Filipino, with a heavy accent. He told me he wanted to be a lawyer.

One day, our second year in, I told Mike all of that. We were out shopping for groceries. He fondled the ginger and the cabbage and the bacon.

Halfway through my story, he stopped me to ask around for some kombu.

He said, Your folks sound like real angels.

And you, said Mike, you're like a baby. Just a very lucky boy.

And then one morning Mike had already

left our place for the restaurant. He'd forgotten his phone by the sink. I didn't mean to touch it, but it flashed, so I did.

I did not and do not know the guy whose cock blipped across the screen.

Just for a second.

But then it disappeared.

You see these situations in the movies and shit, and you say it could never be you. Of course you'd be proactive. You'd throw the whole thing away.

When Mike knocked on the door, looking for his cell, I pointed silently toward the sink.

Wait, he said, what's wrong?

Nothing, I said.

Tell me, said Mike.

It's cool, I said. I'm just tired.

You're not drinking enough water, said Mike, and he actually sat down to pour me some.

I never said shit about that photo. But I guess you could say it nagged me.

Mike figures we'll make a bed for his mother on the pull-out.

Tomorrow you'll get the bedroom, he says to her, looking at me.

His mother doesn't say shit, but by now she's stopped crying. She sets her bag on the counter, crosses her arms. We lift the mattress from the sofa, layering it with blankets that Lydia gave us, and when I slip into my room for some pillows I decide not to come back out.

The thing about our place is that there isn't much to clean. Most of what I make goes toward half the rent, and Mike spends all of his checks on food. Which, when you think about it, leaves plenty for a ticket. That's plenty of cash left over to fly halfway across the world.

They're still shouting in the living room when I settle into bed. Something heavy falls out there. I don't jump up to look. And once Mike finally comes in and shuts the door, I hear his mother sobbing behind him.

She's taking it well, says Mike.

You hardly gave her any warning, I say. She flies in to catch you and you're fucking flying out.

That's unfair. You know exactly why.

It's not fair to her either.

It's fine. She'll be fine.

You're easy to love.

Ma's low-maintenance, he says. You won't have to do anything, if that's what you're worried about. After a few days, you won't even know she's around.

I start to say, Does she even speak English?

And then I swallow it.

And then I ask.

You're joking, says Mike, throwing off his shirt.

I'm not, I say.

I'm not gonna call that racist, says Mike. But it's fucked up. For a second there, I thought you actually gave a shit.

He kicks off his pants, toes them into his duffel. He's gained more weight, but that's nothing new. It's never been an issue, never been something I look down on, but for the first time I sort of gag.

Mike catches me. He keeps quiet.

You can teach her, he says. If you care that much. Word by word.

You're joking, I say.

I'm packing, says Mike.

My sister met him accidentally. It happened during Halloween, at a bar off Westheimer. I'd wandered away from him to take a piss, and when I made it back to the table, Lydia was stirring her Coke beside him. She wore some witchy getup, a costume with too many straps. Mike had on a toga. I'd gone as myself.

I was just talking to Mark, said Lydia.

You didn't say you had a little sister, said Mike.

They went on like that, back and forth. Lydia ordered more drinks. When I asked if she didn't have a date to get back to, she smiled and told me she'd just have to reschedule it. *This*, she said, was special. She'd never meet her baby brother's boyfriend for the first time again.

Lydia was Mike's age. A few years older than me. She wrote copy for the Buffalo Soldier Museum downtown, and if you told her you didn't know Houston had one of those, she'd say that's because it's for niggas.

But that evening, she played it cool. Laughed at our jokes. Paid for more beer.

Just before last call, Lydia gave Mike her number.

Wow, said Mike. This is a first.

Life is long, said Lydia.

Cheers, said Mike.

Later that night, Lydia texted me.

He's funny, she said.

Too funny for you, she added.

Between the four of us, my father and Lydia are the darkest. Whenever we ate out as kids, she and I always sat on the same end of the table. If we didn't, we ran the risk of waiters splitting the check, the sort of thing our father bitched about for months. We never ate at those restaurants again.

It's late when Mike touches me, and I'm not thinking about it until we've started — then we're mashing our chests together, jumbling legs and elbows.

His tongue touches mine. My nose strafes his belly button. There's a point when you're with someone, and it's all just re-action. You've done everything there is to do.

But once in a blue moon, they'll feel like a stranger, like this visitor in your hands.

So it's the first time we've kissed in weeks, and then I'm sucking Mike off when he lifts up his knees.

I point toward the living room.

Grow up, says Mike.

And before he says anything else, I've got one finger in there, and then four. Like I'm kneading dough. He laughs. He stops when I'm inside him.

He's tight, but I fit.

I wish it takes me longer.

Afterward, Mike waddles toward the toilet, and I'm staring at his packed duffel. When I wake up, he's back in bed, asleep, arms wrapped around his shoulders.

Now would be the time to wake him up and ask him to stay, but I don't do that.

I watch his chest rise and fall, rise and fall.

A few dates in, Mike told me a joke. I'd just let him fuck me at his place. We hadn't made it past the sofa. And it was fine, mostly, except for a few things, like his putting his thumb in my mouth, and me spitting that out, and my grinding too fast, and his saying *slow down,* and my laughing, and his coming immediately, and my taking forever to come.

But eventually it all happened.

Afterward, I rubbed a palm on his thighs. He held my head in his lap.

So, said Mike, a Jap and a nigger walk into a bar.

Hey, I said.

That's it, said Mike. That's the joke.

2.

Slamming cabinets wake me up. I reach for my pills. Then I reach for Mike, and he's not there.

His duffel's gone, too. He left the bathroom light on. It would've been too much to ask for a note, but of course I look for one anyway.

There's a text though: MITSUKO HARA

And then: MAKE SURE SHE TAKES HER MEDICINE BC SHE FORGETS

And then: IT'S MY FATHER, BEN. IT'S REALLY NOT YOU

Mitsuko's in the kitchen, opening things and looking into them and closing them back up again. Water's boiling on the stove. There's a mug on the counter. She's cooked rice, sliced a cucumber, and poached an egg when I step on the tile, and she doesn't look up, doesn't even acknowledge that I'm around.

Then she nods my way.

Do you work, she asks.

What, I say.

You don't work, says Mitsuko, shaking her head.

I do, I say. Mostly in the afternoon.

And what does that look like?

I'm at a daycare.

So you're a teacher, says Mitsuko.

More like a babysitter, I say.

And Mitsuko doesn't say anything to that. And I don't prompt her.

Mike's mother is compact, like him, but nimble. Sturdy. She finishes her bowl and turns to wash the dishes. I tell her she doesn't have to worry about that, and she doesn't even turn around.

When she's finished with everything, she wipes down the sink, setting everything back in their cabinets. I couldn't tell you where she found the rag. But as she reaches for her jacket, lifting her shoes at the door, I ask if she's taken her pills, and Mitsuko finally looks at me.

You're joking, she says.

Mike just mentioned them, I say.

Incredible, she says. That's what he tells you.

I'm sorry, I say.

And now you're apologizing, says Mitsuko.

Well, she says, you're too late.

And loud, she says.

Both of you, says Mitsuko before she shuts the door. The whole night. Like dogs.

My mother's new husband is Nigerian. He's a pastor. They've got this Pomeranian and two boys. She lives in a neighborhood with a gate, hosting potlucks and block parties, but the first time I showed Lydia their Christmas photo, the one they sent my father in the mail, she shrieked.

The *dog,* she said.

It's fucking *hideous,* she said.

I usually bike to work. Mike owns the car. It's in his name, but he's gone now, so I drive it just to see what that's like. His steering wheel's worn and warm on my fingers, and the fabric's torn against my thumb, and the seat's indented underneath me, probably from Mike's ass. I try to settle into it, but something still feels off. After fucking around with the rearview mirror, I give up, drive the whole way blind.

Most days, it's the same eight kids at the aftercare center. There's Hannah, with the straightened hair. Thomas with the twists.

Xu and Ethan are twin brothers, and Marcos has a sister named Silvia. Then there's Margaret, who's a year or so older than the rest of them, and Ahmad, the lone Black kid, who's something like two years younger.

I work with another guy, named Barry, who's big and white and scruffy. And then there's Ximena, who is none of those things. We're something like a team. Our boss comes by in the evenings, but she mostly just handles the money and our schedules, and unless she's handing us checks, she's generally MIA.

When I stumble through the doors, Ximena waves. She's watching Ethan and Xu on the swings. As Ahmad runs from the sandbox, pointing at nothing behind him, I pick him up by the elbows. He laughs. It's our Thing.

I tell Ximena about Mike.

You're joking, she says.

Nah.

Well, says Ximena, have you talked to the mother yet?

She's talked at me, I say.

At, says Ximena.

Around.

And?

I don't know, I say.

34

She's Mike's mom, I say.

No, says Ximena. There's mothers, and then there's moms. Then you've got ma*mas.*

Ximena lives with her mother, and they're co-parenting her kid. That's what she likes to say: that she's raising a six-year-old with her mother. She used to go to med school, but then she stopped doing that, and whenever the aftercare dads come around, they linger with her by the counter.

A while back, I asked Ximena why she entertained them at all. She asked if I'd ever seen a cadaver.

Doesn't matter if it's fifty years older or twenty, she said, a body's a body's a body.

But Ximena's getting married, again, in a few weeks. To some whiteboy who cleans teeth for a living. I've met him exactly once.

Before I take my lunch, Ximena touches my elbow.

At least there's a bright side, she says. It could've been Mike's father.

Mike could've left you with some man, she says.

On the seventh or eighth or ninth date, I asked Mike about his parents. I'd started spending some nights at his place. We ordered single-topping pizzas and drank gas station wine.

He looked at me a long time before he finally answered.

Ma grew up in Tokyo, said Mike. Got knocked up in the city. Had me there, moved here, and eventually she went back home.

To Japan?

Sure.

But you didn't want to go back with her, I said, and Mike made this face.

No, he said. This is where I live.

But Ma's adaptable, said Mike. That's where I get it from.

And your father, I said.

What about him, said Mike.

You didn't mention him.

I didn't mention him, said Mike.

One night, Mike told me that his father hit Mitsuko. We were at the Warehouse, watching his friends strum guitars in some band. They slumped onstage, a little fucked up, tinkering at amps already way too drenched in reverb. Some kid in a mariachi suit blew into a trumpet. A sleepy crowd nodded behind us, bouncing around on the 1 and the 3.

I didn't know whether I liked this scene. Mike had told me his ex was playing. I'd

36

tried picturing what the guy might look like, wondered which one he was up onstage, but eventually Mike yawned and asked if I was ready to leave.

Already? I said.

He saw us, said Mike. Or I think he did. He had opportunities.

So we were vaping outside by the entrance when he told me about his father. This couple walked their pit bull to the intersection behind us. When it growled at the two of us, Mike bared his teeth, and the dog shut up and looked at his owners, who looked at Mike, who looked at me.

Ma hit him back with this pan, said Mike. We were in the States by then.

Shit, I said.

Knocked him over and everything, said Mike. I thought she'd killed him. Then she shouted at me for not helping her. But she was yelling too fast, in Japanese, and I couldn't understand.

It was like something out of a movie, said Mike, vaping. I still don't think she forgives me.

When the streetlight turned, the couple kept walking. The pit bull nipped at a biker, who almost busted his ass.

Movies are based on life, I said.

Not always, said Mike.

■ ■ ■ ■

Mitsuko's flipping through a magazine when I make it back from work. She stares at my shoes when I step inside, so I turn around and slip them off at the door.

I figure I have to try.

So, I say, how was your day?

How was my day, says Mitsuko.

My son leaves the country the morning after I arrive, she says.

He leaves me with I don't know who for I don't know how long, she says.

I haven't seen him in years, she says, and he's off looking for my ex-husband, who is rotting from cancer as we speak.

My day was fucking phenomenal, says Mitsuko.

I shake a little and smile. Tell her I'm only stepping into the bedroom for a minute. But then I lay down, and I fall under a blanket, and I don't get up again for hours.

Around midnight, I'm awake. The lights are out in the living room.

I start to text Mike.

I type, We're done.

I type, Fuck you.

I type, It's over dickhead.

I type, How r u, and that's what I send.

My mother told me about her new husband first. She trusted me, or at least that's what she said. So I didn't tell Lydia. Didn't tell my father. I watched him walk in and out of his house, occasionally with a woman he was seeing and occasionally not.

Her name was Carlotta. Sometimes she'd stay over. When that happened, she'd crack eggs and slice queso fresco the next morning. She was from San Antonio, living with her brothers by the high school, always saying she wished I was straight because I'd be perfect for her daughter.

She only goes for bad boys, said Carlotta.

I'm no good either, I said.

And Carlotta considered me for a second, before she went back to chopping cilantro.

It's different, she said, grinning.

I don't know when my father found out about my mother, exactly, but eventually Carlotta stopped coming around. And then my father didn't leave the house for a while.

He mostly sat on the porch.

He started saying *please.*

One morning, around that time, the doorbell woke me up. It couldn't have been past four. These two guys were holding my father, in a tank top and briefs, slumped on their shoulders and looking uncertain.

Es tu papa? said one of the guys.

Sí, I said, lo siento.

Lo encontramos por allá, said the guy, pointing across the block and over some trees.

Es not safe, said the other guy.

Lo siento, I said again, and they handed him off.

Necesitas cuidarlo, said the first guy, scratching at his shoulder.

Afterward, my father laughed and hiccupped the entire morning, speaking all sorts of gibberish, before he suddenly, thoroughly, knocked out that afternoon.

The next day, he called me downstairs before breakfast. He said he had something to tell me. Something about my mother.

I tried to make the appropriate face of surprise.

3.

It's still dark when I'm up the next morning, but Mitsuko's mincing shrimp. She's hunched over the cutting board, beside eggs, flour, and honey.

Do you eat, she says.

I tell her I do.

We don't say shit while she's working. Mitsuko blitzes everything in a food processor. Drops the mixture in a skillet, dabbing everything with soy sauce, folding the batter gradually. I take my pills, watching her do all this, and she ignores me the entire time, working at her own pace.

When I sit on the sofa, Mitsuko stops rolling. I stand to set the table, and she starts rolling again.

Once she's finished, she fills a bowl with some pickled cucumbers, with a plate for the omelette, leaving another one out for me. We chew hunched over the counter, hip to hip.

So, Mitsuko says, how long have you been sleeping with my son?

Or is it casual, she says.

Not really, I say.

I don't know how it works, says Mitsuko.

I think it's the same for everyone.

It isn't, says Mitsuko.

She says, I'm sure you can tell that Michael and I are very close.

We've been together for four years, I say. More or less.

More, Mitsuko asks, or less?

A little more, I say.

But just a little, she says.

Mike's better with numbers, I say.

It occurs to me, out of nowhere, that my posture is entirely fucked up. Mitsuko's is impeccable, even at a lean. So I straighten up, and then I stoop, and Mitsuko raises an eyebrow.

She snorts, and says, My son could not be worse with numbers.

After that, we eat in silence. Scattered Spanish filters in through the window. The kids next door kick a soccer ball against the wall, until their father steps outside screaming, asking which one of them has lost their minds.

While Mitsuko's focused on her food, I really look at her. It's clear that, at one point, she was a startlingly beautiful woman.

Then she meets my eyes. I blink like something's in them.

She says, I realize that this must be strange for you, too.

No, I say, it's fine.

So you're a liar, says Mitsuko.

I'm being honest. Really.

I'm fluent in fine, says Mitsuko. Fine means fucked.

Did my son tell you how long he'd be gone, she says.

A month, I say. Maybe two. I don't know. We didn't talk too much about it.

Of course not.

But did he tell *you*?

Tell me what?

How long he'd be gone, I say. Or that he was leaving?

Mitsuko looks me in the eyes. She cracks her knuckles on the counter. No, she says. My son neglected to give me that information. But this could be a good thing. I needed to get out of Japan for a while. No sense in rushing back to Tokyo to look at a dying man.

So, I ask, you're staying here? Until Mike gets back?

My voice cracks, just a bit. But Mitsuko spots it. She grins.

43

Would that be a problem, she asks.

No, I say. That's not what I meant.

Then what did you mean?

I'm sorry, I say. I really was just asking.

It's enough for Mitsuko to cross her arms. She leans on the counter, and her hair slips down her shoulders. I make a point to slow my breathing, to let my shoulders droop just a bit.

Then I think staying here is exactly what I'll do, says Mitsuko. I could use the time off. Your place is filthy, but it'll work until Michael makes it back.

And that's absolutely okay, I say. Totally perfect.

Remember, says Mitsuko, you're the one who let him leave.

You're right, I say. I'm the one who let him leave.

How generous, says Mitsuko, but then she doesn't say anything else.

Once Mitsuko's finished her bowl, she drops it in the sink. She turns on the faucet. Reaches for mine. The omelette was delicious, the sort of thing Mike would cook, because he did everything in the kitchen, and I think that this could have been the problem to begin with.

Nice chat, says Mitsuko, and I apologize, but I'm not sure why.

At some point, Lydia and I started talking about our mother's new family. I never asked when my sister found out, or from who. But she never asked me either.

4.

The next day, Mitsuko's cooking potatoes and okayu and a sliver of fish. She sets a bowl aside for me, with some scallions dashed over the porridge. Then she sips tea by the counter, and I drink water like a drowning man, and I never see her take a pill or check her blood pressure or anything else.

Once she's finished, Mitsuko slips on a jacket and shoes. I don't ask where she's going. I won't make the same mistakes twice.

At work, Ximena asks where I think Mitsuko heads during the day. We're looking at photos of the reception venue. She's opting to skip the actual wedding. A while back, Ximena told me that she's already walked down the aisle, and it didn't do much the first time around, so why the fuck would she try that again?

Mike's mother goes wherever broken-hearted mothers go, I say.

The laundromat, says Ximena.

The mall, I say.

The dog park.

The spa.

The market.

The gym.

The bar.

No way.

What, says Ximena, you think you're the only one who needs to fuck?

I try not to think of Mitsuko like that at all, I say.

And that's why you're stuck, says Ximena. She's not human to you. Go figure.

As opposed to an angel, I say.

As opposed to anything else, says Ximena.

You're really calling me a misogynist.

I'm calling you a man, Benson.

Before I can open my mouth, Barry sprints around the corner with Ahmad. He's got the kid by his shoulders, and Ahmad's hanging tight to Barry's stomach.

Barry is actually married himself, to the woman he's been with since high school. She's a surgeon. And here he is, cleaning playpens with us. Whenever his wife drops by the building, she smiles at nearly everyone, but one day Ximena told me that she

47

never actually touches anything. To just watch and see if she did.

And Ximena was right. It never happened.

When Ahmad tugs Barry's neck, he nearly drops the kid.

Your son is having a *day,* says Barry.

He's not my son, I say.

Benson's son needs a haircut, says Ximena.

Stop, says Ahmad. I'm not *his.*

Here's the running joke: as the most child-ambivalent employee in the building, the one who thought he'd only be flipping through paperwork, it turns out that they don't much mind me at all. That most of the kids we take care of actually *like* me. And I'm the only one, really, that Ahmad tends to bother with. So whenever Ximena and Barry had an issue they couldn't handle with our charges, I was their last resort. And then things usually worked out. I still don't know how I feel about it. But one day I told Mike about this, and he said it made sense and that I just couldn't see it myself, that this was a part of the appeal.

Eventually, I ask Ahmad what's happened, what is the problem, and he tells me that Marcos slapped him.

You mean Marcos slapped you *back,* says Barry. You started it.

He started it, says Ahmad.

You hit him first, says Barry.

Yeah, says Ahmad, but he *started* it.

I could tell Ahmad that, in his own way, he's right. You don't have to hit first to start it. And I'd like to tell him that, as young as he is, it doesn't get any easier.

But instead, I pick him up and flip him over my shoulder. And he looks around at me, a little suspicious. He lets out a grown man's laugh.

At one point, Mike started staying out. Heading who knows where after his shifts. Or maybe he was still at work. Or maybe he sat in his parked car, biding his time, chewing his fingernails. But, in any case, I started camping out on the sofa, which is a thing I probably picked up from one telenovela or another.

One night Mike stumbled through the door, drunk. He set his phone on the counter. I leapt from my blankets and threw that shit against the wall.

The cell cracked clean in half. We watched it pop in silence. Then it started ringing, and before it stopped, Mike looked at me and asked if he should answer it or what.

When I told Ximena about it afterward, she wouldn't stop shaking her head. We were at her place. Her mother was out. So we watched Ximena's kid, Juan, sprint from wall to wall, giggling at nothing, waiting for the delivery guy. Her fiancé was out of town, at a conference for incisors, and we'd ordered pad thai with some cash he'd left behind.

It's like we're in some fucked-up rom-com, I said. It's like we're both fucked-up rom-com villains.

Juan ran into the coffee table, bounced off, and careened into a bookshelf. I thought Ximena might stand to check on him, but she just sat there until he jumped up.

Way back when she was still with Juan's father, Ximena drove herself and the kid to me and Mike's place. She was crying, a mess, with a half-stuffed backpack for Juan. Mike made her tea while I sat with her on the sofa. Ximena told me she wasn't ever going back, that this was the last straw, but it was still another month before she finally broke up with the guy.

Now we watched her son attempt a crab-walk across her carpet.

Ximena said, Everybody's somebody's villain.

5.

Mitsuko and I form something like an evening routine: She cooks. I set the table. We both eat at the counter. Later, I wipe it down while Mitsuko hits the dishes.

Otherwise, we mostly keep to ourselves. It's probably better that way.

But I've learned a few things. Little things.

Like how, back home, she works at a jewelry store in Shimokitazawa.

Or how she flies to LA three times a year, to meet a man, or to meet a friend, or to meet a man who is also a friend.

And she's hardly flashy, but all of her clothes are *nice.* Every sock and skirt and earring is clearly part of a larger, varied whole.

Mike, meanwhile, wears the same three things seven days a week.

He has no patience for schedules, routines, or patterns of any kind.

Before me, he saw whoever he wanted,

whenever he wanted, fucking them however he wanted, and then he'd leave when he got bored.

Living with Mitsuko is, in other words, entirely unlike living with her son, whose gayness she is comfortable with, or at least not entirely uncomfortable with, or at least less disagreeable toward than my own parents, probably.

When Mitsuko asks about laundry detergent, I tell her it's in the cupboard under the sink.

When she asks where we do laundry, I point to the laundromat across the street.

When she asks where we buy groceries, I give her a few names, but she looks skeptical at all of them.

Will they have natto, she asks.

I say the H Mart just might.

You know what natto is, asks Mitsuko, frowning.

Soybeans, I say, right? Mike uses it.

And for the first time in our acquaintance, Mitsuko looks confused.

Here in Houston, she says. The city where you could hardly find daikon a few years ago?

Yeah, I say.

And *you* eat natto, she says.

I do, I say.

I don't believe you.

Because you don't think I could like it?

How the hell would I know what you like, says Mitsuko.

That night, I hear the television from the bedroom. Mitsuko's scrolling through movies. She settles on *War of the Worlds,* and I listen as Tom Cruise chases after his son. The kid's gone to join the resistance or some shit, although the viewer knows he's a goner. But Tom doesn't see that. He goes after the kid anyway.

So I'm dozing off when my phone dings. I'm thinking it's Ximena, but it's actually Mike.

He's sent a picture of his face in front of what looks like a train station. He's not quite smiling. The background is clogged with bodies.

And he's texted: HOW ARE THINGS?

I type: How the fuck do you expect.

A few minutes later, Mike sends another selfie. There's the backdrop of a neighborhood. It looks quiet, bookended by telephone poles.

If you adjust the brightness and squint hard enough, you can see up his nose.

looks cool, I say.

IT IS
found him yet?
YEAH
and?
HE'S DOING FINE
HE'S NOT REALLY DOING FINE
IDREK

Mike sends another photo of some trees. And then one of some other train station. There are plenty of things we should be talking about, but here we are, talking around exactly all of them.

So I text: where can you get natto here
Y?
Your mom says she wants to make some.

And Mike's response is immediate, possibly the fastest he's ever replied to me: WHAT THE FUCK?

6.

The next morning, for the very first time, Mike's mother knocks on my door. She's fully dressed, while I lean on the doorway in a tank top and boxers.

Take your time, she says.

Jesus Christ, she says.

We leave five minutes later. Our Black neighbors wave from their porch. There's a question on the grandfather's face, and I wonder if he'll ask it.

But Mitsuko doesn't look away. If anything, she walks slower. Staring him down.

Mike's car is filthy with clothes: our hoodies and socks and a loose pair of shoes. The whole thing smells like him, and I know his mother smells it, too. When I toss a pair of shorts behind us, she grunts, and there's a jock strap in the back seat, and I pray to no god in particular that Mitsuko doesn't catch it.

We've pulled out of the neighborhood, and into town, when she says, You're sure they'll have what I need?

They should, I say. You and Mike make the same things.

Maybe similar, says Mitsuko. Not same.

We drive through the mix of locals beginning their day. Whole swathes of Houston look like chunks of other countries. There are potholes beside gourmet bakeries beside taquerías beside noodle bars, copied and pasted onto a graying landscape.

At a stoplight, these two smiling guys walk a toddler across the street, holding the little girl's hands on either side. One of the men is white. The other one's brown. They look like something straight out of *OutSmart*. I glance at Mitsuko, and her face doesn't tell me much.

So, she says, you're Black.

You noticed, I say.

Just barely, says Mitsuko. And how did you find my son?

Accidentally, I say.

Let me guess, it was Grindr.

It wasn't.

You found my son on the internet.

No.

We met at a get-together, I say. An acquaintance introduced us.

Sure, says Mitsuko.

Once the couple crosses the road, their daughter looks up at them, beaming. She is the happiest that a child has ever been, ever. If Mike had seen them, he'd feign some sort of choking, or he'd honk his horn, or he'd grow sober, not saying much at all.

On Sunday mornings Mike drove us from market to market, all over the Northside. He juggled onions and guanabana and garlic and pineapples. He'd haggle with vendors in his shitty Spanish, and those evenings he'd cook three versions of the same fucking meal. I'd take a bite of one, and then a bite of the second. Then Mike would motion me toward the third. I usually went with the second.

Mike said this was practice for him. It was how he'd get better. I told him that not everyone did this, and he said there was a reason for that.

I didn't grow up with their palates, he said. They can assume a lot of shit that I can't.

So you force it on me, I said. Down my throat.

You'll miss it when it's gone, said Mike.

60

■ ■ ■ ■

Our local H Mart is, inconceivably, closed
for the day, and the next grocery store I
bring Mitsuko to instead is objectively filthy
— but there's natto. There's also a metal
detector by the entrance. The doorway is
flanked by a fried chicken vendor in scrubs.
Older women and their children finger carrots on our left, and a little girl wandering
the aisles wears a branch of parsley like a
crown.

I drift around looking for a shopping cart.
I find one with three wheels. We end up filling the whole thing, and also the basket,
and also the crooks of Mitsuko's elbows.

At the register, I feel for my wallet, and I
wait for Mitsuko to stop me. But she
doesn't. So I pull out my card slowly, and
that's when Mitsuko plucks a bill from her
bag, shaking her head.

The girl behind the register laughs, tugging at a braid.

Just like a nigga, she says.

Isn't it, says Mitsuko.

In the parking lot outside, a pair of women
in hijabs are yelling. Everything they say is
punctuated with a gasp. Everything is hor-

rible. They're both close to tears, but then they fall on top of each other, laughing until they're breathless.

7.

At the daycare, Ahmad pushes Ethan to the ground. When he sees his brother struggling, Xu wrestles them both in the sand. I spot it all from the window, and Ximena sees them, too, and I wait for her to intervene, but it turns out that she doesn't.

By the time I'm outside, Barry's already on it. He grabs Xu by the waistband and Ahmad by the elbow.

I sit Ethan down. Ask him what happened. He says he was ambushed, and when I ask why, he cocks his head like how couldn't I know.

When I step inside to check on Ahmad, Barry's stationed him at a coloring table in our tiny little computer room.

He won't say why he did it, says Barry.

We know why he did it, I say. He does it every day.

Sure, says Barry, but there's always a

reason. Headache. Stomachache. Something at home.

If you asked him then he'd tell you.

He only fucking talks to you, says Barry.

In the computer room, I hand Ahmad a juice box. He blinks before he takes it. Then I sit on the carpet beside him, and I start to say something, and he looks like he appreciates it when I finally don't.

We watch Silvia and Margaret watch us from the window. They duck their heads under the sill, resurfacing seconds later.

Whenever there's an altercation, it's our policy to chat with the parents. The twins' father shows up in basketball shorts and a Texans hoodie. Once we've finished telling him what happened, he frowns.

I'll talk to them, he says. Could've been worse, right?

Um, I say.

Xu threw dirt in another boy's eyes, says Barry.

Sure, says their father, and is the other kid alive? He couldn't just walk it off?

Ahmad's brother arrives a little later, sweaty and flushed. His name is Omar. He is, I think, some sort of physical therapist. I tell

64

him what happened, and he folds his palms over his face.

So you're saying he started it, says Omar.

Everyone asks that, says Barry.

Ahmad was involved, I say, but we don't give blame.

Maybe you should, says Omar.

Maybe. But we don't.

Then why the fuck are my parents paying you guys?

I don't say anything to that. Barry only winces. Then Omar's shoulders drop.

Sorry, he says.

It's fine, I say.

It isn't. Really.

Things have been rough, says Omar. Ahmad's living with me. Our folks are going through some things.

Totally understand, I say.

Omar's lighter than his brother. He's built like a baker. Standing next to each other, they look nothing alike — except for their noses, which are indistinguishable.

Does this mean I can't come back, says Ahmad.

Omar and I both say, No.

Nothing's wrong, I say.

Nothing, says Omar, glancing at me.

Ahmad looks between us. He obviously

doesn't believe it. But he accepts what we've told him, for now, jogging outside.

I tell Omar I get it. And he thanks me, extending his hand, smiling real wide. When I watch them walk out, I half expect him to box Ahmad on the head, but he doesn't do anything like that. He rubs Ahmad's hair, shepherding him toward the car.

Eventually, I ask Ximena why she didn't stop the fight. She looks at me for a long time before she finally answers.

I was going to, she says, but how often do you get to learn that lesson? That sometimes you just lose?

Better here than later, she says, when it actually matters.

Once, I asked Mike if he wanted kids. We were at a pub in the Heights, watching two drunk whiteboys fall all over each other. One of them would stand from his barstool, and the other guy would catch him. Then the other guy would stand, and they'd repeat the performance again.

Mike had already finished his beer, but he managed to spit some up anyways.

It was around this time that we had the

monogamy conversation. Mike's the one who brought it up.

I didn't refuse him outright, but I never affirmed him either.

I'm just saying we should think about opening things up, said Mike.

There's nothing to think about, I said.

I wouldn't care what you did, said Mike, as long as you came back home.

You aren't in a relationship with yourself, I said.

Just consider it, said Mike. Really. All I'm saying is that it's a big world out there.

World? I said. What the fuck? What world? We live in one place.

You know what I'm saying.

And the thing is, I did know. I knew. And I'd thought about it. But I was less worried, at the time, about what Mike would do than how I'd handle it: If I opened the door, even just a crack, would I still have a reason to step back inside?

We didn't actually decide anything, between the two of us. But a non-decision is a choice in itself.

Growing up, my sister was the disciplinarian. Our father was always working or drinking up all the booze downtown. Our mother compensated by staying out on the town herself, racking up credit on handbags.

So Lydia gave me my first cigarette, shaking her head when I inhaled and choked.

And Lydia told me how, and who, to plug for beer by the pharmacy.

And Lydia taught me how to drive, and she paid for my first speeding ticket.

And Lydia handed me my first joint, allowing me to sit in the smoke with whichever acquaintances she'd assembled.

Lydia also taught me how to kiss. She actually brought over a girl from her school. They talked in her bedroom, sipping gin from my parents' liquor cabinet, until my sister called me up from downstairs.

The girl had dark hair and mermaid earrings. She touched my forearm, slowly, and when I jumped, she frowned.

She asked if I didn't want to. I told her I did. Then I turned to Lydia, who looked deeply disappointed. She asked if I needed her to demonstrate, and her friend made a face, but I told her that wasn't necessary, for real, I was good.

Years later, Lydia reminded me of all that. She lives in the museum district now. Her place is stuffed with plants. The floors are a sheened wood. Our mother used to ask her when she'd bring back a husband, and our father used to ask her when she'd find a real job, but one day Lydia told them that it wasn't their business. They'd shot their shot. Played their game. And then I came out, which took the pressure off her for a while.

Mitsuko's chewing vitamins when I make it back to the apartment, and I'm ducking toward the bedroom when she calls my name.

Can you cook a chicken, she says.

You mean boil it, I say.

I meant what I said.

Like, frying wings?

Absolutely not, says Mitsuko. Come here.

She's more comfortable in Mike's kitchen than I've ever been. He'd arranged everything to his liking, but Mitsuko's reorganized all of it. Everything in the drawers, all of the ladles and spatulas and sticks. The bowls were a certain way, and now they are not. Plus, all of Mike's spices. And the utensils, too. I never knew where he'd kept his chopsticks — they just materialized whenever we needed them — but now the place looks unrecognizable. She's flipped it on its head. It's entirely disorienting, but for once I can actually settle in.

Mitsuko grabs the chicken by one leg,

balancing the other with a cleaver. In one fluid motion, she slices it entirely in half.

Jesus fuck, I say.

Quiet, says Mitsuko.

She proceeds to break down the carcass, bone by bone, stuffing the remains in a pot on the stove for stock. When she's finished clipping the fat, Mitsuko shakes each limb with a flick of her wrist. Her seasonings are lined up. She douses the meat in what looks like a pool of salt. But she doesn't say shit about it, and eventually she pirouettes to the side, flinging the chicken into a pan. It sizzles like a sheet of rain.

If I were at home, I would've marinated this, says Mitsuko. But I'm not at home.

Once she's finished and the meat's cooked, Mitsuko sets two bowls on the table, which is new. I sit across from her.

We eat, mostly in silence.

Did you get that, says Mitsuko.

Well, I say, bits and pieces.

She looks me over a little coolly.

That's all right, she says, but you're going to learn.

You have to, she adds.

My parents didn't cook. Neither did Lydia. They ordered everything from this Vietnamese spot a few blocks from the house or we went out to eat. But after the women in my family bounced, I made my hungover father simple meals for breakfast: scrambled eggs, grilled cheese, fruit bowls. A mangled guacamole.

Once, a little beside myself, I cooked chilaquiles. I'd watched a man on the internet fry a batch the night before. Foolproof, he called the recipe. Impossible to fuck up.

So I sprinkled too much cheese. Cut myself chopping tomatoes. My father glazed in the living room while I mashed the chips and the eggs. He groaned, eyeing the weather, when I passed him a paper plate.

We sat on the couch, chewing slowly, tracking a storm. My father winced while he ate. But he didn't spit it out.

Mike texts me that night. His father's doing worse.

worse? I say.

CAN'T SLEEP, WON'T EAT, BREATHING HEAVY, says Mike.

i'm sorry

YOU DIDN'T PUT IT INSIDE OF HIM

When I ask Mike what the next steps look like, he tells me they don't know yet. He tells me his father is stubborn. But the one certainty Mike has is that he's glad he flew over, or he thinks that he's glad, or he can't really imagine having not flown over.

It's too much to parse over the phone, over a screen. I tell Mike that I dismembered a chicken with his mother.

Mike writes, ???

i know, I text. i'm shocked

YOU ENJOY IT?

I survived

HA. THINK YOU'LL TRY AGAIN?

we'll see

I wait for Mike to ask about his mother. Or how we're doing in Texas. But he doesn't. The dots on my screen appear, and disappear, and reappear again, but nothing comes through.

So I ask him how *he's* doing, how he's really doing, and he sends me a selfie.

He's shaven, wincing in the photo. I can see his whole face for the first time in a year.

8.

When I'm up the next morning, Mitsuko's already gone. Her jacket is gone. Her shades are gone. I check for her shoes and they're gone.

I look for a note, and Mitsuko's left one on the table.

It's written entirely in kanji.

I could pull my fucking ears off.

But then I finally notice that she's taken the laundry baskets. Hers, and mine, and all of the detergent.

At work, Ahmad sits in a corner for hours not talking to anyone.

Ximena tries coaxing him with Legos. Barry offers a basketball. When it's my turn, I ask Ahmad why he's doing what he's doing, and he tells me that he's on strike.

All right, I say. But why?

The rules, he says.

Fascinating. When did you start?

Yesterday.

And how long will it last?

However long it takes.

You could be sitting around for a while, I say.

Okay, says Ahmad.

So I nod, and stand, and Ahmad exhales.

You're leaving, he says.

You're on strike, I say. I'm the appointed authority here. We're at a crossroads.

But you don't have to go.

I think I do.

Nobody has to do anything, says Ahmad. Not even you.

Which is, inconceivably, something that Mike would say.

And because I can't think of an adequate retort, I sit back down.

Over lunch, Ximena flashes pictures of her reception dress. She's in the process of picking the shoes. Her mother won't weigh in on either the shoes or the dress. Her father drove in from Laredo the weekend before, and when he met Noah, he told his daughter the young man was fine, but did she have to choose a gabacho?

Imagine, says Ximena, the fucking nerve.

■ ■ ■ ■

When Omar arrives, I inform him that his little brother's on strike. When I ask if he knows why, Omar smiles.

A better question is why we *aren't,* he says.

That's fair, I say.

If you and I started one right now, says Omar, how long do you think it'd last?

Seventy-two minutes.

That's very specific.

Specificity is important.

I'd like to think we could do better, says Omar.

I don't even know what I'd do, I say.

The same thing we always do, says Omar, palming his brother's head.

But he doesn't say what that is.

That night I'm dicing onions beside Mitsuko at the counter. She strains dashi into a bowl, while I do my best to hold on to my fingers.

Once she sees my vegetables, Mitsuko sighs. Takes the knife from my hands. She chops my halves into quarters, again, and my quarters into halves, again.

Even after we started throwing furniture at

each other, Mike always brought back food from his job. He'd set the Tupperware on the counter. He'd cooked it himself. And it was always, always delicious.

One time Ximena told me that was a sign. We were at her place, watching Juan assemble a Lego train set. I texted Mike that I'd be out late, that I might be gone until the morning, and he'd responded immediately with a solid OK.

Noah never brings me food, she said. Mike's thinking of you.

Noah isn't fucking half of the city.

Wouldn't it be less than half? There aren't that many of y'all out there.

Y'all?

People of the gay, said Ximena.

Eh, I said. There's more of us than you think.

And even if *Mike's* thinking of me, I said, I don't know if they're good thoughts.

But you don't get to control that, said Ximena.

You're taking up space in another human's brain, she said. You're a foreign entity. A parasite. That's a lot by itself.

9.

On weekends with Mike, I'd lay in bed until noon. He'd eat pancakes at the table, three or four at a time, frying another handful for me at midday when I got up.

But now, when I wake, I hear voices in the kitchen. Then I recognize them. The synapses click into place. And I'm flying across the bedroom.

Mitsuko's sipping coffee. Lydia's on the sofa. My mother's sitting beside them with her hands in her lap. They're laughing about something, and Mitsuko's actually smiling, and when I walk in the room, she leaves it on her face, just for a moment, long enough for me to see it.

Lydia's the easiest, so I start with her.

Holy shit, I say.

Holy shit yourself, she says.

You've got some fucking balls, I say.

Yes, says Lydia, more than you.

Stop it, says my mother, standing for a hug.

I don't want to give it. I'd rather just cross my arms. But I cannot even make myself do this.

No hello? says my mother.

Buenas, I say.

Why are you here, I say. *How* are you here.

Why are you here, mimics Lydia, in a pitch two octaves higher.

Also, says Lydia, where's Mike?

Enough, says my mother.

When I turn to Mitsuko, she only shrugs. Her smile's back.

Benson, says my mother, when was the last time you heard from your father?

That can't be what you drove here to ask, I say.

Can you please just answer the question, says Lydia.

I toss a pillow at her. Lydia tosses it back. My mother tells us both to chill the fuck out.

He's not doing well, she says. It's the drinking.

Then take him to a doctor, I say.

Benson, says my mother.

People detox every day. You can all go together.

If you really think it's that easy, says my

78

mother, we shouldn't have come here after all.

That's when Mitsuko clears her throat.

She tells us she's going for a walk.

Mitsuko looks at me, says to leave the door unlocked, and when she's gone, Lydia and my mother exhale.

I mean, she's a little older, says Lydia. Plus you're starting late. But I approve.

Stop it.

You definitely have a type.

I can't talk about this with you. I need to take my fucking pills.

Then you should probably do that, says Lydia.

Tell me what's wrong with my father, I say, and Lydia's cheeks descend.

Honestly, she says, I think he's just lonely. Like, he only needs some company. But my opinion means nothing in this family.

You don't really believe that, says my mother.

Don't tell me you don't see it, says Lydia. There's solitary, and then there's Dad.

If that's true, you did it yourself, says my mother.

We *all* did it, says my mother, looking at her heels, and my sister and I look down with her.

Because, truthfully, our mother looks as

well as I've ever seen her. She's got these bracelets, and these boots, and a jacket that clashes with everything. When she lived with my father, she mostly wore brown. In all of my memories, that's what I see her in.

Look, I say, I'm sorry. Really. But I don't think there's anything I can do. Especially if you've tried.

You're his son, says my mother.

And you were his wife, I say.

I drop that to shock her, but I don't know if it does. My mother just blinks at me. Like she's reevaluating something.

He kept you, says my mother. He didn't have to do that. But he asked to. He wanted you to stay with him.

And now he needs you, she says.

He needs *medication,* I say.

And who better to bring it to him than you, says my mother.

She adds, You clearly aren't doing anything else.

My mother leaves first. She doesn't say goodbye. Just slips on her shades and steps right out the door. But Lydia hangs around and gives me my father's new number. When she asks if I need the address, I tell her I know where I lived.

If you say so, she says. Call me when you

see him.

I'll do that, I say.

No you won't, she says.

There's a beat where I should ask how she's doing, but I let it pass. And she does, too. I don't know if she's grateful or disappointed.

But before she turns to leave, Lydia touches my shoulder.

You never said where Mike was, she says.

You're very observant, I say.

That's what they tell me.

Just like Jesus. Worked out for him, too.

You're a real catch, little brother, says Lydia. Premium grade.

When Mitsuko comes back, I'm lying on the sofa. She takes one look at me, opens her mouth, and closes it again.

Then she says, My son called.

She says, He sounded horrible.

Mike and I once spent the night in Galveston for a long weekend. We hadn't gone on trips together, not a single one, so this was a brand-new thing. But for the first time in months, he'd taken time off from the café. My gig was closed for a holiday weekend. We had a weird energy brewing around the apartment with both of us there, just lying around. And then there were the neighbors, who'd knocked on our door the night before, warning us that they'd be hosting some sort of marathon quinceañera. They spent the entire first night outside in the yard, shouting and dancing and beating a piñata. Around two in the morning, they locked hands to sing a song about Jesus. Once their sixth chorus rolled around, I told Mike it didn't matter where we went, as long as we went somewhere else. But he was already snoring.

So the sand was a grimy pale. Our end of the beach was scarce. A high school couple argued about prom under a makeshift fort behind us. Some girls rolled around in the water in front of us while their mother tucked her head in a Ferrante novel. Every now and then, she'd look up at her girls, and then at us. When Mike finally waved, she wiggled her fingers.

We laid out a towel, took off our shirts, and glazed in the sun for the whole afternoon. For lunch, we drifted up the pier for fish tacos. The woman who sold them was missing an ear. They were delicious, and we ordered four more, and then we watched some boys do somersaults in the sand by the dock. A pair of older couples mimicked them, lounging around the corner, husbands and wives looking round and unbothered.

Eventually, we bought more tacos from the one-eared woman. She said, Buena suerte a ambos, and I asked Mike what that meant.

He told me we were lucky charms. Everything we touched turned to gold.

And we walked the food back to our tiny spot in the sand. I fell asleep with Mike's calves on my shoulders.

When I woke up, the beach had cleared out. Windows glowed from beach houses lining the pier.

I felt around for Mike. He wasn't on the towel. But his trunks were right beside me, and I felt this sort of chill.

That's when he called from the water. He stood in the coastline, far enough out to float away. He yelled my name, waving his arms, with this big-ass grin on his face, and when I started to make my way over, he yelled for me to strip.

I looked to see who else was on the coast. Mike yelled for me to stop.

He said that nobody cared.

And if they did, it didn't matter.

And, sometimes, it helps to think that I was someone who could do that. I could strip buck-naked on the beach, sprinting through the sand, because I felt that strongly about anyone.

10.

I don't visit my father the next day. I don't call.

11.

Or the next day after that.

12.

When the weekend's gone, and I'm back at work.

Ximena ambushes me immediately about her reception.

I watch Barry wrestle with the twins.

I stare at my phone, and Mike hasn't reached out, and all of a sudden the day is over.

13.

Mitsuko buys nine cookbooks from I don't know where. She says we're going to start with the classics. She's been brighter since she heard from her son, a little like Mike's given her a charge — and that night, Mitsuko cooks what she tells me is his favorite: potato korokke, crowded beside onions and gravy, surrounded by sliced tomatoes and lettuce. She mashes the potatoes with pork through her fingers, drizzling the mixture with salt and pepper, molding tiny patties and flipping them in flour and egg yolks and panko. I watch them crisp from the counter, and Mitsuko watches me watch them.

It is the most personal thing she's shared with me so far, and I tell her that.

She looks at me for a while, then says, Don't be stupid.

14.

We play *WALL-E* for the kids. They sit enraptured in front of the television. We're not in the habit of turning it on — that's the one thing we're paid *not* to do — but none of them have seen it before. Silvia and Marcos park themselves on the rug. They're followed by Ethan, who's trailed by Xu, and then Thomas and Margaret and Hannah. The only kid who hasn't joined them is Ahmad, who's sitting at the table, sketching tiny skyscapes in crayon.

No wonder, says Barry.

The screen's like fentanyl, he says. Shuts them right off.

Ximena and I don't ask him where he found that analogy, or why.

When Omar comes for Ahmad that afternoon, he asks if he can talk to me.

Better day? asks Omar, palming his brother's head.

Strike's over, I say.

At least for now, says Omar.

Every day is a gift, I say.

You don't look religious.

I didn't know you could or couldn't look religious.

I know, says Omar, smiling. Aren't people mysteries?

Ahmad twists the bottom of his jacket in front of us, squirming with his feet.

Listen, says Omar, I have a question. But I don't want it to be weird.

Then I guess you'll just have to ask.

You know my brother really well, he says.

Sure.

And I'm trying to learn him better. Figure out this thing he's got going on.

So do you think you'd want to grab a drink one day, says Omar.

Not like a date, he says. But, you know. Just to talk.

I look at Omar, and then at Ahmad. He's staring at the clouds above us, and I can't tell if he's internalizing any of this or not.

I decide that they look nothing alike.

I tell him that it's fine. That I'll accompany him on this not-like-a-date.

I ask if there's anywhere he wouldn't recommend.

No, says Omar. But I can't text you.

Should I not use your name, I say.

Only if you give me the wrong number, says Omar.

Of course Ximena sees everything. She bites her lip, and then she un-bites it.

I tell her it's nothing, and she tells me she hasn't said a word.

Instead, she shows me pictures of the shoes she's chosen. What her mother's wearing, the venue, the suit for her son. She finishes with photos of her dress, a glowing, golden thing. Apparently, she's already shown her fiancé.

I know you're not supposed to show them, says Ximena, thumbing her screen. But it's *okay.*

That night, my mother calls, and I don't answer.

Lydia calls, and I don't answer.

Mitsuko has me frying pork cutlets, directing my hands at the stove. I burn the first batch. The second one's even worse. But she takes a bite from both, and neither of us says anything about it.

And then, out of nowhere, Mitsuko asks about my mother.

She used to be a divorcée, I say. Now she isn't.

So we're halfway in common, says Mitsuko. Have you met the new husband?

Once. He's rich.

Does that surprise you?

In a way.

Why, says Mitsuko.

I don't know, I say. He's just nothing like my father.

Wrong, says Mitsuko. You're all like your fathers.

And then, later, as we're washing the dishes, Mitsuko clears her throat.

She says, It's none of my business. But my son crossed the ocean for his.

One day Mike cooked me a meal and I told him I hated it. I said that just to say it, just to see what would happen. We'd fought that afternoon, about nothing, about money. He'd told me I couldn't understand because I'd grown up *with,* because my parents *had.*

We lived in a *box,* said Mike. Slept with fucking roaches on our fucking *faces.* We didn't fucking dine out on fucking Elgin. My folks couldn't be fucking *frivolous.*

You don't know what you're talking about, I said, although really, he did, and that conversation ended the only way that it could've — with fucking, hastily, half-clothed, on the counter, because we just didn't have the words.

He'd cooked a pork stew. You could smell it from around the block. I took one sip, and sort of frowned, and told him it wasn't for me.

In the end, we both stood bare by the kitchen counter. Mike smiled real wide, like he was going to cry.

I couldn't help but apologize.

15.

So, the next morning, despite everything, I'm at his door.

My father's door.

And then I am knocking. Waiting.

It's hard to head home without succumbing to nostalgia, standing where so many versions of yourself once stood, one of a suburb's magical properties. There's the bakery on the cul-de-sac, with the Korean lady who'd always slipped me donut holes. There's the chicken sandwich shop by the gas station. The pasta restaurant by the Tex-Mex joint. And everyone's lawn is sort of glowing, because it's the middle of the day in Katy, and every couple of seconds a minivan materializes behind me, and I'm thinking of just turning around and calling the whole thing off when the door juts open, just a crack.

My father's eyes.

Who're you, he says.

Stop it, I say.

My father squints a little deeper.

I think, just for a blip, that this could be worse than I'd thought.

Kidding, he says, opening the door.

Learn to take a motherfucking joke, he says.

The house is a sty. It's almost unbelievable. My father's got takeout cartons on the carpet, and the counters give off a musk. The windows are dewy from the inside, my father's sweatpants are stained, and I have to wonder if things were this way when we lived together or if Mike's standards just rose my own.

My father sits on the couch. An open beer stands between us. He eyes me, and then the beer, and then the ceiling above.

Go ahead, I say. I'm not the cops.

Might as well be, says my father. Showing up at the crack of dawn. Out of the blue. You even take your meds yet?

Don't worry about me, I say. Ma says you're not doing well.

You're right here. You tell me how I'm doing.

She says you're not taking her calls. She's worried.

Then tell her to come out here her damn self.

When my father gets like this, there's no talking to him. No point. So I pick up the burger wrappers around the couch, which gets me looking for a bag to put them in. After a while, I've made my way through the foyer. Then the kitchen. I leave his bedroom alone, but my old room's open beside it.

I look inside, and it's the one place that hasn't been trashed. The posters haven't been touched, Bowie and Hendrix and Ultraman Tiga. Vinyl records lay scattered on the desk. Below them, in the desk drawers, there's still probably some faded, printed-out porn.

When I'm back downstairs, my father's dozing. I reach for his beer, but he grabs at it before I do.

He drinks, looking me in the eyes.

I can count the number of times my parents touched each other in front of me.

Once, after my father's promotion at the station. A hug.

Once again, after his mother died, before a two-day drive to Columbia for the funeral.

And then again, after my mother's mother died, during a five-hour drive to Dallas.

96

A fourth time, the night Lydia told them she was done with their shit.

And once again, before our lunch at the deli, after our last big argument. I watched them from the house's driveway, through the window. I'd flipped a dresser on my way out, knocked over a generation's worth of photographs. When my father put his hand on my mother's back in the dining room, it happened briefly, instinctively, I think. And then my father took his palm back, squinting through the glass at me, and neither of my parents said shit about it.

When I'm finished, the house isn't clean, but it is cleaner. My father tinkers with his shirtsleeves. He frowns at my fifth bag of trash.

Nobody asked you to do that, he says.

But here I am, I say.

You ever think that's the problem? says my father. Niggas voluntarily doing things I'm not asking them to do?

That's my cue. I grab my shoes by the door.

Bye, Dad, I say. Call Mom. She's worried.

And then I'm back outside.

And I'm maybe, what, three steps from Mike's car when I hear the door open behind me.

My father stands there, watching me. I lean on the car's window.

When do you think you're coming back, he asks.

You want me to come back? I say.

Can't answer a question with a question, says my father, and I look at him, and he really does look lonely.

For a while, this was a man whose guffaw commanded entire newsrooms. But now, here he is. Or was. I hadn't even asked him when he'd last subbed for a class. I hadn't asked how he was on money. Not that I could've helped him.

Soon, I say.

Approximate, says my father.

I don't know, I say. In a few days. Next weekend.

Hunh, he says, you still working with those bad kids?

I'm still working with those bad kids.

I figured.

Promise me, says my father, playing with his hands.

Whatever. Fine. I promise.

I'll believe it when I see you.

Then I'll see you, I say, stepping in the car, turning the ignition, gone.

■ ■ ■ ■

Lydia figures our household's lack of intimacy is why I have trouble connecting. She told me that, in those exact words, when we were packing up her last apartment. She was moving, again, to another spot a few blocks up the road. Her place was all portraits of friends, pictures of the places she'd been.

How the fuck would you know what's wrong with me, I said.

Baby brother Benson, said Lydia, I literally watched you take your first steps. Of course I'd know.

We were smoking something entirely too strong on the stairs of her new place, this walk-up behind a gaggle of bars in Montrose. I'd asked Lydia if she was worried about her new neighbors, and what they'd think of her, and she made the tiniest shrug.

Who gives a fuck what they think, she said. I pay rent every month.

They do, too, I said.

Exactly. We both know our roles. So there's nothing to debate.

How's that one guy, I said. The one you were seeing?

Nice try, said Lydia.

You never tell me anything.

You're one to talk about discretion.

You know what I mean, I said, kicking at the steps, and that's when Lydia put a hand on my shoulder.

She said, You'll know when there's something to hear about.

We could all be dead and gone before then, I said.

That's not impossible. The coastline's rising.

Guess I'll just stockpile love stories between the two of us.

It wouldn't hurt, said Lydia. You've got a good one.

I don't know, I said.

There's nothing for you to know, said Lydia. I'm telling you. Mike's a good guy.

She kicked her legs out behind me, stretching toward the ceiling. I mimicked her, and she tapped the back of my head with her palm.

Mike's a wild card, I said.

He must be the affectionate one, said Lydia.

That's the last word I'd use for Mike, I said.

You're too close to see it.

I think I know him a little better than you do.

And yet, said Lydia. You're both soft.

Because you're so tough, I said.

Brother, said Lydia, you literally have no idea.

I'm stuck on I-10 when I dial my mother. The trucks beside me weave through the lanes like ducks in a pond.

Before she answers, I get another call, from an unknown number. I don't even think about it.

Mike, I say.

What, says Omar.

Oh, I say.

Who's Mike, says Omar.

Don't worry about it, I say. What's going on? What's wrong?

I was calling about our date, says Omar.

I mean, he says, I know it's not a date. Really. But I have to cancel it.

Okay, I say.

Okay, says Omar.

A lane opens slowly in front of me, clogging itself with a pick-up truck and a Porsche simultaneously. The drivers flick each other off.

Then Omar says, Can I ask what you're up to?

At this moment? Traffic on Allen Parkway. I'm sorry.

Me too.

But, says Omar, believe it or not, there's actually this happy hour I like in that area. By Greenway Plaza? It's hot dogs, you know? Maybe one day we c—

How about right now, I say, before I even think about it, before he codifies the implications into existence.

Oh, says Omar. Wow. Yes. Do you eat meat?

I eat everything.

And then Omar gives me the address.

And then Omar tells me where to park.

I promise it's still not a date, says Omar.

I know, I say.

Good, says Omar.

The happy hour is actually at an icehouse. The patio's oversaturated with white people. Six or seven televisions blare reruns of the same college football game, and Omar's sitting on a bench in the back.

He looks oblivious. A little dopey. And he's smoking a cigarette. But when I walk over, he stomps it right out.

I promise I won't tell on you, I say.

No, says Omar, this is good. I'm trying to quit.

Looks like that's going well.

It was until today, says Omar, grinding

the butt with his toe.

We both order hot dogs. His is a reasonable size. Mine is obscene, a bratwurst, topped with way too many garnishes. The guy who brings them over is pale and tattooed, asking us once, and then once again, if we want anything on tap. But we don't.

A few bites in, we haven't really spoken. Omar glances at me, and then over my back.

Ahmad's a weird kid, says Omar.

All kids are weird, I say. They're kids.

Go figure, says Omar. I guess you'd know. I was pretty weird.

And now?

I'm a therapist, says Omar. Stretching people who didn't stretch themselves. A little less weird.

Just a little, I say. Does your brother live with you?

My brother lives in his own world, says Omar. He checks in with me from time to time.

I'd join him if I could, I say, and then I take a sip of my water.

Omar finishes and looks like he wants to lick the crumbs from his fingers, but he doesn't. He twiddles them instead.

I should be thanking Ximena, says Omar. My parents could never afford you guys if not for the discount she's giving us.

Xim's the best, I say. You met her fiancé?

Yeah. He's cool.

He's all right, I say.

And then, all of a sudden, we've exhausted our list of things to talk about.

It occurs to me, briefly, that if Omar knows Ximena well enough for a discount, he probably already knows about Mike.

The whiteboys behind us are starting to get rowdy. When one of them busts his ass on the concrete, the others raise their beers and cheer.

Thank you, says Omar.

For what, I say.

For this.

I already paid, I say.

No, says Omar. For coming out here. You didn't have to.

I needed to sit down with someone else for a while, he says. It just gets to be a lot. It *is* a lot.

Don't worry about it, I say. Anytime.

We watch the whiteboys behind us.

Tomorrow? says Omar, and for a moment I can't tell if he's joking.

Any other time, I say.

An indeterminate time, says Omar.

A time and place to be determined, I say.

Cheers, says Omar.

■ ■ ■ ■

When I make it back home, Mitsuko has already cooked. There's miso soup on the counter. She's watching television on the sofa. Her eyes are red, like she's been crying, and when she sees me, she doesn't say a word. And then I hear her sobbing, and then I see the television.

She's watching *Maid in Manhattan*.

She's bawling at *Maid in Manhattan*.

Jennifer Lopez sits on the stoop, and Mitsuko's leaking her eyes out.

When she catches me staring, she asks what the hell I'm looking at.

That night, I text Lydia about our father. Then I call my mother. She answers on the third ring.

I'm a little busy, she says, and her new life erupts in the background.

There are children laughing. The Pomeranian's barking. I think I can hear a man.

I saw Dad, I say.

Something pops on the other end of the line. There's more laughter from my stepbrothers. We've only met a handful of times, and I can never match their names with their faces.

I said I'm busy, says my mother.

I saw Dad, I say again.

Hold on, says my mother, shifting over the speaker, away from the noise.

Okay, she says. Okay. Was he drinking?

He wasn't drunk.

Good, says my mother. That's better than when we stopped by. But you've got to stay on him.

I can hear a screen door shutting behind her, and then the click of a lighter.

Are you smoking, I ask.

I am, says my mother.

I thought your husband wasn't into that?

You can use his name, Benson.

I could.

It wouldn't kill you, says my mother, taking a drag.

Ever since she got remarried, my mother's toggled between her old vices and her new life: She started going to church again, because of her new husband's profession and the need to show face. But she also picked up her cigarettes again, because she loved them, and my father couldn't stand them. She changed her entire wardrobe. She started swearing. She started smiling, deeply and widely.

Lydia says my mother and I are the same. She says that this, too, is something that

I'm too close to see.

You never told me how you were doing, says my mother.

You didn't ask, I say.

I did. But I'm asking again.

Things are fine. Nothing's changed.

You're taking your medication?

That's not something you have to worry about.

You can't stop me from worrying about you, says my mother. And how's Mike? I didn't see him.

Mike's away, I say, and I can hear my mother start to say something before she stops.

Is that something you want to talk about, she asks.

No, I say.

It's okay to talk to people about these things, Benson.

You don't have to keep saying my name.

You're my son, says my mother. I named you. I love saying your name.

I watch some flies dance outside my window. They connect and reconnect.

Let me know if you need anything, she says. Whatever it is. I'm here for you. Whatever this thing is that you're going through, you don't have to do it alone.

And I start to thank her, but then the kids

start yelling, and the dog starts barking, and my mother's husband calls her name, and everything on her end dissolves into noise.

16.

Another dream about Mike: This time, we're in a nightclub. The sort of place you'd never actually find us. Only, he is a stranger, and I am a stranger, and we are flirting at the bar.

Hey, stranger, says Mike.

Hello, stranger, I say.

And then we are laughing together. Our shoes kiss each other's soles.

And then we are in a bathroom stall, biting at skin, hands in each other's pants, grunting like otters against a dingy, dented stall.

It's a little past midnight when I clean myself up in the bathroom, because it's been literal years since I've had a wet dream. The television outside is at a low murmur. Lydia's texted me back.

She says: Nigga u really went? LMAO.

17.

The next morning, before I head to work, Mitsuko says she needs a ride downtown. She'd mailed herself ingredients from Japan to the FedEx building by the Marriott.

So we pull out of the neighborhood, and off I-45, dodging the never-ending construction on Elgin. As I hook a right at a stoplight under the bridge, a disheveled guy in a Rockets sweater sips from a paper bag. He's seen better days, but the sweater's brand-new. It's got the tags and everything.

He nods our way. I nod back. Then the light changes, and we both turn back to our lives.

Tell me something about my son that I don't know, says Mitsuko.

Well, I say.

But, the thing is, I've got nothing.

Mike is irritable.

Short-winded.

He does this thing with his tongue.

For the first few months, he'd trace shapes across my back in bed. Whenever I got them right, he'd chew on my shoulder.

Mike knows a little bit of Spanish, I say.

That's nice, says Mitsuko.

He has to. For his job.

Also, I say, he's really into food.

Thank you for that, says Mitsuko. Really. You're a wealth of knowledge.

But tell me, she says, when did you know you were gay?

I take my eyes off the road, nearly swerving onto the sidewalk. Some loiterers in shades hop away from the curb. They flick me off through the rearview window.

Never mind, says Mitsuko.

Sorry, I say, it wasn't you.

Of course it wasn't me, says Mitsuko.

We resettle into traffic.

If it helps, she says, I had no idea Mike was that way.

He never told me, says Mitsuko. Or his father. I had friends whose children are gay. Sons who sleep with sons. Girls who sleep with boys and girls.

But not mine, says Mitsuko. I didn't see it.

And then one day, she says, I just knew. Before he left home, it clicked. Everything finally made sense.

There was nothing to say after that, says Mitsuko. We both understood.

Cruising into the parking garage, we find a spot just across from the elevator. Once I've settled the car in park, we sit in the darkness.

What kind of guy did you think your son would end up with, I say.

Is that your real question, says Mitsuko, or are you asking something else?

Are you asking if I thought the man would be Japanese? she asks. Or if I care that you're Black?

A white dude emerges from the elevator in front of us, looking extremely distressed. He fumbles with his keys for a second. At the sound of his car alarm, his whole body relaxes.

If you put it that way, I say.

Well, says Mitsuko, I didn't think about that. That wasn't my business. Isn't. I'm his mother.

Or are you really asking what I think about *you,* she says.

Another white guy in a suit unlocks the car beside us. He peeks into my window, frowning above his tie.

I'd tell you, says Mitsuko, but you might drive us into the wall.

■ ■ ■ ■

I trail Mitsuko as we walk past each suite, up an escalator, and over a crossway. The staff in the FedEx are mostly women, mostly Black.

They look at Mitsuko. They look at me.

A light-speed calculus blips across their eyes.

Once we've reached the front of the line, I smile as wide as I can. Mitsuko still hasn't taken off her shades. She hands one woman a card and receives an armful of envelopes. When she's asked if she needs a basket, Mitsuko declines.

That's what he's for, she says, nodding at me.

My kind of woman, says a lady behind the counter, chuckling.

On the drive back, I ask Mitsuko what her home in Tokyo's like. She raises an eyebrow.

Quiet, she says.

18.

Ahmad corners me at work, jumping all over my back. Marcos and Ethan see him do this, and they follow suit, hanging from my knees. Then Barry stumbles over to try to help, but I wave him away. The boys and I slog from the copy machine, to the dumpster by the playground, to the broken door in the hallway.

When I tell them I'm tired, they dislodge, standing around.

When I finally stand up, they latch on to me again.

Ahmad seems to be doing better, says Ximena.

I ask what makes her think that, and she raises an eyebrow.

Driving home, I nearly hit a pigeon in the road — the brakes kick in just before we connect.

Luckily, there's no one behind me. So I leave the car and walk up to the bird. It looks me up and down, and then at the ground, scrutinizing something: a quarter in the concrete.

The bird examines the coin. Glances at me. Then it grabs the quarter with its beak and takes off, flapping its wings.

19.

The next time I see my father, he insists that I take him out.

So we go out. There's a crawfish spot not too far from his house. The business is an anomaly for the area, with the very old and Black commingling with the very young and white. The property was bought by a Pakistani guy last year, and he tore up the floor and put in some new walls. He gave the menu a sheen. Stocked the fridge with craft beer, tacked flat-screens on every wall.

My father sips one of the beers.

You drink IPAs, I ask.

They're essentially piss, says my father. Means I'll drink a little less.

When our waitress comes by, my father asks for another beer. She's a pretty white-girl, and she asks if I'm still good with my water, and my father says that no one is good with just water.

But I tell her I'm fine. She smiles, tilting

her head.

Once she's gone, my father whistles.

Your mother told me you're living with a woman, he says.

For now, I say.

I hope it isn't homophobic to call that a significant development, says my father.

So you and Mom are speaking now, I say.

We've always spoken, says my father. We just don't say anything. Does this mean you're not gay anymore?

No, I say.

It's never too late to change, says my father.

From him, this is typical. I've stopped trying to shout him down.

Our hands are full of crawfish. Their entrails seep through the newspapers below us. When the waitress stops by our bench again, my father smiles and asks for more water. Even though my glass is topped off, she adds a little for me anyway.

Let me guess, says my father. That was an insensitive comment.

I'm over it, I say.

You know I don't mean it, says my father.

You're a grown man. It is what it is.

I just don't know the rules, says my father. They keep changing on me.

They'd be mandates if they didn't, I say.

There's a reason dictators do what they do, says my father.

There's no way we'll finish our food. The crawfish has overcome us. My father says he'll eat more later, and I know that he won't, but we wrap the leftovers in classified ads anyway.

As we walk through the parking lot, the waitress waves again. When I wave back, my father thumps the roof of Mike's car.

We take the long way back. Every few miles, my father gives commentary.

There's the house your mother and I almost bought.

There's the church we went to for years, the one with that cheating pastor.

There's the complex your aunt almost leased.

There's your chemistry tutor's lawn.

There's the pharmacy.

The pool.

The park.

I slow down for all of it, but I never actually stop.

And then we're back home.

You know what, says my father, I never cared who you fucked.

I know you think I do, he says. But I don't.

Your mother cares, says my father. A lot. But not as much as you think.

And then he grabs his sack of crawfish, whose guts have bled all over the car floor mat.

20.

That evening, I catch Mitsuko sharing a mug of something with our Venezuelan neighbor. It's one of the rare moments that I've seen the woman without her children. She and Mitsuko aren't laughing or smiling or anything; they're just drinking over the fence, silently, together.

Every now and again, one of them looks up, like they've suddenly heard something. But they don't say shit about it.

21.

Here is the root of the problem, our problem: the night before Mike left, in bed, before we fucked, he asked if I thought we were working.

What the fuck kind of question is that? I asked. Working? Are you saying we're done? Right after we bring home your fucking mother?

I'm asking a question, said Mike. That's all.

Just say it. Don't be a little bitch.

Benson, I am literally only asking what you think.

I think you should just come out and say what you're trying to say, I said. If you think we're done, just say it. I'll pack my shit tomorrow.

It's not that simple, said Mike, and then he put his face in his palms.

But it is, I said.

You are the only one that's been fucking

121

around, I said.

This again, said Mike.

Yes, I said. Again. Again and again and again. And now you're leaving for who the fuck knows where. For who the fuck knows how long.

You're not being fair, said Mike. That isn't fair. It's my dad.

A man you couldn't give a fuck about!

That won't matter when he's dead.

We'd been whispering. We hadn't looked at each other. I felt Mike's body relax beside me.

Look, said Mike. Just because something isn't working doesn't mean it's broken. You just have to want to fix it. The want has to be there.

Tell me, I said. Do you want to fix it?

I guess that's what I'm trying to find out, said Mike.

22.

I'm cooking with Mitsuko when I get a call
from Omar.

It's Ahmad, he says. Shit.

What's wrong, I say, and Mitsuko gives
me a look.

I don't know what he's doing, says Omar.
I don't know what's —

You need to call an ambulance, I say.

No, says Omar. It's not that. Nothing
wild. He's just being strange, you know?
The way he gets sometimes? But you've
seen it before. I couldn't think of anyone
else to call.

We hang up. I tell Mitsuko that I think I
have to go somewhere.

She looks at the pot still simmering in
front of us, a seafood curry swimming with
scallops and shrimp and carrots, just waiting for rice. Her hair is down. She's not
wearing makeup. For the first time since
she's lived in this apartment, Mitsuko's

starting to look comfortable.

Only if you tell me that you're taking this food with you, she says.

When I open my mouth to protest, Mitsuko grimaces.

We're not wasting it, she says. We don't *do* that.

Which is how I end up at Omar's door with an armful of curried rice and katsu.

When he sees that it's me, he buzzes me upstairs. He opens the door in basketball shorts and this tank top that's too long.

Sorry, he says.

Don't worry about it, I say.

No, says Omar. It's really nothing. I shouldn't have called.

We walk through the apartment — which is bright, with good lighting — and Ahmad is lying facedown on the floor. He's lodged in the hallway, arms to his sides. Legs splayed out like some sort of performance piece.

When I call his name, he looks up.

Hey, kid, I say.

Hey, says Ahmad.

What's going on, I say.

I'm thinking, says Ahmad.

What about?

Stuff.

Sounds rigorous.

I take a seat beside him, and then I look up at Omar. He looks at his brother, and then at me, and sits awkwardly behind us, bouncing on his ass.

And that's how we stay. Saying nothing. Which gives me a chance to look around.

There's no art on the walls, but there's a bookshelf. Some throw pillows. A cowboy rug is draped across the wood, and the room smells a little like cinnamon.

Omar squirms, working to get comfortable.

Nothing's really changed. Ahmad hasn't moved much at all. So what I do next is kick out my feet, get flat on my stomach, and join him.

Once we're parallel, Ahmad turns his head to give me a look.

All of a sudden, he begins to cry.

After he's put his brother to bed, Omar meets me back in the living room.

It's the divorce, he says. Kids take it a lot of different ways.

This isn't the worst one, I say. Trust me.

He hasn't talked about it since he started staying with me.

Just hug him every once in a while. Make him feel seen.

That's the thing. I don't think he wants that.

Unfortunately, he doesn't have a say. Ignoring him is the one thing you *can* do wrong.

And then the two of us sit there in silence. I wonder if we're thinking the same thing.

There's a pair of work shoes by the door, and also a child's sneakers, and also mine. They're followed by six pairs of sandals, bear-size, all of them frail at the toes.

Wait, says Omar, you brought food.

You can cook! says Omar.

A friend made it, I say.

A friend, says Omar.

A friend, I say.

If you say so.

Trust me.

Well, says Omar, should we eat it now?

And then he says, Maybe this could be that date, you know?

It comes out boyishly, as if Omar isn't entirely sure. Then he crosses his legs on the sofa. He props up an arm, looking objectively ridiculous.

Honestly, I say, you should save the food for Ahmad.

He'll be hungry, I say, and the words feel like weights in my mouth.

He won't eat it, says Omar. No offense,

but it's french fries or bust with him.

I should go, I say, because of course I really should, and then I start to stand, because that's where gravity's leading me, and then, out of nowhere, for no reason at all, or maybe for every reason that's already clearly presented itself, Omar leans over and kisses me.

It's brief. Just lip to lip.

There's this smooshing sound, like we've just shucked an oyster.

And then, Omar's sitting again. Hands in his lap like he's been scolded.

I say, Ha.

I say, I should still go.

And then I stand up.

And then I grab my shoes.

And then I am gone.

I've literally just parked by the apartment when my cell rings.

Ben, says Mike.

Godfuckingdammit, I say.

It's been a minute, says Mike.

I agree that it has.

One of our Black neighbors is sitting on her porch. She's rocking in her chair, watching the streetlights flicker. The block's quiet, for once, and the mosquitoes are out, and the woman swats her elbows from time to time, wiping her mouth with the crook of her arm.

Well, I say to Mike.

How are things, I ask. Are you at your father's?

I am, says Mike. Or we were. We're out now. Took a little trip.

He's not doing well, says Mike.

I'm sorry, I say.

And instead of Mike's usual You Didn't Do It, or his You Don't Have to Say That, he just says, Thank you.

That's when I understand.

But how's my mother, says Mike.

Just lovely, I say. Still adjusting to our shared proximity.

That's what she told me.

Go figure.

But it's a compliment, says Mike. Could be worse. Ma says you've been cooking.

We play house together, yes.

I can't even imagine it.

Just because the neighborhood's snoring, that doesn't mean it's asleep. There's a house party going on a few houses down. Some whitegirls stumble onto a lawn, laughing with red Solo cups. They glance back at the door they came from, and one of them covers her mouth, and her friend latches on to her shoulders, balancing them upright.

Hey, I say, when are you coming home?

Scattered voices slip through the phone, and also the sound of motion. For Mike, it's midday.

That's the question, isn't it, says Mike.

It is.

Mike asks if I want him to come back, and I don't say a word.

We're both silent. Both holding the line.

I owe him a lot, says Mike.

Not everything, he says. But I think I should see him through this, you know?

I know, I say.

So when he's gone, says Mike, I'll come back.

When he's gone, I say, you'll come back.

The whitegirls up the road stumble into the grass, laughing all over each other. The streetlights keep flickering. A chill settles in. And our neighbor, as if snapping out of a reverie, smiles and waves my way, putting her whole shoulder into it.

And you, says Mike. How are you doing?

The other day I saw a pigeon fly away with some cash, I say.

Go figure. It's probably for booze.

You think so?

Duh, says Mike. Don't overthink it.

I shut the door behind me as quietly as I can, but Mitsuko's already asleep on the sofa.

There's a bowl of rice on the counter, covered with a paper towel. It's still a little warm.

23.

One day, Mike asked me what I wanted. This happened a few months back. Before the photo. We were standing beside a taco truck in the Heights, since Mike had driven by it, and he'd noticed me staring, admiring the sign, and just like that he turned the car around. It was the most spontaneous thing we'd done in a while.

A guy and this lady stood on the other side of the window. The man leaned over the stove, beside the space heater, and his partner played with their credit card reader. When Mike and I ordered in Spanish, her eyes sort of fluttered, but then she smiled, and we waited for our food under a flock of trees. It was winter. They were dying.

This should fill me up, I said.

That's not what I mean, said Mike.

Then what do you mean?

Like, what do you *want*?

I looked at the truck. A little bit of steam

slipped through the windows, and it teetered from the breeze.

I mean, I'm fine right now, I said.

Okay, said Mike.

I don't need kids, if that's what you're asking.

I'm a fat Asian gay, so I wouldn't be able to help you there.

Exactly, I said. Or not exactly. You know what I mean.

Not sure if I do, said Mike.

I'm saying I don't need a ring. We don't even need to be exclusive. I'm okay.

I want you to be better than okay.

Then learn to code. Make us some money.

I'm being serious, said Mike, and when I saw his face, I knew that he was.

He shuffled around with his hands in his hoodie, stepping all over the leaves. They cracked underneath his sneakers, and then mine, until we'd formed a crooked graveyard of their stems.

Look, I said. Okay is good. All right is *good*. Most people don't get more than that. That's a myth.

I don't think it has to be, said Mike.

If something happens, it happens. We'll deal with it.

That's what everyone thinks until the thing actually happens.

You're good enough for me, I said. Our situation is good enough for me. And everything that comes with it.

So you're saying you don't know what you want, said Mike.

I think you're making a problem where there isn't one.

But, said Mike, and that's when the lady called us over from her truck.

She handed us our sack, smiling. Mike tipped her a five-dollar bill. She told us to be well, and I told her we'd try, but Mike had already started walking back to the car, already stuffing his face.

24.

At work, we watch the kids climb each other's backs like mountain lions. They make it to three levels before they topple. And on the gravel, they point fingers, make blame, and complain — but then they brush their hands, steadying themselves for another go.

Ximena schools me on the reception's venue. She and Noah chose a taquería on Airline that they eat at all the time. They're planning for a mariachi band, and a fuckton of sombreros, and Ximena's mother disapproved until she learned the groom's family was paying for it.

Now it's all smiles, says Ximena. Suggestions. Gentle critiques.

She asks if Mike will be back in time. I tell her I don't know.

Let me know, she says, so I can warn the bartenders.

Eventually, the kids have built an unsteady sort of tower. Marcos, the child on top, raises his hands in triumph.
Ximena and I clap, and clap, and clap.

I spot Omar when he picks up Ahmad. He basically pivots his whole body to avoid making eye contact, but he lingers to talk to Ximena.
Later, once he's left, she asks me what's wrong.
Why does something always have to be wrong, I say.
It doesn't, says Ximena. That's why I'm asking.

25.

A few years after the divorce, my mother drove me to her new home. Everyone else was out that morning. She'd offered to show me the place. I'd said that was fine, but we'd made it to the driveway before I told her I couldn't go inside. She looked at me for a long time, and then she opened the car door and sat on the hood. I watched her pull one cigarette after another from her purse, smoking them down. Eventually, I joined her. She offered me one, and I took it.

We smoked through an entire pack before she stepped back inside the car. I followed her, and we drove back to my neighborhood. She dropped me off. I never went back to her new place, and we never brought it up again.

26.

Nearly three weeks in, it's almost astounding how little Mitsuko and I have talked about her son. When I tell her this, she shakes her head.

What is there to discuss? she says. What could *you* possibly tell me? I asked you once already and you gave me nothing.

He came out of my body, says Mitsuko. He's a homosexual. He left his mother with a stranger. I've already got everything I need to know.

She's sitting at the table, scrolling through her tablet. I'm in the kitchen, leaning over the stove.

I don't know, I say.

Exactly, says Mitsuko. You don't. So don't worry about it.

Maybe you could tell me a story, I say, and Mitsuko actually laughs.

A story is an heirloom, she says. It's a personal thing.

Okay, I say.

You don't ask for heirlooms. They're just given to you.

Okay, okay.

Check the rice, says Mitsuko.

I figure she's just cutting me off, but then I look at the stove and it's bubbling.

But here's a story: Once, my father drove the entire family to Dallas. There was some sort of work convention. He figured we ought to come along. Our mother fought it — she was already on her way out by that point — but our father won her over, or he won the rest of us over, and then we bugged her incessantly.

Even if this was only a last-minute thing, we never actually went anywhere, and of course our mother didn't trust my father to drive us kids on his own. So the four of us ended up in his Corolla, driving hours on the 10, out of the city, in the middle of the week.

I spent most of that week by the hotel pool. I made eyes with one whiteboy swimming laps in the mornings — some college kid, a few years older than me — and another one manning the lobby, and a third in the café, but by the time I'd decided they were feeling me, too, it was already time to go.

Things hadn't gone well for my father at the conference. He'd missed out on some accolade or another. And we were halfway back home, driving five over the limit, which was twenty less than the line cruising in the lane beside us, when a cop pulled us over by a gas station in Huntsville.

The cop was young and blond. He explained to my father about speeding. He said he hadn't wanted to stop us, but that was his job, and the law was the law — but my father was irate.

He slapped the window. He yelled. It was the most upset I'd ever seen him, shaking like he had something to prove. My father called the cop a motherfucker and a narc and a pig, and before I could even think about it, the whiteboy put him in handcuffs.

My father told the cop he didn't know what he was doing. He'd sue him. His family. The whole fucking department. And this whiteboy held my father loose by the wrists, looking at the rest of us like why didn't we jump out and help him.

So it was my mother who opened her mouth.

She told the cop our father didn't mean it.

He was just scared, she said, for his family. His insurance. You know how it is.

The cop looked at her like she'd given him permission to let things go.

He smiled. She smiled back.

He let us off with a warning.

When my father got back in the car, he didn't say a word. And we were already a few miles down the road before I realized I'd squeezed Lydia's hand the entire time.

But he didn't speak to my mother for the rest of that ride, or the rest of that week, or the rest of that month.

Mike is the only person I've ever passed that story off to. It took me two years.

We were at an arcade bar on Lester. He was hunched over *Tekken,* tapping the same two buttons.

He didn't say anything when I finished. He just kept tapping.

Then Mike said, I get it.

You get what, I said.

I just get it, said Mike, and he fed the machine another coin.

27.

Now, sitting on the sofa with my father, we're watching one of the Fast and the Furious movies. I made him a bowl of instant noodles, blanketed by some sliced cheese. He's picking at them with a spoon. I spent ten minutes looking for chopsticks in the kitchen, nearly calling it quits before I found some shitty takeout disposables.

During a monologue from the Rock about defying gravity, my father says, He teach you that?

I ask him what he means. My father pantomimes with the chopsticks.

You never ate like that in my house, he says.

I want to say that I had, and he was too drunk to see it.

Or that it wasn't just *his* house.

I taste the words and swallow them.

Who's *he,* I say.

You know, says my father.

I really don't.

Your beau. The nigga you're shacking up with.

You don't know what you're talking about.

Lydia told me, says my father, but we don't have to talk about that.

One dude on-screen drives his car off a bridge. It explodes in midair. A group below him gasps.

You've been talking to Lydia?

All of my children have found me in my time of need. You've all panned out.

Then why am I here, I say.

My father only shrugs, and then he nods at the television.

There's an ad for a weight that shakes you into some semblance of fitness. The man on the screen doesn't do much; he holds it and sits. But he already looks healthier, happier, better.

28.

Omar drops off his brother and asks to speak to me. Ximena overhears, shooting me a look, but she doesn't say anything about it.

Before I can open my mouth, he says, I just wanted to apologize.

You have nothing to be sorry for, I say.

I didn't know, he starts, and I cut him off.

You're right, I say. You didn't. Water under the bridge.

So it's just sitting there, says Omar.

Waiting for a current, I say.

Truce? says Omar.

We shake on it.

29.

I watch Mitsuko crack an egg with her palm in the kitchen. I think it's a fluke, but then she does it again.

Wait, I say. Wait!

What, says Mitsuko.

How did you do that?

Do what?

Mitsuko gives me this look like she's entirely exasperated. But then she does it again, executing the cleanest of breaks.

30.

A few days before the reception, I get a call from Omar.

He says, What the hell do people wear to these things?

Suits, I say, but this isn't really a wedding.

That's what I keep hearing.

It's the truth.

But if we don't treat it like one, says Omar, are they still married?

Of course, I say, although I don't know how sure I sound.

So I say it again.

Awesome, says Omar. Thanks.

I'm going now, he says.

But he lingers on the phone. And I don't hang up either.

Hey, he says, listen. I'm sorry.

We talked about this, I say.

But I *am,* says Omar. I didn't know.

Or I only sort of knew, he says. Ximena sort of told me.

145

But you didn't *know* know, I say. Not from me.

Right, says Omar. And now I do.

Then it's all right, I say.

Isn't that what they say? I add. That you've gotta try to find out for sure?

That only works for white people, says Omar.

We don't have to tell any of them, I say.

Right, says Omar. It'll be our secret.

31.

I text Mike in the evening, thinking he'll just be starting his day, after Mitsuko and I finish an elaborate collaboration: udon cooked in a hot pot, beside abura-age and kamaboko and spinach and two chicken legs.

When Mitsuko cracks an egg into the pot, tasting a spoonful, she actually doesn't grimace.

It's edible, she says.

Really?

Really.

Once we've brought everything below a simmer, I take some photos. All of them are blurry. But when I send them to Mike, he responds immediately.

Nice! he says.

Mike has never, not once, used an exclamation point in our correspondence. Ever. He's not one of those people.

I ask if he's all right.

The next message he sends takes a little longer to arrive.

I'll call soon, he says.

Everything will be OK, he says.

I promise, he says, and that's what I take to sleep with me.

Mike's never promised me anything. Only delivered or didn't. He always said that promises were only words, and words only meant what you made them.

It's late when I hear the front lock jiggling.

I slip on basketball shorts, some sandals, and dip into the living room. Mitsuko's sliding into a jacket and her pair of graying sneakers. She gives me a look when I cough in the hallway.

You can come, she says, but keep your mouth shut.

We walk from the apartment to the next street over, and then a few blocks more. The air is mild for Houston. A little too crisp for February. Plodding behind Mitsuko on the sidewalk, I wonder what we look like to anyone peeking from their windows.

Eventually, we stop in front of what looks like a church. Something something Methodist. I look at Mitsuko, and then at the signage, and she waves me over to the building's entrance, which is unlocked.

There's a light on by the pulpit, but otherwise the altar's empty. The aisles are cleared. The seats are clean. The church's windows are stained with various highlights from the Old Testament.

Once we've reached the head of the pulpit, Mitsuko takes to her knees.

I feel ridiculous standing behind her, so I settle into the space on her right.

We stay like that for a while. Mitsuko mutters gently, quietly, in Japanese. Her hands are clasped. Her head is bowed. At one point, I hear Mike's name, and then once again, but that's all I get.

It's been at least a decade since I've stepped in a church. I'd been baptized, as a teenager, because my mother had insisted. The pastor dunked me in the water and everything. Afterward, I came out soaking, feeling brand-new, like money, and I ate a wafer and drank some wine and never went back again.

I wonder how long Mitsuko's been doing this.

I wonder if it's even legal. If we're trespassing somehow.

But once Mitsuko's finished, she nods toward the choir bleachers at no one at all.

Then she stands beside me, steadying herself on my shoulder.

Hurry up, she says. We're leaving.

Back in the apartment, I pour us both a glass of water. Mitsuko doesn't thank me, but she takes it anyway.

In case you're wondering, she says, that's what it's come to. It's absurd.

I don't think it's absurd, I say.

It's absurd, says Mitsuko.

I watch her drink her water. That's all she has to say. So I take my glass back to the bedroom, draining the rest on the way.

32.

And then there's the morning of the reception.

I wake up to two texts.

The first one's a photo from Ximena, smiling with Juan in tow. She's written It's the big day!!!!!!! with about nineteen different emojis.

The next one's from Lydia, asking if I've heard from our father.

I'm already typing when my sister sends another one, clear out of the blue.

False alarm, she says. I'm handling it.

Have fun at prom, she says.

When Mitsuko sees me in my tie, she gasps, jumping from the couch.

Oh, she says. It's you.

Just me, I laugh.

Even after my protests, I end up leaving Mike's car at Ximena's place. I tell her it's

151

imposing to ride along with the newlyweds, but she says denying her invitation on the wedding day would be gravely rude.

But you're already married, I say.

Exactly, says Ximena. You're fucking with a real-life *wife*.

Her mother's standing by the door, on the phone. She raises a finger when I wave. And in the living room, Ximena's husband sits on the sofa, legs crossed, bouncing her son on his lap. The kid looks enraptured, and the man does, too, and they're both already dressed for the evening.

They look up at the sight of me.

Noah raises the kid's arms.

Ben, says Noah.

Noah, I say. Hey.

And congrats, I add.

Thanks, says Noah.

That means a lot, he says, especially from you. You know how much Xim thinks of you.

Only on paydays.

At least you're a good sport about it.

Noah rocks the kid on his lap, making ridiculous faces at him. Ximena told me that he's from Amsterdam, that he'd lived there most of his life. They met a few months after Noah arrived in Houston, after he'd rear-ended her at a gas station. He hadn't gotten insurance yet, and of course Ximena was pissed, but she gave him her number anyway. It only took a few weeks.

She's still getting dressed though, says Noah. The makeup thing. I tell her it all looks good, but she has to get it right, you know?

And she's supposed to be the one who doesn't care, I say.

Everyone cares, says Noah.

You think so?

Trust me, says Noah. My family? They're the least sentimental people on this planet. They all work in the woods, making babies with whoever's closest.

But I just got off the phone with my brother, says Noah. They'll be here today. The ones that are left. And I'm grateful.

Juan lets out a burp, shaking his hips, and Noah opens his mouth to catch it. The kid laughs a little bit, and then a lot, and then he's burping again.

But hey, says Noah, where's your better half? Is Mike coming?

He's out of town, I say. He sends his best wishes.

He'd better, says Noah, rubbing his nose against Juan's.

The kid can't stop laughing, like he's the luckiest boy in the world.

■ ■ ■ ■

Ximena's mother informs us that we're all going to make her late. Her ex-husband, Ximena's father, stands beside her, smoking a cigarette by the doorway in a cowboy hat. They're both wearing this formal red, nearly matching from top to bottom, and I wonder if they've planned this or if that's just what sharing a life with someone does to you.

But when Ximena finally pokes her head around the corner, she really does look beautiful in her dress. It's a purple gown. This lace-up thing.

She shouts at everyone from the bathroom, a volley of Spanish I can't understand.

A few days back, I'd asked Ximena if she was worried. We were smoking at lunch, which Ximena never does.

Noah's a good dude, but what if it doesn't work out? I asked. What if you don't know?

Nobody ever knows if it'll work, said Ximena. That's why you do this shit. To find out.

Once, I asked Mike about his parents' wedding, and he didn't know much about it.

154

He told me they'd had it in a living room. Mike's father shouldn't have even been the groom, but the story behind that was messy, too.

Messy how, I asked.

Who fucking knows, said Mike. I can't exactly ask now.

My folks got married in a living room, too. But they didn't have a grand reason. They were young and fucking broke and they thought it was a good idea. That's it.

When I told Mike about that, he just shook his head at me.

That's the thing, said Mike. Most ideas are good at the time.

We don't find out that they've gone wrong until they actually do, said Mike.

The wedding reception is a wedding reception.

Ximena and Noah kiss.

Ximena and Noah smile.

Ximena and Noah take a fuck-ton of pictures for IG.

We're on the taquería's patio, a wooden deck laced in Christmas lights, and the staff stands around with their cell phones, recording the whole thing. Three old men and a kid strum a warbling "Amor Eterno." You'd think the arrangement wouldn't work, but it does. When the youngest one opens his mouth to sing, it's almost shocking how beautiful it is. We all cry.

After the performance, and a couple of first dances, the reception devolves into people talking to the folks they already know.

I know Ximena and Noah, who are otherwise occupied.

And that's how Omar and I end up beside each other.

I don't think either one of us means to. His coat is frumpled. And also a half size too small. But it's fitting, still, like I couldn't have imagined him in anything else.

Why are you even here again, I ask.

Friend of a family friend, says Omar. Friend of a friend of the family. Steward of the bride.

Well, I say, at least no one died.

There's still time, says Omar.

True. But they'd have to make it quick.

Maybe they could feel too much, says Omar.

A sweet death, I say.

Yeah. That might work.

Before we can veer the conversation anywhere more sensible, my phone starts buzzing.

I nod at Omar, touch him on the shoulder.

Hello, son, says my father.

Whoa, I say. What? What's wrong?

It's nothing, says my father. Or just one thing. A tiny thing. I'm having a little trouble breathing.

I ask where he is, what he's doing. I'm already trashing my plate.

I'm at the house, he says. Sitting down. I read something about squeezing concrete things whenever this happens, so that's what I'm doing.

You're having a panic attack, I say.

If you say so.

I tell my father I'm on the way. He says that isn't necessary. I give him twenty minutes, tops, and then I hang up.

That's when I remember that I have no speed, no wheels.

Ximena's sitting on Noah's lap. They're already drunk. Already smiling too wide. Ximena's mother is holding the kid, sharing a drink with her ex-husband, and together they look like a family, or the closest thing to a family that any of us gets.

Out of nowhere, Omar asks if everything's all right, and I give him a look. I tell him what's happening. I tell him it'll be fine, I'll get an Uber. But then he's already walking toward his table, grabbing his keys, telling me to follow him outside.

We glide across the freeway like bats. Traffic is light.

Omar doesn't play any music while we drive, which I appreciate.

He doesn't ask questions that aren't navigational, which I also appreciate.

When we pull through my father's neighborhood, to my old house, I tell him I'll figure out a ride back to my place.

You're sure? says Omar.

One hundred and ninety-nine percent, I say.

Eighty-five would be more believable, says Omar.

But he doesn't argue with me. He rolls up the window and waves me away.

My father sits on the carpet. He's choking down a bottle of water.

I told you not to come, he says.

When have your kids ever done as you've asked, I say.

Figures. And if I'd told you it was urgent, I'd still be here by myself.

Probably, I say. Can I have a sip?

My father says he doesn't know where my

mouth's been, but he passes the bottle anyway.

The house looks dainty, and unperturbed, which is infinitely more terrifying than if it had been trashed.

I'm seeing a man about it, says my father. This whole thing.

You too?

You've always thought you were funny, says my father. I mean a shrink. He's mostly good, I guess, and the insurance covers everything. He says to focus on solid objects. Things you can touch in the room.

That makes sense.

Of course it makes sense. I'm fucking paying for it.

But does it always work? I ask.

Ask me in an hour, says my father.

The two of us sit with our legs kicked out. We haven't done anything like that since I was a child. Every few seconds, my father wiggles his toes, and they waggle in intervals, like a fountain.

After not very much time at all, there's a knock on the door.

Shift's over, says Lydia, to me, holding a greasy sack of food. You can go back to prom now.

Prom's over, I say.

Then try the after-party, says Lydia. Unless you weren't invited.

Our father lights up at the sight of her. My sister kneels across from him.

They unwrap their cheeseburgers on the coffee table, spilling all the fries.

I open the ride-share app once I'm out on the sidewalk. The block's quiet in that way suburban neighborhoods get.

Then, I have a thought.

I make another call instead.

It isn't five minutes later before Omar pulls around. A Whataburger sack sits on the passenger seat.

I got hungry, he says, through a mouthful of sandwich.

He takes the long way into the city. We never pull off Westheimer. Omar just cruises beside the highway, cutting through back alleys and suburbs. When we emerge from the other side, it's already midnight, on a weekday, which means the streets are mostly empty, except for the people waiting for buses and all the folks with nowhere to go.

Omar's a steady driver. There's no jolt when we hit our stoplights. He just slides into them, until we ease our way out.

Eventually, finally, soon enough, I am home.

I owe you one, I say.

You really don't, says Omar.

I ask about Ahmad, and Omar says he's with their parents.

Just for the night, says Omar. He didn't want to go. But I wasn't bringing him to Ximena's thing to act out.

You probably could've, I say.

Definitely not, says Omar.

Definitely not, I agree.

Omar's car is tiny, but not in an obnoxious way. It fits the two of us snugly. The interior doesn't smell like much of anything at all.

I'm not the most experienced man in the world, but a beat passes when I know that something should happen.

I also know that if I let it pass, then I can leave, and nothing will have happened.

And nothing will have gone wrong.

And we could both just move on.

So the moment passes.

We sit looking out the window.

A raccoon darts across the road.

Okay, I say, and then I set my hand on Omar's thigh.

His leg stiffens, immediately, and it doesn't relax. His pants won't unzip, until he finally maneuvers the seat belt — and he's hard when I grab his cock, jerking him off with one hand and squeezing his chest with the other, and then we are kissing, and then he comes. It happens in spurts, and he jolts, rocking the seat. Looking entirely bewildered.

And then he looks at me. Like something has opened that he hadn't intended. I tell Omar it's fine, that I really have to leave, but he reaches for me, and of course I am hard.

Omar unbuckles my seat belt, collapsing a little onto my lap.

Wait, I say, we can't do that.

What? says Omar.

I need a condom. We need condoms.

It's fine.

No. I'm poz.

Omar looks me in the eyes.

That's why, I say. So we can't. I'm sorry. We just can't.

Okay, says Omar.

Then he says, I get it.

I'm sorry.

Don't be, says Omar. But you're on medication?

Of course I'm on fucking medication.

Good. Then hold on a second.

He unbuttons my shirt, drops his slacks, and slips me between the crease of him. Just enough to create some friction. And then we're rocking, at his pace, and it can't be comfortable for Omar, and there's hardly enough room for our rhythm. But I tell him I'm almost there, does he want to shift his weight so I don't ruin his suit. And Omar declines, he says that it's fine, he'll survive, just keep going, so I do, until I don't, and then we're both moaning, and then we're done.

Afterward we're just two guys in a car, performing an impossible yoga.

Despite everything, I smile at Omar, because I can't do anything else.

Omar smiles back.

We clean up with the wrappers from the food he'd been eating.

I tell him I'm leaving, right now, for real, and Omar says goodbye, good night, for real.

I watch him drive away.

And now I'm at my door.

And now I'm in my living room.

I don't see Mitsuko, she isn't in the kitchen, and I chalk that up to luck. But then, as if on cue, I hear wheezes coming from my bedroom.

Mitsuko's on my mattress. Gasping. Wiping her face on the sheets.

Shit, I say, fuck. What is it?

Nothing, says Mitsuko.

What's wrong?

Nothing.

Then she whispers something in Japanese, under her breath. And she's crying again. Slapping at both of her cheeks.

I reach out to touch Mitsuko's shoulder, and she immediately jerks away. But then she grabs my hand, squeezing it.

It's fine, she says. It doesn't matter.

We should both get some sleep, she says.

And since it isn't a suggestion as much as a demand, I nod along. I tell her I'll be around if she needs me.

Mitsuko purses her lips, standing up to lay on the sofa, but I'm not entirely sure that she hears me.

When I check my phone, there's a text from Omar, some emojis.

There's a text from Lydia just saying hi, everything's okay.

And then there are texts from Mike.

But there's also a voice mail, which is something Mike never leaves, and I'm sitting on the bed when I open it.

His voice is calm. I can actually picture him speaking.

He says, We're cremating him tomorrow.

He says, My father, I mean. He's dead.

And after that, says Mike, I'm headed back to Houston.

Mike says he'd appreciate it if I could pick him up from the airport. That would really mean a lot.

MIKE

My fam's last apartment was the largest. Once we'd made it to the States we bounced from Alief to the South Side to the West Loop, settling wherever Eiju could keep a job, and this new spot off Bellaire was way way way way way over budget. We weren't skipping meals or anything but my folks were always strapped. Neither of their families in Japan were helping us. As far as they were concerned, we'd left. We had to figure shit out on our own.

The new complex had us parking under these busted-ass streetlights. You'd push a buzzer to open the gate but the gate just wouldn't budge so the Filipinos smoking by the basketball court would drag it open for whatever quarters you kept in your car. Ma told Eiju that something had to change. Had to be him, or our surroundings. I'm realizing all of this later. You don't see any of that shit when you're a kid; you don't have the context to flesh it all out.

I hadn't started expanding yet, eating the entire world, but once my clothes stopped fitting Ma just stuffed me into Eiju's. They were the fits he'd brought from Osaka. All baseball jerseys and tank tops and mesh shorts, and Eiju never thought he'd need them again but Ma wouldn't let him trash anything and here they were, eleven years later, halfway across the world, and every now and then I'd catch a blip of myself in the mirror, thinking that this is what my father must've looked like as a kid.

That summer in Bellaire, Ma and I lazed around the new spot. Eiju didn't want her out in the world. That shit had less to do with tradition than with his very particular vanity — but Ma entertained it anyway. At least at first. Less out of allegiance to her man, I think, than something else entirely.

The place was big but our pipes stank. Our carpet stank. The tap water stank. Eventually cash got even tighter than it already was. Eiju's shouting turned physical, shoving and pushing and squeezing, and Ma started planning her escape, but we spent that season revolving around our living room.

I picked up cardboard boxes left over from the last move and set them back down. Ma watched soaps on the television — *Days of Our Lives, The Young and the Restless;* Ma swore that shit was bad for me but I'd still post up on the sofa beside her. She'd mouth phrases in Japanese — the Tokyo Japanese she'd grown up with — and ask me to spit them back at her. When Eiju overheard, he'd ask Ma, in Kansai dialect, why I wasn't speaking fucking English.

Some days, Ma and I kicked our bare feet under the kitchen table. That was our thing. I was still twelve. I'd touch my heel with her heel and her toes with my toes. We'd keep them there until one of us pulled away but the one who gave up was always me. Ma could stay stone-faced through anything. Which was a sign, I think. Even then.

But again: hindsight, 20/20.

Eiju lost his gig that fall. He'd been prepping at this Chinese restaurant on Dashwood. Some strip mall enclave. He blamed his fate on the Mexicans, who cooked longer hours for less pay, and Eiju joined the tiny constellation Ma and I had con-

171

structed — but our orbit couldn't support him. He threw everything off.

Whenever we sat at the table, he'd ask why we were wasting time.

Whenever we flipped on the television, he'd flip it right back off.

Then he'd drink up what little we saved. Had Ma counting coins at the end of the month. One night, I knelt beside her, sorting dimes into piles, sprawled on the carpet, and when I found a quarter lodged in the sofa, my mother actually collapsed in tears. She straight-up wouldn't stop shaking. Eiju had no idea. He was still snoring from yesterday's binge.

Eventually Ma finessed a situation selling discounted jewelry by the Galleria. You rarely found anyone speaking fluent Japanese in Houston. The manager was a Hawaiian transplant, an older Black dude, and he hired Ma on the spot, and eventually Eiju found another job bartending for white people around West U and their incomes were enough to keep us mostly afloat. But we didn't know all that would happen.

So every glare and shove and yell between my parents felt irreparable. Intolerable. Like the craziest shit that'd ever occurred. And one night, after an argument that sent Eiju flying right out of the house, I asked Ma why we didn't just move back to Setagaya, as if everything would've been better if we simply went back home.

She looked at me for a long time. Her makeup was smeared. Her cheeks were patchy.

Then she said, That isn't your home.

Ma said, We're here now. This is your home.

She didn't sound too sure about it, even then. Maybe she hadn't quite convinced herself. And, of course, about a decade later, a while after Eiju split for good, she'd pack all her shit and fly to Tokyo and my mother would not come back.

But before that — our apartment with the gates.

Roaches on the carpet.

Our feet under the table, grazing in the heat.

Ma would set her lips on my earlobe, whispering all sorts of shit in Japanese, enunciating in the most ridiculous tones, until I fell out of the chair from laughter, only having picked up like half of it, and it was only later on that I'd think about what she was actually saying, that it was all just

173

the same thing, frantic and unending: *I love you, I love you, I love you, I love you, I love you, I love you, I love you!*

After a week in Osaka, I came up with something like a routine: I'd make it out of the apartment around eight in the evening, to prep Eiju's bar. It sat a few minutes from his busted walk-up in Tennoji, beside a bakery and a tattered bookstore and another walk-up and two parking lots and like sixteen love hotels. The streets were always quiet except for the other third-shift folks running last-minute errands before work. You didn't have to walk too far from the nearest station to reach us, but it wasn't like we ever actually opened before ten and most guests stayed well past midnight either way.

I spent hours mopping and scrubbing and wiping. Or at least I'd start to, until Eiju popped in. He'd put me on the broom until it clicked in his head that I could actually help him, that this was my area of fucking expertise, and then he stopped showing up to the bar until he absolutely had to.

This was probably the only reason he didn't send me back to fucking Houston.

Or at least before he finally got sicker.

But then the fucker didn't have a choice.

■ ■ ■ ■

When I first showed up in Osaka, Eiju asked how I planned to spend my time. I'd just dropped my shit on the wood floor of his apartment, this ugly one-bedroom thing. The luggage made this cracking sound. I asked him to repeat the question.

You heard me, he said, in English this time. Your ears aren't broken yet.

You're not making any fucking *sense,* I said.

Fucking, said Eiju. So you're grown now.

I flew here for *you.* I came down here for *you.*

Which is fine. But you need a job. And I need extra hands.

You want me to *work* for you? I said.

I'm here to spend *time* with you, I said. Before you fucking *die.*

Sure, said Eiju, and we'll spend more time together if you make yourself useful.

He told me about the bar. About the money he'd made off it and the blood he'd thrown into it. Eiju called it his baby, the one thing he had left — which, by itself, had me curling my fucking toes — and when I asked him for its name, my father said it, and I blinked.

175

No, I said. The bar's name.

You heard me, said Eiju. Mitsuko.

I made a fist and then I unmade it and I watched Eiju watch me do that. I wiped my eye sockets with my palms.

But I also took stock of the liquor. I chopped the daikon and rinsed the rice. Eiju didn't serve many meals — the main thing was booze — but his regulars made requests, and he was a big fucking baby about turning them down.

I didn't ask Eiju what made him so amiable with his patrons or what those motherfuckers had that his family didn't.

I didn't put up a fight.

At the end of the day, he was terminal. Pancreatic cancer. That was his diagnosis. Playing along was the absolute fucking least I could do.

The bar's stairs were busted as fuck. So I usually heard Eiju as he scaled his way up the railing. Whenever he opened the door, he wore this big-ass smile on his face. The sounds of Osaka seeped into the cracks, disappearing altogether when the lock clattered behind him.

Gonna be a good night, he said, tossing his jacket.

I'd catch a sleeve before it hit the ground and stash it under the counter. Eiju'd start rearranging bottles behind me.

The entire bar was about the size of my living room in Texas. We kept six stools across one counter and the place usually found itself fucking packed. Eiju's clientele came from all over the neighborhood: businessmen on benders, and hostesses on their breaks, and college types, and taxi drivers, and singles wasting the witching hours.

They all knew Eiju and his bar.

But none of them knew he was dying.

I'd ask if he'd taken his meds in the morning, and Eiju would say, What meds, and I'd say, Fuck, and Eiju just waved that off.

Shut up, he said. Didn't you come here to relax? Stress'll make you even fatter.

But later on, I'd find my father's prescriptions in that jacket. I'd count them out on the bar top. He was always up-to-date.

One night, early on, we were cleaning the bar side by side. Mondays were pretty slow but that didn't shift our routine. So we swept and we wiped and we dusted and we shined and Eiju whistled the whole time, or he'd play D'Angelo or Sade or Toni Braxton or the Isley Brothers or whatever the fuck else he'd been feeling for that day.

Eventually he asked if I'd prepped the sandwiches. I told him they were done.

And the limes? said Eiju. The potatoes? The batter?

Finished, I said. Oil's out and everything.

Good. What about the cheese?

What cheese?

We're frying cheese tonight.

You're fucking with me, I said.

I am most certainly not fucking with you, said Eiju. It'll be tonight's American special. We're celebrating our American guest.

Then he started laughing, a rolling thing that blanketed the bar.

The laugh morphed into a cough.

The cough sloped into a hack.

Eiju started choking.

I've never been the guy to hop a bar top but I did that anyway.

When he finally settled down, I sat by his side, rubbing at his back. Eiju winced, and I told him to breathe easy, to inhale.

But then, out of nowhere, the coughing stopped. And his grimace led to tears. And the tears slipped into a laugh.

Eiju started laughing again.

He pointed at my face.

You should've seen yourself, he said, still laughing. Holy shit!

So concerned! he said. Where the hell's my actual son!

Eiju stood half a foot shorter than me. Already looking thinner than the day I'd flown in.

He treated everything like a joke but the punchline was that he'd reached stage four.

No surprise sat waiting in the wings.

I knew what to expect.

I knew how this would end.

My first morning in Japan, I asked Eiju if he knew he was dying. Did he truly, functionally, see that? Did he understand? Did he know the stakes?

He stood across from me in pajama pants, yawning, tugging at the drawstrings. His breath smelled like cigarettes.

Of course, he said.

But so are you, he said. So is everyone else.

Think of it as a race, he said. I'm winning by a mile.

That's bullshit, I said. You're bullshit.

Maybe, said Eiju.

I would've called Ben when I landed at Itami, but my phone died. And then I missed the first rail into the city so I had to grab another ticket. And I was so worried about blowing that train, too, that I didn't touch my charger, didn't look away from the clock, and I just plopped down by this German family standing on the platform, arguing between themselves, while a Korean couple stood beside them, and this white lady cried into her hands and out of nowhere a pretty Black woman zoomed by us with this rolling suitcase, like, she was walking sprint-fast, in heels and a blue dress, and I was still wondering how that was even possible when I barely caught the train and I made it to Shin-Osaka station, but then, like, two minutes later I missed the next line to Namba, and then I caught a line headed the exact opposite way, toward Kyoto, and then back down toward Tennoji, which is when rush hour hit, and about thirty minutes later I got off on the wrong stop, again, but I was less than a mile from Eiju's apartment, the man I hadn't seen in a decade, the dying one, and I'd been traveling for over twenty-four hours, so I was spent, out of my fucking mind, and I wasn't thinking about much else by then, or anything at all, really — but that was a mistake, the whole fucking thing was a mistake, I'd left Ben with Ma, and I'd left Ma in the middle of nowhere, and I hadn't called my boyfriend at home, and home was the only place I wanted to be, even if, technically, I was already there, I had already made it, I was finally back home.

We met at this party. I'd already seen him on an app. And I walked right up to him, squeezing his shoulder, because Ben had exactly nothing to drink and of course I'd had way too much.

He'd been laughing in his profile pic. It hadn't look forced.

And now, here he was. IRL. In a flannel and khakis.

When I asked who he'd come to the party with, Ben nodded vaguely at the crowd.

The mob carried you over?

No, he said. Just one mobster.

Well, I said, are you fucking this particular punk?

And that's when he finally looked at me.

Ben made a face, one I would learn the mechanics of in the future. I'd recognize what brought it on and how long it lasted. I'd figure out how to defuse it. Each of its nooks and crannies.

But at first, I didn't know shit.

So I just tilted my beer, cheersing him.

I'm a little fucked up, I said.

Don't worry about it, said Ben, raising his water.

My day off and all.

Ah. Go figure.

And our conversation should've ended there.

I should've drifted back toward the kitchen, and we should've gone on with our lives, however the fuck they would've unspooled.

But then, Ben said, Does that mean you don't get many?

Many what, I said.

Days off.

Let's just say I make them count.

Ben considered me like he was solving some sort of equation.

My friend is the host's cousin, he said. I wasn't doing shit tonight, so she dragged me along.

Well, I said, as far as drags go, you look just fine.

You'd be surprised, said Ben.

Or maybe you wouldn't, he said, more to himself than to me, and he looked back at the crowd, but before I could jump on that, Ximena waved from around the corner.

She winked at me, smiling. Glowing in a skirt and this letterman jacket.

Ben made another new face.

Looks like we've got mutuals, I said.

Just a friend of a friend, I said.

An ex, I added.

But you got Ximena in the divorce, said Ben.

I think she dabbles between the two of us.

Kanpai, said Ben, clinking my bottle with his cup, before he slipped around my shoulder, into the living room, and right the fuck out of my life.

That night I drove home with another guy. I don't remember much about him, but he was definitely white. He told me I was his first, and I said, First what, and he said, You know, except I genuinely did not. Sometimes, you forget how people are. And then he reminded me. But before this whiteboy fucked up the rest of my evening, I put my mouth on his mouth, and my palms on his ass, and he jammed his knuckles in my khakis, and the two of us were off.

We fucked. It sucked. He came once, and then once again, and I jerked off on his stomach until I decided nothing was happening.

When I woke up the next morning, he was still knocked out on the mattress. I slipped into his kitchen thinking I'd fix us some omelettes. Scramble some eggs. Maybe he kept scallions. Peaches. Fuck. You never know, sometimes folks surprise you.

But this guy didn't. He was predictable. All I found in his fridge was a tub of protein and half a Hershey's bar stuck in the wrapper.

Back at my place, off West Alabama, the kids next door played tag on the driveway. They were chasing this cat and the cat was letting them. They'd named him Bruno, but also Gabriel, Victor Hugo, and Señor Gato. When their father, a heavy dude, came outside for a smoke, he called the cat over. It sat on its ass while he rubbed its belly. Once the cat looked my way, so did everyone else.

I showered and got my shit ready for work: the apron and the T-shirt and the jeans. I held a part-time gig at one restaurant and a part-time gig at a coffee bar. On weekends, I played cashier at the grocery store. None of it was bearable. But the money wasn't atrocious. That shit gave me something to do.

Afterward, still soaked, I sat my ass on the sofa. Checked my phone, opened the app. Scrolled to Ben's profile.

But it was gone. I'd starred it and everything.

I closed the thing and opened it up again. The only thing left was a gap in its place. Not even a digital memory.

My first morning in Osaka, Eiju didn't even speak to me. I spent one hundred and twenty-two minutes looking for his shitty little apartment by the train station. Once I'd passed the same fucking alley a fourth time, this lady smoking beside a Family-Mart waved me down from the corner, and later, I figured out that she owned a bookshop by the complex and she'd known Eiju for years. Sometimes, she brought him eggs from the market behind their building.

But that day, she was just some lady.

She wore this big-ass scowl.

You look lost, she said, in Japanese.

What? I said.

You look lost, she said, again, a little slower.

Oh, I said. I feel lost.

When I pulled out Eiju's address, her features softened. She pointed above us.

You're kidding, I said, and the lady laughed.

You've already made it, she said.

But you're still lost, she said.

■ ■ ■ ■

And then, like some Netflix Original shit, while I stood warming my hands by the steps, I watched Eiju lock his door through the railing, rooting around in a messenger bag, fiddling with his key chain, peering at the sky over my head.

For a long fucking time I had this dream where I'd spot the man and he wouldn't recognize me but I never thought *I* wouldn't recognize *him.* That's just a thing that would not have happened.

It started once he split from our apartment in Bellaire.

I dreamt about my father back when I was a kid, snuggled beside Ma, when I couldn't sleep by myself for the first year after he left.

I dreamt about my father while I slept beside who knows how many fuckers.

I dreamt about my father in my own bed, hanging off the mattress, snoring beside Ben.

I dreamt about him the night I left Houston.

I dreamt about him on the plane ride over.

And now, here he was.

Here.

186

Here here.

Here here *here*.

Right there. In front of my dumb fucking face.

Solid as the ground below me. And I recognized him.

I watched Eiju pat his pockets for keys.

I watched him tug on his hoodie.

I watched him reconsider.

He gave this little wince. But that was it, nothing else.

I leaned on the stairs. Waited for him to crash into me.

My father nodded my way as he passed.

Then he walked a little farther, nearly turning the corner.

And then I watched him shake his head.

Flip right around.

There wasn't any anger on his face. Just the barest confusion.

Then, recognition.

And *then* he was pissed.

I thought he'd hug me or grab my arm or punch me in the face, but none of that happened.

My father's first words to me in sixteen

years, in his loud Kansai dialect, were: What the fuck?

Eiju's bar didn't get its first customers until around ten. That's when the streets were at their apex. A few hours before the trains finally stopped for the night. The temperature dropped to a chill and you couldn't see your breath but I'd blow on the windows anyway, tracing my name or a plane or stick figures fucking until Eiju finally told me to cut that shit out.

One night, we ran through that very same routine. I was mopping the tile. Eiju wiped at the counter.

You're not a fucking child, he said.

I'm *your* fucking child, I said.

Hana and Mieko usually arrived first. They were coworkers at some advertising joint. They'd sit side by side, ordering two rounds of sake apiece, showing up straight from the office, where they worked into the evening, throwing faded jean jackets over their blouses, and whenever they stepped through the bar's sliding door, without fail, they laughed and laughed and laughed.

My first night at Mitsuko's, Hana asked me, straight off, if I was my father's son.

Eiju shined some glasses beside me. His

face said, Say no.

Everyone asks me that, I said. Think of me as a nephew.

Shit, said Mieko. Eiju's got plenty of those.

All nephews and no sons, said Hana. Like some sort of gigolo.

But you're not from here, she added, turning back to me.

It's that obvious?

No offense, said Hana.

It's fine, I said.

Your Japanese is blocky, said Mieko. Like you learned it from a book.

But good for a foreigner, said Hana.

Should be better than good, said Eiju, pouring the women another round.

No excuse, he said.

There are *plenty* of excuses, said Hana. I dated an *American* once.

Shit, said Mieko. You did.

He was the worst, said Hana.

Holy *shit,* said Mieko. The *worst.*

He thought he knew the way things worked here, but he didn't. Not really. And I wanted to say, it's okay! You don't have to pretend! I appreciate it, but don't.

You couldn't take him *anywhere,* said Mieko.

He'd cause these scenes, said Hana. He had to know *everything.* And he *needed* you

189

to *know* that he knew everything.

Both women ducked their heads for a moment, reminiscing.

I glanced at Eiju, who'd crossed his arms.

So why'd you stay, he said. If this man was so terrible?

Hana made a face. Mieko jabbed her with an elbow. Eiju poured them both another glass, nodding at me to replace the bottle.

After a while Mieko said, I know why.

He was good at *that,* she said.

What, said Eiju.

You know, said Mieko, raising her palms a respectable distance.

Anyways, said Hana, in the end it couldn't work. He had to go.

All I'm saying is that you shouldn't break your back over it, said Hana, looking at me. Don't stress out. Your uncle's friends don't bite.

You're not my friends, said Eiju.

Bullshit, said Mieko. I don't know what you'd do without us.

He'd just sit in here by himself, said Hana. Wiping those glasses like a turtle.

He wouldn't survive, said Mieko. He'd just fall over and die.

They both pantomimed the action, the collapsing, and the thud, and Eiju just laughed and laughed.

■ ■ ■ ■

This was the same man who, a decade ago, threw our apartment's landline against the wall when Ma got a call from another man.

The man was her boss. He was calling about her schedule at the jeweler's.

Eiju asked why he had our apartment number, why my mother was fucking around.

And Ma said that if only he could see himself, then he wouldn't have to ask.

Hana and Mieko were usually followed by a trio of salarymen: Takeshi, Hiro, and Sana. Three blind fucking mice. We were all around the same age. They'd stumble into the bar, already wasted, though sometimes it was just Hiro who was fucked up, and other nights it was one of the others. They kept some sort of running system about who got the drunkest each night, I could never figure it out, and they were jovial, always asking if I could fix one of them a sandwich. When I told them bread wasn't on the menu, they told me 7-Eleven was right up the road. When I told them that I didn't fucking do that, that I wasn't their fucking maid, Hiro or Takeshi or Sana called bullshit, clapping, and then they'd pivot their tone, saying, Sorry, and Please, pursing their lips and fluttering their eyes and pawing my elbow, creating a big fucking production.

I'd glance at Eiju and he'd just shrug, like, You asked to be here.

Eventually Hiro told Eiju, You should've hired this fucker earlier.

He's just moonlighting, said Eiju. Apprenticing.

Like a child, said Takeshi.

A child star, said Hiro.

Children mean work, said Eiju. Sana would know.

Sana groaned behind his bottle. His two friends slapped his back.

Twins, said Takeshi, when he saw my face.

Finally decides he's gonna leave his girl and then she pops out two sons, said Hiro.

We decided *together*, said Sana. Nobody popped out *anything*.

You're drunk, said Eiju.

Two boys, said Sana. When they grow up they'll be just like Mike.

They'll make *sandwiches*, said Sana, from *Texas*.

No shit, said Hiro. Must be nice for Mike's girl to have a cook around.

The three guys looked my way, fingers laced across the banister. They'd been drinking, but they weren't drunk enough to miss a response.

When I finally opened my mouth, Eiju started coughing.

He leaned over the banister. Grabbed at the counter.

The four of us watched him. The guys at the bar looked my way, concerned.

When Eiju recovered, wheezing, wiping at his mouth, I handed him a napkin, and he waved it away.

Hiro and Sana played with their thumbs.

Then Takeshi let out a laugh.

Shit! he said.

We thought you were done for! yelled Sana.

I felt a chill. But all Eiju did was grin.

Nope, he said.

If that happened, said Eiju, who else in this stupid city would babysit you?

After the guys took off, Eiju started closing up shop. He wouldn't meet my eyes. For once, he looked like the old man that he was.

It isn't like Takeshi was lying, I said.

About what, said Eiju.

I *don't* have a girlfriend. Won't ever have one.

I *am* gay, I said.

Eiju kept scrubbing the counter. Threw his whole back into it. Looked like he'd all but toss his fucking shoulders out, but then he finally sat down, feeling around under his apron.

He pulled out a box of cigarettes.

You are fucking kidding me, I said.

Shut up, said Eiju. So you're a fag.

That's fine, he said. Whatever.

And you're just gonna kill yourself faster, I said. I guess that's your response?

It's nothing you haven't already done to me, said Eiju. My own son.

Didn't you call yourself childless? Isn't that what you just told your fucking customers?

And, at that, Eiju slammed his fist on the counter.

You little fuck, said Eiju, in English.

There it is, I said, in English. There's the man I remember.

You don't get to parachute over here and do this, he said. Not now. Not in this life. You don't get to do that.

But even just saying that took his breath away. Eiju started to sit, nearly missing the chair. When I jumped up to help him, he waved me away.

Fuck off, he said.

But I guided him toward a stool.

After a few days, I found a busted notebook by the apartment's toilet. Threads fell from the seams. Everything in it was written in English. My father had scribbled a bunch of lists, all of them in the tiniest handwriting. Grocery lists. Train routes. Practical shit. But then there were other things.

Like, a brief list of things Eiju didn't believe in: *socks, fate, predetermination, promises. Chili oil. Locked doors. Christmas cards. Christmas. Savings accounts. Birthday parties, gifts. Ultimatums. Last strikes. Luck.*

Most days, Kunihiko passed through the bar to help Eiju.

He was a little younger than me. Thick but not as thick. And his clothes were always two sizes too big, but all he did was smile. When we met, I was chopping vegetables in the nook behind the bar, skinning sweet potatoes and straining dashi, and Kunihiko wandered in the back, looking lost as shit. But it would be a while before I realized that's just how he was.

The first thing he said was that I looked just like my father.

If you say so, I said.

Really, said Kunihiko. It's the eyes!

He'd started working for Eiju after wandering into the bar one night. His job at some local bank had dumped him. Apparently he'd made an astronomical fuck-up with the wrong person's account. Something big enough that he didn't want to share it, big enough that his boss dropped him super quick, big enough to lead Kunihiko on a three-day bender. Eiju's bar was the only spot he actually remembered drifting into — he woke up drooling on the counter, with Eiju slapping him awake.

I was lucky, said Kunihiko. If Eiju hadn't hired me, who knows what the hell I'd be doing.

You'd be doing the same shit everyone does, I said. Something else.

Something else, said Kunihiko, laughing with his chest.

He was goofy. Always rocking his shoulders. Kunihiko showed up late every evening, forever fucking up everyone's orders, but our patrons treated the kid like a mascot, even when Eiju wasn't having it.

He barked at Kunihiko for juggling utensils.

He barked at Kunihiko for abandoning just-emptied beer mugs.

One time, Kunihiko's elbow brushed the edge of the bar, catapulting a stack of plates, scattering them across the wood, and Mieko clapped at the show from her corner by the door, and Hiro, that evening's drunk, let out a whoop, and Eiju grabbed the towel he kept wrapped around his waist, slapping it hard against the barstool, sending Kunihiko leaping into place. He told the kid those plates were coming out of his check.

I really don't think I can cover that, said Kunihiko.

Of course you can't fucking cover it, said Eiju. So we'll work through your tips, too.

Kunihiko bit his lip. He quivered, just a little bit. But at the sound of that, Hana slapped a five-hundred-yen coin on the counter, while Takeshi and Hiro reached in their pockets, extracting some grubby bills.

Give the kid a fucking break, said Hana.

Tough love breeds competence, said Eiju.

Bullshit, said Hiro.

A full gut of it, said Takeshi.

Fuck outta here with that, said Mieko.

But Kunihiko raised his hand, smiling.

It's really all right, he said, reaching through his own pockets.

He pulled out some hundred-yen coins of his own, adding them to the pile.

I totally understand, said Kunihiko, smiling, shrugging, emptying his pockets, and we all sort of pitied him. But we envied his devotion, too.

The thing is, if you knew my father, you'd know he wasn't really upset.

None of this was true anger.

These weren't the shouts that I'd heard in our apartment with Ma.

They weren't the hands he threw at me, asking why I was so soft.

They weren't the yells he'd given my mother once she'd started making more bank than him, once she began climbing the rungs leading out of his life.

What Eiju showed Kunihiko was endearment.

It looked a lot like love.

Ben popped up on the app again a few weeks after the party.

He wasn't there, and then he was. I hadn't exactly been searching.

When his face blipped on the grid, I was shelving hot sauce at the grocery store. The gig was easy money. Mostly, I unpacked crates of tomatoes, shepherding white folks through aisles of artisanal bread. No one could ever pronounce what they were looking for, and I'd guide them through the syllables — gram masala, coriander — but that day, some whitelady scanning the shelves took a peek at my phone.

He's cute, she said.

Excuse me?

Your boyfriend. In the picture?

I must've made a face, because the whitelady smiled a little too enthusiastically. She started stepping away, already pushing her shopping cart down the aisle. A little girl sat in the basket, juggling zucchini and kicking her legs. The kid made a face at me, scrunching her nose and biting her lip.

Not a boyfriend, I said. Just a boy.

Well, said this lady.

If it helps, she said, that's how they all start out.

And then, Boom, said the lady, opening a palm toward her daughter, flinging her fingers, which the little girl caught with glee.

Eventually, I messaged him.

Just couldn't help it.

I wrote: STILL SOBER?

Then I jammed my phone in my pocket.

After a minute or two, he didn't respond.

Fifteen minutes later, my inbox was still empty.

A few hours later, I told myself it didn't matter. If this guy reached back then he reached back. If he didn't then he didn't. So I chalked it up to fate, messaging five other guys across the grid.

Two of them hit me back immediately. One of them asked how big my dick was.

Immediately, unthinkingly, I typed, BIGGER THAN YOURS, and then I blocked him.

I kept yet another job at a deli by the rail-stop on Pease. Right on the edge of midtown. A twenty-minute drive from the Third Ward. This was months before the pop-up was even half of a thought, and Tony was still chopping veggies at this overpriced taquería on Shepherd. He was always bitching that he could make better food for a fraction of the cost, and one day I told him, on a whim, that we should go ahead and do that, and at first he'd waved me off, swearing we'd both found ourselves good situations, but eventually Tony changed his mind.

In the meantime, at the deli I was frying avocado spreads on flatbread, with olives and Gruyère and basil. And on that afternoon, I'd just taken this whiteboy's order when he slapped his sandwich back on the register.

It's the tomatoes, he said. They aren't *quartered*. That's how they should be.

You serious?

I'm serious enough to ask your boss about it, he said.

I was, incidentally, the manager on duty. More or less. The motherfucker who supervised me hardly ever came in. So I started to bring that up, but I felt a buzz in my pocket.

Let me go see if he's back there, I said, cheesing, dipping right the fuck out of there.

The buzz came from Ben.

He'd written: still sober

And that was it.

It wasn't much. Or even anything.

But he'd responded.

When the whiteguy out front called, clearing his throat, I let him simmer a bit before I came back. Once I passed him the sandwich again, he asked what someone had to do for decent service in Houston.

Move to Austin, I said.

Another of Eiju's regulars was this couple: Hayato and Natsue.

They'd roll up to the bar on bikes, leaning them against the staircase. Hayato was basketball-player tall — a weird fucking sight for a Japanese guy. Natsue kept her hair in this tiny bun. She'd slip just under the arch of his elbow whenever he held the

201

door. They'd order a beer apiece, with a bowl of rice on the side, while Natsue tugged on Eiju's ear from over the bar.

We've been coming around since the old man opened this hole, said Natsue.

We watched him take his first steps, said Hayato.

He's like our baby.

Our big fucking baby.

Everyone likes to think they discovered something, said Eiju.

We didn't find you, Eiju-kun, said Hayato. We only shepherded you along.

All you needed was some direction, said Natsue.

I wouldn't know shit about that, said Eiju.

And all three of them laughed.

One morning a few weeks after I'd landed, Kunihiko was washing glasses and I was drying them off. Once he'd finished, Eiju set a hand on his shoulder. He told the kid to try showing up on time for once, and Kunihiko grinned, bowing a little, slamming a shoulder into the doorframe on his way out.

After he'd left, Eiju and I locked up. The walk back to his apartment was short. It was just before five in the morning, and some stray lights flickered around us, but mostly nothing moved except for the cabs idling by. The sun hadn't risen yet. All we had was this dark sheen above us.

I asked Eiju if Kunihiko knew about the cancer.

Does he actually know you're dying, I said.

Have you fucking told any of these people, I said.

Eiju kept walking. Didn't even look my way.

After a while, he said, You're welcome to stay as long as you'd like.

That's not an answer, I said.

Eiju didn't say anything to that. He just kept walking.

Once we'd made it to his place, he left me on a futon in the living room. There was a light on in his bedroom. I waited for it to dim — but I couldn't. I was asleep before he even started snoring.

A day after Ben reached out, I messaged him back on the app.

What I sent was: SORRY TO HEAR THAT.

It felt like an eye for eye.

Later that night, I'd just made it back to my place from the grocery store, halfway up the steps, when the old Black lady next door called my name. She pointed at my cigarette, waving a hand across her nose.

Her name was Mary. She'd lived in the Third Ward her whole life. From the tail end of its best years, through the bulk of its decline. Her husband went to high school in the district a few blocks away, and she'd been a cheerleader, and he'd been a football player. They met at a school dance. Went to prom. Got hitched a year later like out of some fucking old-timey movie.

A few weeks after I'd leased the apartment, Mary told me her story over dinner. She'd invited me over. Cooked macaroni and yams. She and her guy sat across from me, watching me scarf that shit down, and I know everyone's got their problems but sitting next to each other they looked like they fit. Mary and Harold. Just snug. Like in this way that I hadn't ever fucking seen before.

When I told them it felt strange to eat while they didn't, Mary waved me off.

All that cheese is too much for our pressure, she said. When you get this old, all you can do is watch.

That's what my ma says, I said.

Smart woman, said Mary. Do your people live nearby?

Nah. She's back in Japan.

That's a long way from Houston.

Not too long.

And your father?

Fuck knows.

Mary's eyes flickered. Her husband yawned.

It's hard work to keep a man in one place, he said.

I stared at Harold. He blinked back at me.

Don't mind him, said Mary, boxing her husband on the shoulder.

Harold doesn't talk too much, she said. Unless he's got something stupid to say.

Sounds like a good policy, I said.

It is, said Harold. Gives you plenty of time to *listen.*

And it is *time* for you to listen, said Mary. Lord knows I've heard you out for long enough.

You ought to give people with *sense* the chance to speak, said Mary, winking at me.

I'd found the apartment online. The real estate agent was this whitechick in a sundress. Her agency was based in Katy, but they'd started snatching up property in East End, flipping shit over and brushing it off and tossing it back on the market. It was her second week on the job. She kept fiddling with her wedding ring. She told me the place may have looked like a dump, but the neighborhood was changing. This was the cheapest I'd ever rent around Wheeler again.

The apartment's walls were tattered. The fan looked busted. The floors were wood, but the wood looked discolored and chipped from room to room.

I said it was spacious for the price.

No kidding, said the Realtor.

She asked if I had a wife or kids, and I shook my head at all of it.

Then you can build the nest, she said.

This is a hell of a tree, I said.

It'll grow on you, said the Realtor. If I had this space to myself, I don't know what I'd do.

There's still time for you to grab it.

That'd be nice, said the Realtor, grinning.

But look, she said, trust me. Honestly. It's a deal. Might not look like one now, but this area's the next big thing.

Next big thing or not, I needed a place. I'd just finished a long, messy thing with another guy. It'd take too long to explain. But he'd become something like a roommate with benefits, and he'd actually gotten a new live-in boyfriend, this motherfucker who was always side-eyeing me, and I needed a new situation, so I signed a lease that afternoon and it turned out the newbie Realtor was right: that apartment really was the last deal the neighborhood gave.

Afterward, every spot on the block went to frat kids and professors. The neighborhood's palette changed overnight. The Third Ward was rewired.

My phone pinged just past midnight.

It was Ben. He was online.

don't worry about it, he wrote. i don't drink often

GOOD FOR YOU, I wrote. YOU'LL PROBABLY LIVE LONGER

if you say so

LET'S HOPE SO

i'll do that

And then we hit radio silence. We'd reached the stage where one of us needed to give the conversation a boost.

I'M MIKE, I wrote.

i know, wrote Benson.

?

you know Ximena?

I DO

she told me. we talked about that

SORRY, GO FIGURE

And then, more silence.

And then, on a whim, I wrote: YOU WANNA GRAB A BEER SOMETIME?

Another few minutes passed.

I counted the cracks on the ceiling.

Ten minutes later, Ben wrote:

ur very forward

IT'S WHERE I WAS HEADED ANYWAYS, I wrote. WHY WASTE TIME

To which Ben replied, immediately, i'm not really into hookups anymore

I wrote, THIS IS JUST BEER WE'RE TALKING ABOUT

And then, as if those were the magic words, Benson blipped offline.

The next morning, I had a message:

sounds good, he wrote. u know a place?

All of Eiju's patrons had a story. There was always some convoluted mishmash for how they ended up in the bar.

One night, Hana stumbled in after a breakup. She'd been distraught. On her way out, she ran into a stool, fucked up beyond reproach. And that's how she met Mieko, who was also drinking away the end of a relationship — but the difference was that she was celebrating. They came back into the bar and toasted each other. Afterward, the two were fucking inseparable.

One night, in the middle of June, Sana met

Takeshi at the bar. And then Takeshi met Hiro. And then Hiro met Sana. A few weeks later, they figured out that they all worked in the same building.

Natsue was a childhood friend of Eiju's — she'd known him since grade school. Knew him before he married my mother, before he'd even heard of Ma. After he'd told her they were getting hitched, Natsue told Eiju she was happy for his happiness but warned him that living in Tokyo wasn't for him, and neither was marriage. Not that he was hearing it. Eiju called Natsue jealous. He told her to fuck off, and it was the last conversation they'd have before Eiju came back to Japan thirteen years later — but Natsue was the first person he'd looked up when he landed; he spent that first night in Kansai on the sofa in her older brother's living room.

One night, I was shelving beer behind the register when Natsue asked what I had going on in my life.

Hayato sat next to her, sipping from his wife's glass. Eiju'd stepped out to the convenience store. Kunihiko and I held down the fort. Takeshi and Hiro laughed at some too-quiet joke, trying to rope Kunihiko into their conversation — and I realized that, for them, this scene was something like normal. For them, it must've felt like home.

I'm just passing through, I said.

We're all just passing through, said Hiro.

That's the gaaaaaaame of liiiiiiiiiiiife, said Takeshi.

Stop that, said Natsue.

And then to me, she said, You're here for Eiju-kun, aren't you?

I blinked at her.

I mean for support, said Natsue.

You could say that, I said. He's getting older.

He's not too old, said Natsue, but it's nice to see that he's got someone.

That's when a look passed between us. I wasn't entirely sure what'd been exchanged.

Hey, said Hayato, *you've* got someone.

And *I've* got someone, said Takeshi, grabbing at Kunihiko, who flinched.

Sure, I said, and I went right back to shelving.

But when I looked up again, Natsue was still staring.

Seriously, she said. It means something.

Wait until you're our age, she said. See who's still around.

■ ■ ■ ■

Eiju's doctor dropped by every couple of days. The first time I met him, it was too early in the morning. I heard this rapping on the door, and I opened it dazed, shirtless, not even thinking about it.

The man actually gasped.

Oh, he said. Sorry.

Wait, I said.

I'll come back, he said. Didn't mean to interrupt.

Get the fuck out of the way, said Eiju, pushing past me.

And put some fucking clothes on, he said. You're not in fucking Texas anymore.

The doctor, Ryutaro, used to be a regular at my father's bar. He'd been fighting depression for years. His wife and daughter died in a car accident.

A truck T-boned their taxi. They'd caught the cab during a train delay. Hours beforehand, Ryutaro had berated the two of them for showing up late to a hospital function.

In the days after the accident, my father kept Ryutaro company, and, eventually, the doctor cut down on the drinking. He returned to his practice. They welcomed him back. Ryutaro regained the roster of patients he'd built up pretty quickly, and he still visited Eiju's bar from time to time, but now he only drank water.

Once Eiju'd made the decision to give up cancer treatment, Ryutaro was the second person he told.

My mother was the first.

After they spoke outside, Eiju led Ryutaro back through the living room. The doctor took his blood pressure and his temperature and his pulse. I watched from the futon, in a tank top and Eiju's shorts. The heater blew warm air above us, and when Ryutaro brought up Eiju's medication, my father burped.

You know I'm done with all that, said Eiju.

I know, said Ryutaro, but I still have to ask. Are you seeing a difference in your daily pain?

Just the usual. Shortness of breath. Funniness in my gut.

The wheezing, I added, from the sofa.

Both men turned toward me.

He collapsed the other day, I said. At the bar.

I tripped, said Eiju.

Over nothing? I said.

Mind your business, boy, said Eiju.

Eiju-san, said Ryutaro, and it was the gruffest I'd heard anyone talk to my father since landing in Japan.

But then the doctor smiled.

That information gives us a sense of scale, he said.

Look, said Eiju, it's all the same at this point.

Not necessarily, said Ryutaro.

Bullshit.

It's all data. We take what we know, and —

Then you can fix me? said Eiju. Is that what you're saying? This will help you do that?

Well, said Ryutaro.

Then it's nothing, said Eiju, tugging his arm from the blood pressure cuff's sleeve.

Just like that, the checkup was over.

Eiju thanked Ryutaro, and Ryutaro waved him away. The old man shoved past me on his way to the bathroom, and when I heard him lock the door, I ran down the steps to chase down his doctor, and the woman living below us shouted something as I passed her.

But Ryutaro had only made it up the road. He fumbled with a pack of cigarettes.

Mike, he said, smiling.

I'm his son, I said.

213

Okay, said Ryutaro.

His biological son, I said.

Oh, said Ryutaro, smoking.

We stepped into an alley by the building, allowing the flow of traffic to pass us. The doctor told me to just call him Taro. He took a slow drag, waving his pack my way.

You have your father's ears, said Taro.

Most people say they're my mother's.

I've never had the pleasure, but I'm sure that she's lovely.

That's what people say until they actually meet her.

But, Mike, said Taro, you only get one mother.

Look, I said. How is Eiju actually doing? Really?

Taro exhaled smoke toward the road. We watched some girls skip rope by a shopfront. When they turned toward the man sitting on the ledge beside them, he worked his cheeks into a smile. It disappeared when they turned back around.

If you flew all the way here, said Taro, then you must have a general idea of where things stand.

He won't tell me much, I said.

Sure. Your father's a strong man.

But he's just a man.

He's only a man, said Taro. How long do

214

you plan on staying?

However long it takes, I said, surprising myself.

Good, said Taro, nodding. That's going to mean a lot to him.

We watched the dude by the storefront stand, clapping his hands. The girls in front of him protested, pouting. But they each grabbed one of his wrists, disappearing around the corner.

The first time Ben made it to my apartment, he looked around my yard, with its sloping trees, and its half-cracked sidewalks, and the Black people out and about, with the chopped and screwed mixtapes rattling everyone's car windows rolling by, and my other neighbors blasting cumbia from *their* windows, in competition, maybe, or some sort of fucking concert, some kind of impromptu fucking southwestern ensemble, and when Ben saw all of this, the first thing he did was laugh.

He watched my hands when I spoke. His posture mimicked mine. He'd stare at my mouth, reading my lips, like he was looking for the meaning underlying my words. Then he'd sit in silence, nodding along.

Whenever he actually disagreed with something, he'd just smile. Whenever he agreed, he'd nod once, vigorously.

He was stupefyingly shy.

He was the fucking worst to figure out.

But I wanted to figure him out.

Mary watched us from her porch. I waved. She waved back.

You know her? said Ben.

She's a friend, I said. She's my neighbor.

It'd taken three dates to get him back to my place. Ben lived in Katy with his father. He'd drive right back after we closed our tabs. I'd told him that the trip wasn't worth it, that I really didn't mind if he slept over, but Ben wasn't hearing that: he was a guy, I learned early on, who considered shit five times before he committed, before he made a move. And, even then, he was shaky.

We sat on my sofa. I made us both sencha. I slipped a little bourbon in mine, and when I waved the bottle his way, he winced.

So, I said, who are you?

I should be asking you that, said Ben. I clearly don't know.

How so?

I mean, you live in this neighborhood. The Third Ward.

Not what you expected.

I don't think anyone would've expected it.

Because I'm Asian, I said, and Ben smiled.

Because you aren't Black, he said.

So I'm not allowed to live here?

I didn't say that.

But, said Ben, this isn't a part of town that historically takes well to outsiders.

History changes, I said. It adapts.

In the best-case scenarios, said Ben. And this isn't a best-case country.

We sipped at our mugs. Benson took the silence to consider the living room. It was mostly bare, expect for the kitchen — I owned a TV and a rug and a table with a photo of Ma. I kept a tatami mat around the corner. There were a few candles, but I'd burnt down their wicks.

So what brought you here? said Ben.

I stopped fucking the guy I was fucking and I needed a place to live. This one was cheap.

Sounds thorough and well-thought-out.

I thought it was romantic.

I didn't say it wasn't.

The Third Ward's as nice a neighborhood as any, I said. But it's changing.

You say that like it's a bad thing, said Ben.

You think it's a good thing?

I think it's complicated.

The neighbors beside us turned their music a little louder. The chattering Spanish gelled into a ballad. Selena's croon settled over the neighborhood's cacophony, flattening all of that shit, swallowing every other sound entirely.

So what do you think is going to happen here, said Ben.

Are we still talking about the neighborhood?

That's up to you.

Then it's anybody's guess, I said, and I set a hand on his knee.

Ben watched my fingers. We both inhaled. And before I could take my hand back, he laced his hand over my knuckles. When I looked up, he'd started toward my face, so I let him kiss me, and then I was on my back. He slipped his hands under my shirt, squeezing, while mine slipped under his. When we were both topless, suddenly, he sat up to consider me.

This always happened. There was the person I was with my clothes on, and then the other guy. I never worried about my weight until I was just about to fuck someone, and then it hit me in the face, all of a sudden and out of nowhere. One time, I'd made it back to a guy's place, and in the middle of kissing the motherfucker he looked up and laughed. Another time, some guy grabbed my belly, squeezing my waist, until I put my hands on his shoulders and asked if we had a fucking problem.

But Benson just stared. He wasn't an athlete or anything, but we weren't the same.

We can hit the lights if you want, I said.

Why the hell would I do that, he said.

I'm just admiring you, he said, and for the first time, I think, I reconsidered him.

Ben straddled my waist, laying his body on mine, and then he just stayed there, grinding, and I wrapped my arms around him. I felt underneath his jeans, grabbing at his ass, and Benson slipped his hands inside my boxers, squeezing, and I settled under his grip. Eventually he worked a few fingers inside me, and I maneuvered to let him do that, with my legs on his shoulders, until I was looking right up at him.

I took longer than I would've liked. Hit my head on the sofa's shoulder.

When I reached for the zipper of his jeans, Ben blocked me with his palms.

You don't want to? I said.

I'm good, said Ben.

Sure. But I want to make you feel great.

I'm poz, Mike, said Ben.

He turned his face away when he said it. Ben's entire body stiffened, flattening against me. Wouldn't even meet my eyes.

Okay, I said.

I should've told you earlier. I'm sorry.

Don't be sorry.

I should've said something.

Maybe.

No, I should've.

Whatever. I get it. But listen. I want to make you feel good.

At that, Ben looked up. He met my eyes, with his chin on my stomach. The expression on his face looked a little like a grin, and a little like a smirk, and a little like he'd just been stumped.

And, the thing is, I really didn't care about his status. I didn't *not* care, but it just wasn't a thing that I could've possibly minded. This was just another thing about him.

What, I said.

Nothing, said Ben. You're just interesting.

It's nice of you to say so. With my cum on your palm.

And, at that, Ben looked at his hand. He ran his tongue across his wrist, sloping toward his fingertips.

There, he said. Gone.

Now I'll tell you what'd feel nice, he said.

At that, Ben laid down and maneuvered himself into the sofa's corner, pulling my elbow around him. We were, I think, in an impossible angle. My knees jutted from the cushion's edge. Ben lay pressed into the crevice. I didn't think it would work, there wasn't any way we'd fall asleep like that, but then I woke up the next morning with Ben snoring in my arms, and I realized I hadn't slept so comfortably in months.

So our days slipped into a familiar pattern: Ben took the 10 to his dad's place in the mornings. We'd meet at some bar in the evening, wherever we could spend less than fifteen bucks. He'd pay for his shit, and I'd pay for my shit, and we'd take the sloping drive up Scott Street toward Wheeler.

Ben wouldn't say much until we'd made it indoors. After that, we were on our backs, against the wall, loud as fuck.

I was already on PrEP, but we were good about condoms.

Ben always came last. I never knew why that was.

Afterward, we'd lay on the sofa or the wood or the mattress, a whole mess. He'd knock out first, or I'd knock out first, and when I jolted awake in the middle of the night, I'd find the blanket he'd settled over us, tucked just underneath our toes.

One night after I'd fucked him, Ben asked me to tell him a story.

Jesus, I said. That wasn't enough for you?

I'm serious, he said.

How about you go first.

I don't have any.

Everyone's got a fucking story.

I don't have any *good* ones, said Ben. And everyone doesn't want theirs told.

We were naked under this quilt. It'd belonged to my mother's mother. She'd knit the thing in Kanazawa, before her family moved east to Tokyo. Ben's feet slumped between mine, and the TV was on in the corner. But it was only white noise. A stack of commercials. All you could hear was our breathing.

Come on, I said, that's not what you tell the kids you work with.

Calm down, said Ben.

I was born in Katy, he said. Grew up gay in Katy. Stayed at home and fucked around and got sick and got kicked out and dropped out and got a job and then I met you at this party and now here we are.

Your folks kicked you out?

They did.

Because you're gay?

Because they couldn't ignore it once I tested positive, said Ben. That made my gayness something they had to deal with. And they didn't want to. They didn't want to deal.

That's heavy, I said.

222

It's whatever, said Ben.

It isn't whatever.

It's whatever. It's my fault.

You can't honestly think that.

I was being dumb, said Ben. I was fucking whoever. Whoever wanted to fuck, I'd fuck them, and that's just what happens. I couldn't even tell you who gave it to me. I couldn't even reach out to tell them they have it, too.

Ben's entire body loosened at that. I got a little closer, and when he didn't pull away, I squeezed, just a bit. He squeezed back.

Sorry, he said.

For what, I said. What the fuck?

You probably weren't trying to hear all of that. I made it weird.

Bullshit, I said. You let it out. You didn't have to tell me, but you did. Wasn't it invigorating?

You're being mean.

I'm being serious.

That doesn't make a story worth hearing, said Ben.

But you can't just keep it holed up, I said. You can't fucking beat yourself up.

Whatever you say, said Ben.

He leaned over to chew on my neck. The remote clattered onto the hardwood behind us. He stooped for it, nearly taking the quilt

223

with him, and I fell on top of him, and he was under me. And then we were hard, again. But nothing actually came of it. It just was, and we lay beside each other, breathing and feeling and being.

A few of Eiju's favorite things, scribbled in blue ink: *smoked eel, tattered sweaters, the weather in late January. Sex before breakfast. Grapes. Leftover rice. The first steps taken after walking off a train. The first steps taken after walking off a plane.*

One night, Eiju asked if I'd like a drink.

Before I could answer, he nodded at Kunihiko. The kid cheesed at the both of us. It was the end of the evening and we'd been cleaning up the bar; he'd already brought most of the glasses to the back. He'd wiped down the counters and swept the floors and started taking inventory.

Eiju swiped two Sapporo cans from the fridge beneath the bar. He waved me into the kitchen, hunching through the door by the window. A tiny deck stood behind the building, overlooking the alley beside it, and Eiju kept some sandals and a gaggle of plants back there, a tiny garden, but mostly it looked like no one had fucked with it in months.

The neighborhood was quiet. All you could see were the tops of houses. And then there was the moon in the sky, bare up there, something you'd never catch in Houston, and Eiju cracked open our beers, leaned on the railing, and I already knew how the conversation would go: He'd ask how long I was staying. I'd say I wasn't leaving him the way that he left us, and Eiju'd reject that statement, cursing me for it, swearing that I deserved it, or that Ma deserved it, or that we deserved each other, and then I'd leave him to himself on this balcony in his bar, and I'd make the walk back to his apartment, in this city that I didn't know, on this fucking island that was both mine mine mine mine mine mine mine and the furthest thing from anything I'd ever known, but what I did know is that I'd pack my bags, stuffing everything back into the tiny fucking duffel, bringing this whole misguided fucking trip to an end.

I knew that this would happen, because I knew how Eiju argued.

Because I knew Eiju.

Because I was still the fucker's son.

When I opened my mouth to start us off, he put a finger to his lips.

Do you hear anything familiar, he said. Anything you might recognize?

I shut myself up. Despite everything, I strained my ears.

But there was nothing to listen to.

So we stood there, listening to nothing.

As if he'd heard my thoughts, Eiju said, Silence is a sound.

You'll miss it when it's gone, he said, drinking.

I'll miss it when it's gone, he said.

Or maybe it'll all be silence, he said. I don't know if that's something to look forward to. Maybe I'll still be able to listen.

Eiju took another pull from his beer. He glanced at me.

Maybe, I said.

Probably not, said Eiju.

He said, The bar's still gonna be here. I know I haven't given you much. I'm aware. But it's yours if you want it.

Oh, I said.

Wait, said Eiju. Hear me out.

If you don't take it, he said, I'm giving it to Kunihiko. He's young, but he knows what he's doing. I know he'll treat it well. It'll be in good hands.

And you don't know what the hell I'd do with it, I said.

I don't, said Eiju. Because I don't know you. I really, truly don't. But you're my son, and what you do with it would be for you

226

to decide. If you put your mind to it, I think you'd probably do all right. And if you decided to fuck me one last time, you'd make a nice chunk giving up the property.

The two of us leaned on the balcony. Couples walked quietly down the side streets below. Stray bikers pulled into the road, dodging deliverymen on mopeds, and some young women walked home by themselves, clacking in heels down the steps toward the local station.

Eiju said my name, and I ignored him. Then he called me by my Japanese name.

Don't fucking do that, I said.

That isn't your name anymore?

It isn't yours to spit out like I'm a fucking kid.

But you are my kid, said Eiju. And that's your name.

It's a little late for you to come back around to that, I said.

And then we were silent again. Osaka continued to unwind underneath us. My father and I watched a salary dude sprint after a bus, which he'd missed. But then the bus stopped, and the man climbed inside it, laughing and waving his hands.

You'll have a little while to decide, said Eiju. The rent will be paid for the first six months afterward.

Afterward, I said.

Afterward, said Eiju. You can make arrangements in America and fly back, if that's what you need to do.

It doesn't matter to me what you choose, said Eiju.

Sure it does, I said. Or you wouldn't be telling me this.

Don't be simple, said Eiju. I'm saying that I know it's a *choice*. But I want you to know that it's there. That this is an option. That's the important thing.

Once he'd finished, Eiju exhaled, shivering a little. He turned his body toward mine, tapping at his bottle. I knew it was my turn to say something.

I didn't tell him not to give up so easily, because he'd already made his decision.

I didn't tell him that we didn't know he was going to die, because everyone dies.

I didn't ask him why he'd already given up, because I didn't need to know.

I didn't tell him that it was too little too late, that forgiveness isn't something you just hand out whenever you feel like it.

I said, Okay.

A car alarm popped off behind us, breaking the quiet. I nodded, for no reason at all, and Eiju did, too. He watched me drink, silently, and he started to open his mouth, and I started to open mine, but then Kunihiko yelped from the bar.

Eiju gave me a look, like, What can you do? Then he turned around, yelling the kid's name, heading back inside, already gone.

Ma was the one who told me he was sick. We hadn't spoken in weeks, not even our usual check-ins, and those had only lasted something like twenty seconds apiece. She told me she'd been busy with work. I'd been busy with Ben. We'd been too busy for each other.

But this time, my mother called.

We talked.

After Ma said the words, she lingered on the phone.

Say something, she said.

I'd been pushing some shopping carts around the grocery store's parking lot with a coworker, a guy named Rafa, a big Salvadoran dude. He saw me on the phone, and then he saw my face. He put a palm on my shoulder, shooing me toward the sidewalk. I walked toward the neighborhood behind the store, away from the noise, not really looking where the hell I was headed.

After a while, still on the phone, I'd wandered a few blocks away. The neighborhood was rich as fuck, just stuffed with money, full of the fattest houses. This Latina nanny walked a little whiteboy on the sidewalk, and he skipped over the cracks, laughing. She held his hand while he did that. The toddler lifted both arms, and she'd pull him over the weeds. I couldn't read the smile on her face. I wondered if the boy would remember it. Ben would've said something about how kids never really forget.

I said, It's that bad?

It is, said Ma.

And you're just telling me? Just now?

I am. Because it just became that bad.

A silence passed over the line. I could hear the traffic surrounding Ma, the sound of life going on in Tokyo. She'd called me at the end of her workday at the jeweler's.

When did you find out? I asked.

Michael, said Ma.

When?

It's been three weeks.

And you didn't tell me?

You didn't need to know.

Did he tell you? Is that how you found out?

He did, said Ma. It was.

So you're talking again, I said.

It was mid-morning for me. It would've

been well into the evening for my mother. I could see her stepping out of her shop, settling in front of a bike rack, clicking her heels toward the road.

So, I said, you've gone to see him?

What do you think?

I think you should.

It isn't necessary, said Ma. We've already spoken. His doctor's keeping me posted.

That's not enough, I said, nearly shouting into the phone, and I heard Ma choke something back.

Listen to me, said Ma. I didn't call you for advice.

I never said that you did.

No. Stop talking. You need to understand that I'm not asking you what to do, or for your help. I'm not asking you for anything. I'm just giving you the news.

Fine, I said. I'm sorry.

No you aren't, said Ma. But I understand. I get it.

Ma.

It's fine. Your father is dying.

The nanny and the whiteboy hobbled in place beside the intersection. He'd motion to cross, and the woman would tug on his arm. After the third time, he hugged her leg, and she set a palm on his hair.

Eiju told me he's already made his arrangements, says Ma.

So he's not even gonna try to fight this.

From what I understand, he's done fighting. It's over. He wants to ride out the time he has left.

Okay, I said. Then you should come here.

What? said Ma.

You should come back, I said. To Houston. Stay with me for a while.

You aren't serious, said Ma.

There was genuine confusion in her voice. I was speaking before I was thinking.

I am.

You don't have room for me, said Ma.

I'll make room, I said.

And the person you're living with?

Don't worry about that.

I know you don't want to worry about Eiju, I said. So come here and worry about me.

Ma stayed silent on the line. The kid and his nanny looked both ways, before she lifted him by the arms, jogging across the road. He laughed the whole way, and she laughed, too, and once they reached the sidewalk, he stomped at the cracks between them.

My mother told me she'd think about it. I told her the offer was there.

Good night, I said. You can let me know

whenever.

I'll do that, said Ma. Good morning.

Eiju's favorite sounds in this life: *the bridge of Frank Zappa's "Watermelon in Easter Hay." Crickets in the morning. The sound of a fresh beer mug fizzing. A car ignition struggling to turn. A train's doors closing, the hum of a convenience store. Mitsuko humming after sex, just biding her time in the sheets.*

From time to time, strangers wandered into Eiju's bar. They were usually just locals who hadn't known it existed before. They'd spot the alley lights from the road beside it, or they'd hear Hana or Sana laughing absurdly from the window. Or they were wildly drunk themselves, looking for more booze to hold their high. Sometimes tourists passed through because they just didn't know any better, and Eiju was always the harshest with them. Most of his regulars couldn't do shit to temper him.

One time Natsue told him that this was childish. That he'd open his eyes if he wanted to expand his business.

Eiju asked why she thought he was trying to expand anything.

It's called being a decent human, said Natsue. A good host.

Eiju asked her who'd said he was either.

They were backpacking through the country, staying in Osaka overnight. Or they were visiting from BnBs in Kyoto. Or they'd sojourned from Tokyo because they'd heard that Osaka was popping. Or they were in town for business. Or they were visiting a partner's parents. And Eiju was always the gruffest around Americans; he didn't want anything to do with them. One time a guy came through because he was teaching English in Chiba, and this was winter break. Once, an entire gang of British bros stumbled in, stuffing themselves through the sliding doors, and the entire bar fell silent while the four of them talked and talked. One time a mixed chick from California told me she was visiting her father, he'd fallen ill like a week beforehand, and this chill ran all over my fucking back until I asked her more about it. But she didn't want to talk about her situation. She wanted to get fucked up.

Eiju was entirely inhospitable with these folks. Kunihiko did his best, but his English sucked. His boss sent him off on errands whenever they came through. Mieko would call Eiju bigoted, and Takeshi called him an asshat, and Eiju said that had nothing to do with anything, and he wouldn't tell them why he acted the way he did, but of course

I fucking knew.

So they became my responsibility. All of the people passing through. The second I spoke a lick of English, the Americans locked on to me, slapping my shoulder, getting all excited, telling me my English was *so good,* and was I from Los Angeles or San Francisco or Portland or Brooklyn and why was I in Japan and tossing high-fives and thanking me. Eiju would disappear, claiming he needed a cigarette. Sometimes, he'd just leave, silently, immediately. None of the other patrons said anything about it. But they didn't have to. I got it. There was a degree of separation, this sort of wall that popped up, because I was one of them, but I *wasn't,* and I never *would* be, and that's just how it *was.*

But I dealt with them. This was never something Eiju and I talked about or decided or anything like that. Shit was just easier that way.

One afternoon, Eiju woke up feeling weak, stumbling all over the living room, kicking away my futon. I asked if he had a problem, and he groaned, stumbling back into bed. He stood to make some tea and changed his mind after he'd steeped it. Once he'd dropped his mug on the tile, I told him to

235

take the night off, to just stay inside.

You're drained, I said. Go back to sleep.

Bullshit, said Eiju. Don't talk to me like you know how I'm doing.

And that's when Eiju grabbed his stomach. I followed as he hobbled toward the bathroom, and my father barely made it to the toilet before he started dry-heaving, knees spread on the tile.

It'd been happening for a few days now. Sparingly. Just enough to say the tide on his illness wasn't turning.

The second time, I'd called Taro in the middle of the night. He showed up like fifteen minutes later. And he stood, watching over Eiju, rubbing his back, asking me if anything else had been amiss. Had Eiju been finishing his meals? Was he having diarrhea? Sudden loss of control in his joints? Or did he ever feel his legs going out from under him or did he —

At that, Eiju turned around to smile at his friend.

It's all of the above, he said, but it's not as bad as all that.

And Eiju grinned again before he yakked all over the floor.

We'd already put my father in bed, watching him snore from the doorway, before Taro walked me out to the living room. I asked if he wanted anything to eat, and he surprised me by saying yes.

There was some udon left in the fridge. I set a pot to boil, salting the water. Taro sat on my futon until I walked the noodles out, stir-frying them, blanketed by some broth-covered tofu, and crowded around some scallions.

Sorry, I said. This was all we had around.

You've got nothing to be sorry about, said Taro, already chewing.

All of this is normal, he said. Everything with your father. It's all expected.

Expected for death, you mean, I said.

Expected for a man in Eiju's condition refusing medicine, yes.

Cross-legged on the floor, in a hoodie and slacks, Taro was a handsome guy. Most of his hair had slipped into a shining gray. Slithers of black jutted in between. A patch of skin glowed from his waist, by his hip, between his shirt and his pants, and I tried not to stare, and I put the thought away.

And yet.

Still.

It'd been a few weeks.

I let Taro eat a bit before I asked what I could do. He poked the scallions with his chopsticks, stuffing a fingerful into his mouth, and he looked at me, a little pity-ingly, I think, with this smile that said, What *could* you possibly do? But he was gracious enough not to say it.

He scooped more udon instead.

Just stick with the usual routine, he said. No big trips. Nothing that'll exert him too much. But your father should listen to his body, now more than ever. If it tells him to sit, he needs to sit. If it tells him to lie down, Eiju should do that.

I should tell a dying man to spend his last days in bed.

You should tell your father to take care of himself, said Taro. That's what we're here for. At this point, it's all we can do.

Well, I said. Thanks for coming.

My pleasure, said Taro, grinning, and there was something in his grin, and for a moment, I felt warm, from my cheeks to my toes, and the air in the room felt electric.

So, I said, and Taro raised a palm.

I hate to ask you this, he said, but is there any more udon?

The night I convinced Eiju to stay home, I met Tan.

The bar was mostly empty. It was the beginning of the workweek, and I told Eiju he wouldn't be missing out on anything. I'd hold down the fort, or whatever, just for one night, because it's the only thing that made sense — it simply needed to happen — and before Eiju could protest or pick a fight or anything like that, he started coughing on his mattress, and he settled back into his pillow.

Our cops don't carry guns, he said, so if you're robbed give them the money.

Nobody's gonna rob me, I said.

You never know.

I know.

If there's a fire, the extinguisher's broken. You'll have to blow it out. But that shouldn't be a problem for you.

Fuck off.

So Kunihiko and I manned the bar. We worked reasonably well together. Whenever I was looking for something, I didn't even have to ask him, he was already setting it within arm's reach. He'd taken to rewiping whichever cups I'd dried. I didn't put up a fight over it, because it'd occurred to me more than once that Eiju had taught him all of this. I had the feeling Kunihiko knew the shitbag better than I ever would.

Anything wrong, Mike-kun?

Nah. I'm good.

We hadn't seen a customer in hours. Kunihiko talked and talked and talked. But it was all mostly to himself, mostly just for the noise. Every now and again, I'd grunt in affirmation, and he'd take that with a laugh and start in on some other fucking thing. I'd start to ask some questions — about Kunihiko, about his life — before deciding against all of them. And then, before I could open my mouth, Kunihiko would cut me off with some new fucking anecdote.

At one point, he said, How long have you known Eiju?

I looked at Kunihiko's face. He hadn't looked up, just kept wiping away at the counter.

He's like family to me, I said.

Same here, said Kunihiko. More than my actual blood. He always means well.

I don't know if that's true, I said.

What?

Always meaning well. That's a lot to ask of anyone.

You've just gotta get to know him, said Kunihiko.

Not if he shits on me the way he does you.

The last bit made Kunihiko smile. He rubbed a hand over his head. He'd clipped his hair a little while ago into something like a fade, but the barber botched that shit like halfway down his neck.

Give him a minute, said Kunihiko. You

just haven't seen him in a while. How long has it been?

Over a decade.

Exactly. I think he's been going through a rough time.

So I've heard, I said, and that's when the door opened.

The guy in the entrance had a lot of hair on his head. He was a little chubby, and he wore it well, and he wore this hoodie over some jeans. And he looked about my age, and Kunihiko waved him over, asking what he wanted to drink. When the dude answered in choppy Japanese, I ran the same thing back in English.

That had him blinking. He asked for a beer, and I passed it to him. When he took it, the guy nodded slightly, less out of timidity than certainty.

I kept my eyes on him, but he didn't look up. He clearly didn't want to be bothered.

So, said Kunihiko, what brings you out tonight?

The guy turned to Kunihiko, a little warily. He glanced at me before he gave Kunihiko a grin.

Sorry about him, I said in English.

Don't be, he said to me, in English.

And then to Kunihiko, in Japanese, Nothing really. Just restless.

I get that, said Kunihiko.

The guy nodded, taking a sip from his beer. We stood around in silence, until he waved toward Kunihiko for another, and the kid started in on another conversation with himself before I decided that what I actually needed was a smoke break.

I lit up on the deck. Spied some kids on the concrete below me, through the patch of neighborhood poking around this cluster of trees. It was way too late for them to be out alone, and I thought, just for a second, that they were about as old as the kids Benson worked with.

Ben would've been pissed if he'd seen them outside this late. He would've called that neglect. But kids were the same just about everywhere, all over the fucking world.

They bounced their kickball against the wall, flinging it at one another's heads. It ricocheted between their bodies. Their sneakers squeaked through the silence.

Eventually, one of them spotted me. They waved through the branches. I waved back. And when I blew a smoke ring, a few of the little motherfuckers actually cheered.

By my third cigarette, Kunihiko called from the bar. When I'd made it out front, he was throwing his shit in a messenger bag.

The kid said he had to go. He smiled, a little feverishly. Something important had come up. Or he'd forgotten something important. Or something important was on the way, said Kunihiko, waffling a bit, and the guy at the bar looked from him to me and back.

Then I guess we'll see you tomorrow, I said.

Kunihiko nodded, nearly sprinting out the door.

Which left me and the guy in the bar.

I found a glass to clean.

Despite what Ben had yelled a few weeks back, I wasn't actually someone who went after other people. I wasn't the best at starting conversations.

He seems like a handful, said the guy.

Kunihiko? I said. He means well.

Everyone thinks they mean well, said the guy, but I'll take your word for it.

As soon as you do that, I'll end up proving you wrong.

The guy told me his name was Tan. He was Singaporean. When I asked what brought him to Osaka, he said his mother cleaned apartments in the city, and he was here to take care of her.

She's been here for decades, he said.

Does she like it here, I asked.

Doesn't matter, said Tan. It's too late for her to move back now. And Singapore isn't like here. She'd die of boredom in a week.

It can't be that bad.

You'd be surprised.

I feel that, I said, wiping at the counter, and Tan asked for another beer, and I poured two more.

I thought bartenders don't drink on the clock, said Tan.

A drunk bartender probably told you that, I said.

He asked if the bar was mine, and I told him that it wasn't.

You're young, he said.

You aren't exactly a grandfather.

But it turned out he was older than me, by a couple of months.

Fair enough, I said, and no wife?

No wife.

And no kids?

I could ask the same of you, said Tan.

And the two of us sat with that silence. It wasn't particularly uncomfortable.

When I made it back to the apartment, Eiju was awake and smoking. Once he spotted me from the balcony, he gave a single wave.

He asked how the night had gone. I asked

how he was feeling.

Oh, he said, you know.

But Eiju didn't say anything else. So I left him on the railing to his cigarettes and the stinking fucking sunrise.

Ben moved in a few months after we started fucking. I offered to help him bring all his shit over, but he told me he didn't need that.

And anyways, there isn't much, said Ben. It's just me.

You run a tight ship, I said.

Aye-aye, said Ben.

We'd probed each other about our sexual pasts a few weeks before that. That happened at this bar on Richmond, drinking Modelos on their patio. When Ben asked the bartender for the menu, he told us they didn't have one, and when I asked if he could tell us what they served, the whiteboy said he'd be back in a minute. Then he disappeared. The next time we saw him, he was serving these two whitechicks by the entrance.

Was that racist? said Ben.

Depends on how you look at it, I said.

On one hand, it was. And on the other hand, it was.

Then there you go.

In the end, we lifted two bottles from the cooler. Left some cash on the bar.

I wasn't telling Ben about my first, so I started with the phone operator I'd fucked for about a year. Told him about the sneaker store clerk. Told him about the prep cook. And the cell phone guy. And the Apple store guy. And the gas station clerk. And the whiteboys. I told him about the accidental orgy at Numbers, and the grocery store clerk I'd fucked in an H-E-B parking lot.

How does that even happen, said Ben.

The guy was ringing me up. I asked him what time he was getting off.

And then you literally got him off.

Your words.

Perpetuating the stereotype about gays as sex addicts.

Anyone who says that just wishes they were fucking more.

But I think that's it, I said. I think that's everything.

The two of us crossed our legs under the steel table. I drained the rest of my beer, and Ben fiddled with his.

We don't have to do this, I said. I really don't care about this stuff.

If you didn't care you wouldn't have asked, said Ben.

I asked because I wanna know you better.

I don't mind. It's nothing.

I just don't want you to think I'm pressed over it.

Don't lose sleep over what I think.

Ben took a sip from his beer. We watched our not-waiter scramble off the patio and into the building.

Sorry, said Ben.

Don't be, I said. You haven't said anything yet.

There's nothing to say. And definitely nothing as exciting as your shit.

It's *your* life though. That'd be hard for you to judge.

Sure, said Ben, but I couldn't even tell you how many guys I've fucked. One too many, obviously. And then I stopped. And then I met you.

But I'm the best, right?

Sure.

Good. That was the correct answer.

We watched the parking lot's crowd congest and unspool.

After a while, I said, Why'd you stop?

Stop what, said Ben.

Fucking around.

Oh. You know why.

Nah. But I could guess?

Once I tested positive, it just seemed, like, whatever, said Ben. Like, why even do it anymore? It felt like I'd lost something.

I think you're very hard on yourself.

Yeah, said Ben. Well. You're the best.

At that point, the bartender came out. He stopped in front of us, looking like he had something to say. Then, all of a sudden, he slapped the cash we'd left him in front of us.

He said we'd paid too much. Five more dollars than we'd needed to.

I started to tell him that it was a tip, but Ben pocketed the money. He thanked him for his honesty.

The first night after Ben moved in was the first time we actually slept in my bed, the first night he actually let himself do that.

Once we'd settled in, he reached over to touch me. We started to kiss. And then nothing worked after that. At least not for me.

It's fine if you don't want to, he said.

I do.

It's okay, said Ben, but he kept persisting, touching me, and then himself, and then he groaned, and then he was finished.

When he stood to clean up, I watched his silhouette wander across the room.

Here was a new situation.

A new body in my bed.

All of a sudden, out of nowhere, I wanted

him to pack his shit and leave. I wanted him to dissolve. I didn't want him anywhere near me.

By the time Ben came back to bed, I'd shut my eyes. He called my name, but I didn't open them. But he whispered my name again, and he wrapped himself around me, laying his legs over mine. And his shoulders sat on my shoulders. And Ben kept murmuring it, Mike Mike Mike Mike Mike Mike Mike, softly and slowly. Even after he'd fallen asleep, until I was knocked out, too.

After his night off, Eiju was nothing but energy.

I told him to cool it. To remember what Taro said.

Taro's book-smart, said Eiju, but I know my body.

He's a fucking doctor, I said. He knows everyone's bodies.

Eiju slapped my shoulder. It was late afternoon. We'd taken a walk that morning, and Tennoji buzzed around us. We'd gelled into the foot traffic around Namba, until we'd made it back to the complex and the little woman living beneath us shook her head as we clattered loudly up the stairs.

You need to chill the fuck out, said Eiju.

That's hard to do when I'm babysitting you.

No one has to *do* anything.

I guess you'd know that better than anyone.

Are you good? You been laid in a while? Because we've got fags all over this city.

Before I even realized what I was doing, I was already stomping back down the stairs, jogging past the cranky neighbor lady. I crossed the road, took the stairs to the station, and bought a ticket for the local line. But I didn't actually hop on a train. I watched them stop and depart. Our station never got too much traffic in the afternoon, so everyone was either headed toward Umeda, taking a late trek to Shin-Osaka, or coming back from a day out in the world. Some lines formed and dissolved behind me.

Eventually, I realized I'd been holding eye contact with a lady on the next platform. She blinked back at me. Had her hair in this bob, with tight black jeans, and this too-large Toronto Raptors sweater. When I waved, her face broke into a grin, and she waved back at me, until a train severed our view. But then she hopped on and smiled through the window. And neither of us looked away. And the train started up and she was gone.

I used to wonder what Ma meant when I asked her about Japan, because I could only remember so much of that shit from when I was younger, and she'd tell me that it was different from home, but also the same. It was her home, not mine. But it was still home. Whatever that meant.

This was after Eiju left the second time. After their last major break. Sometimes, we'd just be sitting together in some diner by the feeder road, or at the dinner table, or driving, and Ma'd inhale sharply, out of nowhere. As a kid, that shit terrified me. But I got older. I stopped being surprised. Stopped reacting to it.

It was, I figured, just how Ma coped. No one gets to choose what steadies them.

When I asked her what was wrong, all Ma ever said was, Nothing.

Or, I just remembered something.

Or, Never mind.

Or, Don't worry about it.

I always thought it was over Eiju. That Ma missed him. And I was half-right. But at some point, way later, I realized what the gasp was about: not stability, or consistency, but comfort.

The closest place for Ma to find it was home. Her home.

Tan passed through the bar again the next evening.

Eiju glanced up. He'd been feigning interest in whatever Sana, who'd arrived alone for once, was talking at him. Hana and Mieko sat stewing on opposite ends of the counter. They were pissed at each other about something or another, but Eiju teased them both that they'd still shown up to the bar together.

Hana's only here because she has nowhere else to go, said Mieko.

I would, if you'd hurry up and drop your boyfriend, said Hana.

At that, Tan walked in. He pursed his lips at everyone, nodding my way. I went to grab him a beer. And everyone else settled down.

My father gave Tan a glance. Then he looked at me.

Where you coming from? said Eiju.

My mother's, said Tan.

Your actual mother? said Sana.

The one who gave birth to me in Bedok, said Tan.

Lucky mama, said Hana.

Luckiest mama, said Mieko.

All of a sudden, just like that, all was

forgiven between the two women.

What do you do that lets you travel like that? said Sana.

I'm a photographer, said Tan. I take pictures.

Of what?

The city, usually. The site I work for tells me what and when.

Lots of foreigners working in Osaka nowadays, said my father, and Sana hissed at him.

That's a good thing, old man, said Sana.

Never said it wasn't, said Eiju.

I'm sure his mother loves the stability, said Sana.

Stop that, idiot, said Hana.

What? said Sana. Am I wrong?

It's fine, said Tan. What she loves is the bills being paid on time.

And with that, he chugged from his beer.

It didn't take him long to finish.

When Tan stood to leave, I told Eiju I needed a cigarette.

My father gave me a look, but he didn't say anything about it. Tan raised an eyebrow. He paused for me at the door.

Outside, I offered him my pack. He eyed it before taking out his own.

Sorry, he said, in English. If I don't borrow, I'll smoke less.

I tried that a long time ago, I said.

And now? said Tan.

I shrugged, waving my pack at him.

The two of us stood under the railing, rubbing our hands. There was a chill in the air. The streets were clear except for some revelers, and they were fucked up, laughing way too loudly, swinging their arms. When one member of their party nearly slipped and busted his ass, the entire group screamed.

You know Osaka pretty well? said Tan.

I don't know shit.

Ha.

How's it different from back home? I asked.

Tan looked at me. He grinned.

It's softer, he said. Or more present, maybe. Is that what you'd say?

Nah. But English is flexible. Your words.

My words. How long have you been here?

About a month.

That's not very long.

It isn't.

How much longer do you think you'll stay?

I don't know. But eventually, I'll leave.

Do you mind if I ask why you're here, said Tan.

I gave him a long look. He stood an inch

or so shorter than me. Today he'd tied his hair back, and the fur on his chin crept up the sides of his face.

I'm here for my father, I said. The old bartender. He's dying.

It was the second time I'd allowed myself to say that out loud.

Hunh, said Tan, I thought you two looked alike.

I'll take your word for it, I said. Think you'll drop by the bar tomorrow, too?

I might, said Tan, smiling.

I'm flattered, I said.

Don't be, said Tan. Osaka's a small town.

The bar was locked when I made it back. So I walked to the apartment.

When I stepped through the door, Eiju was dozing on the sofa. The news projected variations of the weather across his face. We looked at each other for a moment.

Early night? I said.

Eiju blinked back at me. Then he shut his eyes again.

Hard to compete when your partner's out chasing ass, he said.

Now I'm your business partner?

Don't play dumb. You know what I'm saying.

Yeah, but I don't think you know what

you're saying. I think you're writing checks your ass can't cash.

Eiju stood up so fast that I couldn't anticipate it. He'd definitely shrunken.

And what now, he said, eyeing me. You're gonna teach me a lesson? You're gonna beat my ass?

I was about to respond when I looked at Eiju, standing pantless with a single sock, looking absolutely fucking ridiculous.

I realized, for the first time, I guess, that he really was an old man.

But his fist still connected.

On most days, I wouldn't have fallen. But I was already off-balance. And then there was his uneven flooring, except Eiju must not have expected it either, because he fell into me, or onto me, and all of a sudden the two of us were on the floor.

I lay on top of him. We looked at each other a little dumbly. And then I pushed myself off Eiju and away, jumped up, kicked on my shoes, grabbed my jacket.

Just fuck off! he said. Run away! Just like her! It's all you two are good at!

I didn't say anything to that, because I didn't trust whatever was about to come out of my mouth. Once I'd slammed the door, I stopped for a cigarette on the stairway.

Some dude and this kid stood beside each other on the stairway a floor down, investigating the noise. They could've been brothers. Or cousins. Or maybe a young father and his nephew. Eiju's apartment was a quiet building, in a quiet neighborhood, and I could only imagine what we'd sounded like.

The pair eyed me for a while. The kid picked his nose.

I asked what the fuck they were looking at and the kid said, You.

It was only a few hours past midnight when I came back. I could feel the sleep creeping up my feet. One of the ladies living below us stepped outside to smoke, and when I smiled her way, she gave me a look, like, What the fuck?

Which was a good fucking question. It was time to face facts, or at least catch a few hours of sleep. But when I tried Eiju's door, the handle wouldn't give.

He'd locked it.

Fuck, I said, quietly.

And then, louder: FUCK.

As quiet as it was, I heard the woman below me sigh.

And then, despite everything, I thought about Ben.

So I started to text him.

Deleted it.

Sent him a handful of photos instead.

A chill set in on the rail beside me. It slipped a little farther down my socks. It was midday in Texas, which meant he would've been at work, but I was putting my phone away when the text bubbles appeared on his end.

They appeared. Disappeared. Appeared. Disappeared. And then they were finally, resolutely, gone, but I waited another five minutes, just to be sure.

The bubbles didn't come back.

So I walked.

Tennoji, on a Sunday night, before the crack of fucking dawn, held an entirely different feel. Save for some stragglers, no one else was on the streets. The convenience stores glowed from block to block. The only other people outside were getting ready for the next day, sweeping at the entrances of Lawson's and McDonald's and 7-Eleven. At some point, it started drizzling. And then the rain picked up overhead. And I ducked underneath the awnings beside me, turning into this tiny all-night Chinese diner.

A group of guys sat in a booth, smoking cigarettes over their soup. I nodded, and

they nodded, and the cashier wordlessly passed me a menu. I wasn't really hungry, so what I did was sit there, and it took another five minutes of staring into oblivion before I realized that Tan was sitting at the next table over.

He looked my way, but it was more like he was looking past me. Smoking and staring.

Once we made eye contact, he smiled. Walked over.

Stalker, I said.

I was already here, said Tan. And you spoke first. I thought you didn't know your way around the city?

I don't.

You don't. And yet we've found ourselves at the best Chinese restaurant in Osaka.

Bullshit.

For real.

Is this really the best one?

It must be if we both made it here.

The cashier appeared at our table again, shifting her head at Tan. She set a bowl of noodles in front of me and plate of steamed vegetables across from him. Tan smiled at her, said something in Mandarin, and she said something back, and he laughed.

You're like Google, I said, when the cashier stepped away. All those languages in your head.

I'm not nearly as cheap, said Tan. If that's what you mean.

The two of us ate. The dudes behind us laughed and laughed.

So what brings you out here? said Tan.

A walk.

Fair. It's all right if you don't want to say. Promise you won't hold that against me?

I'll do my very best.

We ate, whispering to each other in English. The guys in the booth behind us burst into laughter again, rattling their table. Our cashier looked up, just once, wiping at her bangs, but once they'd settled down, she slipped back to her phone.

So listen, I said. Who are you?

You really like to talk, said Tan.

I just asked a question.

There's nothing to tell. I work for a dying industry. I live with my mother, and I want her to come home, back to Singapore, and she doesn't want to come home, and I don't know what to do about that. Your turn.

I'm from the States, I said.

Where?

Texas.

With the horses.

Yeah.

The Astros. Beyoncé.

Sure. But I flew here for my father.

Because he asked you to?

Because he didn't ask me to.

I see.

He's stubborn.

Many fathers are, said Tan. Mine was.

And now?

You tell me.

I'm sorry, I said.

Don't be, said Tan. I'm well. My mother's well. For me, home is wherever she is.

You shouldn't make a home out of other people.

Is that right?

I think so.

You speaking from experience?

You could say that, I said.

Maybe you've met the wrong people, said Tan. Or you've met the wrong people for you.

Maybe, I said. But people change. And then you're stuck in whatever your idea of home was.

There's nothing wrong with that though, said Tan. We all change. We'll all have plenty of homes in this life. It's when you don't that there's an issue. That's settling.

And what's the difference between that and settling into one person?

That's not for me to say. We all live our own lives.

Well, I said. Thanks for nothing.

It's all I'm good for, laughed Tan.

When the group of guys behind us stood, our table jostled just a bit. The cashier hustled over to their booth.

No girlfriend to go back to? said Tan.

You already asked me that, I said.

I took a bite of rice, and he nodded.

And for you? I said.

With the beginning of a grin on his lips, Tan rose his bowl to his face, inhaling half of the broth.

When we stepped out of the diner, we walked for twenty, thirty minutes. Didn't say much to each other.

At some point, I realized we'd been wandering in loops.

Looks like we've made a perfect circle, I said.

It's only perfect if you end up where you

started, said Tan.

That's what we did, I said, and Tan looked up at me, reaching for my hand.

He held it while we walked. His thumb looped across my palm, rubbing until he reached the edge of my pinky.

I've been thinking about what you asked, said Tan, about home.

Really, I said.

Really, said Tan.

And what have you decided?

That loving a person means letting them change when they need to. And letting them go when they need to. And that doesn't make them any less of a home. Just maybe not one for you. Or only for a season or two. But that doesn't diminish the love. It just changes forms.

I don't say anything to that. Tan and I walk from one street to the next. His thumb grazes my knuckles, and I massage his palm, and we keep letting each other do that.

And now, said Tan, swiping his finger, we split.

Tan squeezed my shoulder, turning away. Leaving my ass to watch him cross the road and dip into a train station.

Overhead, it'd gotten a little brighter. A little closer to morning. Osaka was rousing itself awake, and when I looked up, I realize he'd walked us back to Eiju's bar.

This time, my father's apartment door was unlocked. It was nearly five in the morning by the time I made it back.

Eiju dozed outside of it, by the doormat, hands stuffed under his armpits.

I squeezed the top of his head until he opened his eyes. Once he'd finished blinking himself awake, Eiju squinted up at me.

I could've been anyone, I said.

Where the fuck did you go? said Eiju.

Could've been a robber. An arsonist.

Nonsense.

A serial murderer.

I'm going to bed, said Eiju, hobbling.

He couldn't stand by himself. So I grabbed his elbow, easing him inside. And he didn't shake me away. I locked the door behind us.

The first few months living with Ben were fucking mundane. Fucking domestic.

I went to work, he went to work.

We came back.

Drank.

Ate dinner.

Dishes.

Laundry.

Napped.

Fucked.

One night, I asked Ben what he wanted. We steeped on the top of our mattress like tea bags. The A/C wheezed overhead.

Ben sat up. He smiled.

Honestly, he said, I hadn't expected this to be anything.

Oh, I said.

Yeah. Whatever happens, happens. Isn't that what you wanted?

I want whatever's best for both of us, I said.

There's no best. Things just happen.

I don't know if that's true.

Ben blinked at me, looking weary all of a sudden.

Whatever happened, happened. That was the same attitude Eiju had carried around. It's what he'd told my mother, so I knew exactly what it got you.

Nobody's assurances were permanent. I wasn't a fucking dummy. But, the thing is, they were *something.*

Whatever happened, happened.

And then there was something I noticed about Ben, a small thing, a nothing thing: he never acknowledged our neighbors.

The Latino kids played on the stoop,

releasing their fucking cacophony of music, grabbing at their poor cat. The Black couple across from us always sat on their porch. Everyone slogged through the business of living, getting through their shit, and whenever Mary or Harold waved our way, Ben never even waved back.

One day, I asked him why. We were sitting in my car. Our problems were just on the horizon. We hadn't gotten it up for each other in weeks, which had turned into months. And now, whenever we touched, it was just a passing thing. Like an idea you know you've had and then you lose it before the fucking thing comes to fruition.

I hadn't started the engine. Ben gave me The Look. He said he didn't know Mary.

So you can't wave back when she waves at you?

Why would I? Would that make you happy?

I'd be overjoyed.

Then you can do it for the both of us, said Ben, and he opened his door, shuffling out of the passenger seat, headed back inside.

Another story about Mary and Harold: their daughter passed through town every now and again. Her name was Janet. Her folks were always telling stories about her, always showing me pictures from kindergarten, from high school, from dropping her off at College Station. She was getting her MBA at Bauer, and then she would move back home, and Mary and Harold had other children, and grandchildren, with baby photos on the mantle, but they never really talked about those, didn't bring them up like they brought up Janet.

One day, they invited me over to meet her, and from the moment Janet walked through the door, it was clear that she'd thought it was a set-up. Some sort of surprise date. But when we actually sat down at the table, there was a shift in her body language. And her tone. At one point, she just totally fucking relaxed.

We ate some yams I'd baked, and this slow-roasted ham by Harold. When Mary brought a pie to the table — double-layered in caramel and pecans — she said her daughter and I should share it.

And that's when Harold stood up to leave. He didn't say shit about it. Then, Mary said she'd make the coffee, and she disappeared, too.

That left me and Janet in the parlor. With her parents gone, she sighed. She crossed her arms, and then her legs, setting her elbows on the table.

Do you do this often, she said.

What?

You heard me. Freeloading off the elderly.

You've got this whole thing screwed up, I said. I'm their neighbor.

So you're just randomly over here, said Janet. Just because.

Just because, I said. Your parents are cool. We eat together. Sometimes we talk.

You're joking.

We went walking the other day and Harold almost caught this toad.

Nobody does something like this for nothing.

Look, I said, do you want me to leave? Because it's not that serious. And they're *your* parents. If you want, I'll go thank them and I won't fucking come back.

You wouldn't? Not ever?

Your call.

I don't know if I expected Janet to flare up at that or what, but she didn't. She actually laughed.

You're a bullshitter, she said.

I talk a good game, I said.

No, you don't. But it's cute. Mom must not know you're gay though.

Who said I was gay?

Please, said Janet.

I've got this sister, she said. As much as

269

you talk to my parents, you'll never hear about her.

Let me guess, I said. She's the one on the mantel.

Yep. She's got a wife and this kid and a house and everything. They're cute together. But none of that matters.

Because she's queer.

Because my parents are old, and change is hard.

That's not an excuse, I said. It's never an excuse.

But here you are, said Janet. So you'll never come back again now that you know?

And I started to say something — although I still don't know what it would've been — but that's when Mary stepped back in the room. She asked if we wanted any coffee.

I looked at Janet. Her face wasn't giving me anything.

I told Mary that'd be great.

That's what I thought, she said, smiling.

One day, I told Ben all of that. We were at a bar in the Heights, out on the patio, and he'd been staring at the beers beside me. Once I'd finished my bottle, Ben folded his hands behind his head.

Of course that's how she's gonna react, he

said. People don't just do things like that. Eating other people's food like it's no big deal.

I did.

And you're a weirdo. But they're her parents. They're old.

And, I said, waiting for the next thing.

And what? said Ben.

You know what. You almost said it.

Ben smirked at that, a rare sight from him.

That's just not something *we* do, he said, laughing.

The skyline glowed under the patio's lighting, an assembly of Christmas blinkers. A patch of traffic snaked around the cars parked bumper to bumper beside us, stacked like haphazard dominoes across one another's backs. Some dog wandered between them with its tongue batting the concrete.

Then tell me, I said, what would *you* do?

I'd mind my fucking business, said Ben. But it's not like anyone even lets us do that.

Us, I said.

Black people, said Ben.

All of a sudden, he was serious. He played with his fingers on the counter in front of us. So I grabbed one, making a ring around it, pulling it under the table, stretching it, and sliding my thumb across the whole of his hand. It was the most intimate thing we'd done in weeks. A blush rolled across his face. So I tightened my hold, running my finger across his wrist, which slackened, and then tightened, and then slackened again.

You're annoying, said Ben.

You're blushing, I said.

Shut up, said Ben, but he didn't move his hand.

This is how our second year goes by:

I pull a new gig at this other restaurant.

Ben stays at his job with the kids.

We don't buy a bedframe.

We fight.

We make up.

We fuck on the sofa, in the kitchen, on the floor.

I cook, and cook, and cook.

One neighbor has a baby.

Another has a stroke.

Whitekids invade the block, lining their porches with pumpkins on Halloween and Budweisers on the weekends.

Ma calls me from Tokyo, stalling on the line.

She asks how I'm doing.

I swear everything's fine.

■ ■ ■ ■

A brief list of Eiju's favorite scents: *steamed rice, crisp takoyaki, sesame oil. Laundered clothes. Grated ginger. My mother's wet hair. My wet hair, as a boy, after he'd bathed me, lifting me from the tub.*

One morning in the living room, Taro finished his checkup on Eiju, groping around his abdomen, and the motherfucker yelled out in pain.

I'd been taking a leak. When I ran out of the bathroom, Taro'd pursed his lips, and Eiju'd raised both of his arms.

No, he said, goddammit! No!

Taro stared at Eiju for a moment from the floor. Like he wanted to say something, but he didn't know how the man would take it. He turned to me in the hallway, and then he turned toward Eiju again.

But Taro swallowed whatever he had to say. He rose to his knees, continuing with the exam. Neither man spoke, and Eiju lifted his arms when he was asked to, and he lowered them when Taro said so, and they went through the motions silently — poking and prodding and scooting around.

Once they'd finished, and Eiju slipped his

shirt on, Taro packed up his shit wordlessly. He gave a slight bow to his patient, and his patient grunted him away.

But I cornered Taro outside. It'd become our thing. The block's morning rituals had started up as he waited for me on the street, and I watched Taro wipe his brow with the back of his hand. When I offered him a cigarette, he smiled, waving me away.

I asked what went wrong, what the fuck I'd just witnessed, and Taro cracked the biggest grin.

Oh, he said, you know how men are.

Eiju never asked me what I talked about with Taro.

When I asked him why that was, he just shook his head.

What will it change, he said.

But I noticed that he'd started moving slower. Sometimes, Eiju dozed off in the middle of the day, grimacing himself awake. Whenever I asked what was wrong, he said it was none of my fucking business, although that didn't change the fact that it was happening.

So we slowly, wordlessly, adjusted course.

I took off from the apartment by myself.

Eiju came late, or he left early.

Or he didn't make it to the bar at all.

Or, if he did, he'd pull up a chair in the back room, tugging a baseball cap over his eyes.

Our patrons noticed. They didn't say shit about it.

When I told Eiju that, if nothing else, what he needed was sleep, he laughed right in my face. He said that we both knew he had a big one coming up.

Hey, I said.

But I didn't have the rest of the words.

Here's something that changed about Eiju as he got sicker and sicker: anger. Or the lack thereof.

He stopped knocking cups off of tables.

He stopped smashing doorknobs on his way out of the apartment.

He didn't raise his hand at the first sign of a disagreement.

Now, what he did, mostly, was sigh.

He rolled his eyes.

He asked if you were done.

I guess it could've been his sickness. Or it could've just been his being an old fucking man.

Or, maybe, Eiju was just tired.

■ ■ ■ ■

One night, Kunihiko flubbed an order for a group of American tourists. They were the first white people I'd seen in weeks. And they were fucking loud, asking for sake and sushi and karaage, which wasn't on the fucking menu, and never had been, because there was no fucking menu. But Kunihiko still ran to the Lawson's down the road.

Eiju was outside, smoking. Now he only stopped in the bar for a few hours at a time, mostly to get out of the house. For the most part, Kunihiko and I were in charge of nightly operations, although when Sana pointed that out, I told him to go fuck himself.

But it's true, said Hiro.

Hardly, I said.

We're not blind, said Sana. We see Eiju. We get it.

Nobody said that was a bad thing, said Hana, and I just fucking waved them off.

Now Kunihiko sprinted back up the stairs. Exploded through the bar with three sacks of convenience store chicken, cheesing from ear to ear.

And the white folks were too confused to say shit.

They eyed the karaage, greasy in their sacks.

Eiju stepped inside just as they fumbled with their napkins, dabbing at the wings. He looked at the white folks, and their food, and then, out of nowhere, Eiju froze, stiffening up.

But what happened next is not the thing that I expected to happen: Eiju began to laugh.

At Kunihiko, and then at me.

Then Kunihiko started to laugh.

And I started to laugh.

We were all laughing together. Eiju asked the tourists if they were enjoying their chicken. And this fat white dude told him, in the blockiest Japanese, that everything was wonderful, that they couldn't have been having a better time if they'd tried.

When I was nineteen, before Ma left the States for Japan, she sat me down to talk about it.

By that point, we lived together most days of the week. I was out in the world for the rest of it. I fucked guys and I'd shack up with them, for a little while, whenever that worked out. When I finally got bored or they got bored or they dropped me for some skinny sparkling whiteboy, then I made my way back home. It was hardly ever complicated. I spent whatever cash I made, and I threw Ma a little bit for the apartment, but by then she didn't need it. She'd moved up in the jewelry shop, working alongside the same manager who'd hired her. She brought home more money, most months, than she and Eiju raked in collectively when they were together.

And it showed: now Ma lived out by Greenway Plaza. She always looked way too comfortable. My mother only ever wore the nicest dresses, the nicest shoes, with jewelry on her neck, hanging across both wrists. An ankle. Every few months, I'd hear murmurs from her about some man, but I never actually saw them — if anything, by the time I heard about those fuckers, they were already gone.

Every few weeks, Ma still took me out. The restaurants were always entirely too nice. I was working at a gas station. Not fucking with college or anything like that. Our meals together cost more than I budgeted for food most months. But my mother didn't spend money frivolously, and it was around this time that I noticed, whenever we sat down together, to eat or to drink or whatever, there was something entirely different about her. I couldn't really place it. Until I finally did.

Ma had, literally, let her shoulders down.

That night, she told me she was going back home. *Home* home. Home to Japan. She'd lined up a few job interviews, and Ma would stay with her brother in Setagaya for the first few months — a guy I'd met only once when he visited Houston, short and thick like me. Afterward, she'd find a spot of her own a little closer to the city. And I could visit every now and again. And she'd be willing to front the ticket.

Or, said Ma, you could just come live with me.

In Tokyo?

Where else?

I don't think that's a great idea.

We both chewed at our salads. Our waiter, this older white guy, set some pasta across from my mother. I asked him for another beer, and he glanced at Ma, who nodded.

Well, said my mother.

Yeah.

Do you have anything keeping you in Houston?

Or any*one* keeping you here? said Ma, and my skin froze for a moment.

It wasn't like she didn't know I was gay. She knew. But it wasn't something we ever spoke about. Not with actual words that you could feel and see between us. It was just a feeling in the air, whenever we interacted, like a pothole in the road. Something we didn't have to acknowledge every time, all the time. Because that shit was implicit.

Not really, I said.

Not really? said Ma. Or no?

No one worth mentioning.

Ma and I looked at each other for a moment. We weren't smiling, but there wasn't any malice either. The air was exactly empty, aside from the diners beside us, clinking their glasses and going on about whatever the fuck went on in their lives.

I have no reason to go back to Japan, I said.

Of course not, said Ma. You're only Japanese.

Stop.

I'm just saying. What will you do with yourself here? And don't say it's whatever little job you're working, Michael.

That's pretty fucked up.

All I stated was a fact. That's it.

Whatever, I said. I'm thinking of switching jobs anyway. I've got a friend at this shop.

A shop?

A deli. Sort of.

So you'd cook. Like your father.

What?

Eiju cooked. Cooks. And it sounds like you want to, too.

This has nothing to fucking do with him.

That's not what it looks like.

Whatever. I probably won't even do it.

Calm down, said Ma, playing with her napkin.

What if I said that I wanted you to come with me, said Ma. What if I wanted you to come home? Would that sway you at all?

If that were the biggest deal to you, I said, we would've gone back earlier.

And I suppose I'm not a big enough reason, said my mother, smiling.

And I'm not important enough for you to stay, I said.

We sat with that for a moment. Before I could open my mouth again, my mother signaled the waiter for our bill. He nodded, smiling even wider as he handed it over, and Ma slipped him her card. She didn't even glance at the numbers.

Then there isn't much else to talk about, she said, standing, reaching for her coat.

When Eiju left us for the final time, it was entirely unceremonious.

The sky didn't fall.

The clouds stayed in place.

We'd grown used to him taking off for a day or two. He'd reappear a few nights later, in the same clothes, smelling like piss.

A few days passed without hearing from him. And then a week. And then the place where he tended bar called our apartment asking about him.

I don't know how long Ma knew he'd gone back to Osaka or if she'd just needed to confirm or what, but the next thing she did was call my father's sister.

I'd never met her. But I'd heard stories. And I knew about the history between their families, or the complete lack thereof.

Ma called her once in the morning, their time, and nobody answered.

Ma called her again in the evening, their time, and nobody answered.

Ma called her again the next morning, their time.

No one answered until the final ring.

Eiju's sister told Ma that he'd been home for a few days. He was sleeping.

You didn't know? asked my aunt.

I didn't know, said my mother. But now I do.

And then Ma hung up.

I told Ben all of that one night in bed. This

was the week after he'd put his hands on me. I'd shoved him back, not even thinking about it, and neither of us knew how it'd happened. But the only thing we could do afterward, to clear the air, was to fuck. That became our routine whenever we fought. Whenever things got bad. Like we were fucking away the thing that'd sat itself on our chests.

Afterward, Ben said, Shit.

Yeah, I said.

And you stayed.

I'm looking at you right now.

Well, said Ben.

We both sat cross-legged on the floor. Ben thumbed at the waistband of his boxers.

What about your parents, I said.

What about them? said Ben.

You know what I mean. How'd they split?

It wasn't anything like that. They just got sick of each other. There's no story to tell.

That's a whole story right there.

If you say so, said Ben. But my parents weren't surprised. They knew it was coming. It'd been building up for a while.

And y'all had money, I said.

What the fuck does that have to do with it?

It has everything to do with everything.

Ben shifted onto his elbow, staring at me.

He'd been letting his hair grow out.

Sure, he said. They had money. I grew up middle-class. But we're Black. So that cancels everything out.

If you say so.

I say so.

That wasn't an attack, I said. It's not a competition. It's okay to grow up okay.

Fine, said Ben. Sorry.

Don't be sorry.

All I'm saying is that my folks knew who they were when they settled in with each other. The only ones blindsided were me and my sister. So maybe that's the funny thing. The surprise. We were the ones who ended up having to find out.

I don't think so, I said. Nobody knows what the fuck is going on. Maybe everyone's parents are like that.

Not everyone's, said Benson. Just most of them. Many. And then they end up with us.

And we didn't say much after that. We listened to the dogs barking next door, and the corridos humming from the next window over. And the neighbors outside chatting and smoking, and the white kids blaring trap music, and Harold stepping onto his porch, eventually, to tell them to shut the fuck up.

No matter how it felt at the time, we were

just one part of the neighborhood. A cog inside the whole thing. But in sync, regardless.

One morning I woke up and Eiju was sitting beside me. Eyes closed, snoring, with his arms slack. Ass on the floor. I didn't know how it happened, but I wasn't about to shake him awake to ask.

I'd never really looked at his face before, and definitely not since I'd been in Osaka.

But now, here he was.

I saw the creases on his forehead. I saw the bend of his nose. His big-ass ears.

All of these were his gifts to me. The only ones he'd given me.

Delayed, sure. Present nonetheless.

A few hours later, he farted himself awake.

Fucking around on my phone, I watched the slow act of his unraveling into himself. The blinking. The gradual, slight tensing of the muscles. The shifting of his body as it registered him coming back to consciousness.

And then, breathing softly, Eiju stared into space.

When he realized I was beside him, he didn't flinch or anything like that.

I thought you'd left, he said.

I didn't leave, I said.

I thought you were gone, he said.

I'm right here, I said. I'm not gone.

And then, that evening, Eiju was himself again. He asked if he could pass through the bar.

It's still your fucking place, I said.

So he walked with me through the neighborhood and up the stairs. Wiping at the stools. Groaning at customers. Mixing his drinks entirely too fast. Snapping his towel at Kunihiko, who'd burnt the rice, asking what in the hell was wrong with him, what on Earth did he think he was doing. And Kunihiko grimaced, but under that grimace there was a warmth, like he was grateful that Eiju was around that night and for the attention, and I honestly don't know how he couldn't be.

Hiro, Takeshi, and Sana sat across from us, clapping and whooping. They'd been buzzed for hours. They were are all on holiday. A thick drunkenness sat in the room, and I'd fucked with a little sake myself, and the night was warm the way it gets in Osaka sometimes.

You're back! said Sana.

I'm visiting, said Eiju.

He's back! said Takeshi, toasting the room.

Shut up. Stop that.

He's back! He's back! He's back!

That night, I closed shop early. The crowd had thinned out. Eiju'd started his walk back to the apartment a few hours beforehand, and when I'd asked if he needed a cab, he asked who the fuck I thought he was.

I'd opened my mouth, and then I closed it. Told him to have it his way.

So Kunihiko started cleaning on one end of the bar. I started on the other. It was inevitable that we'd meet in the middle, eventually, but we always acted shocked when it actually happened.

When our fingers brushed, Kunihiko asked if I knew how lucky I was.

To have him, he said.

I frowned.

He's yours, too, I said.

It's not the same.

It isn't. But you should be grateful. You've seen parts of him I never will.

And then Kunihiko looked at me. Every now and then, slivers of the guy he may've been slipped through his expressions.

But then, just as suddenly, they disappeared again.

I don't know, he said. Eiju treats me like a son.

He *does,* I said.

And I don't know how to repay that.

I don't know if you can, I said.

It was Kunihiko's turn to look a little bewildered at me.

You just have to stick around, I said. That's enough. It has to be.

We just have to stick around, said Kunihiko, cheesing, and then he put his hand on my shoulder, knocking over a bottle of shoyu.

For the longest time, our family could barely afford two meals a day. And a little while later, eventually, we could. But only if my mother purchased it, which meant that all of a sudden Eiju wasn't so hungry anymore. It was rare for him to eat something he hadn't made himself.

But, when Eiju did cook, he made the dishes he'd learned at the Chinese restaurant, and the dishes he made at the Mexican restaurant, and the dishes he made at the Jamaican spot, curry chicken over rice and steamed eggs with okayu and caldo de bistec and fried plantains under fried dumplings, and even in the worst fucking times, when he drank away all the cash, he always found enough to sit us down for a decent dinner. A good one, even.

The three of us sat, picking away at this food. My folks wouldn't talk, but they weren't arguing either.

Once, when I was a kid, Eiju and I both lazed on the sofa, staring at the wall where there should've been a television. We'd sold it a few weeks beforehand. Ma had been inconsolable. She hadn't spoken a word to him since, not even at dinner.

Staring at the nothing in front of us, I asked Eiju how he'd met my mother. I'd never asked before. Hadn't even thought to.

He looked at me, wincing.

It started raining and then she was there, he said.

Things I've cooked for my father, who insists on never eating out anywhere besides his own bar: okonomiyaki, yakisoba, oyakodon, katsudon, mabo don, mori soba, kake soba, kitsune udon, nabeyaki udon, bulgogi, soondubu jjigae, doenjang jjigae, ika-age, takoyaki, lamb curry, chicken curry, creamed salt cod, a Dungeness crab soufflé, poached flounder in tomato sauce, steamed black cabbage, Romano beans sautéed in oregano, salmon, salmon carpaccio, shrimp bisque, garlic-baked squid, grilled tuna in a red onion salad, tempura, grilled asparagus braised in garlic butter, carrot and red pepper soup, soy-braised pork, fried rice, huevos rancheros, huevos divorciados, carne asada, migas, simmered radishes, tatsuta-age, spicy tuna on toasted bread, okayu, fried rice, steamed rice.

Things I've cooked for my father that he's visibly enjoyed:

The next time Eiju asked about my plans, we'd driven out to Nakazakicho to restock the bar. It was usually something Kunihiko handled. He'd make the trip on the days he had off. But that week, according to Eiju, Kunihiko couldn't make it, because he had something or another going on, and when I asked Kunihiko about it later, he said, So I'm not going with you guys?

But I didn't press Eiju on that. We stepped around the tiny little truck he kept behind the bar. I'd never ridden in it, and I asked him why he kept the fucking thing in the first place, and Eiju asked if I hadn't seen *Godzilla.*

Are you fucking kidding me?

Calm down, said Eiju. You never know when you'll need to leave.

That's beyond idiotic, I said.

It isn't, said Eiju. Just watch the news.

I can't even remember the last time I saw you drive.

So you're saying I can't.

I'm saying I don't have insurance. And I'm really not trying to die in a car wreck abroad.

Makes no difference to me how I go, said Eiju.

And besides, he said, fingering the keys, I figured you'd do the honors.

I don't think that's a great idea, I said.

Couldn't be a better one, said Eiju.

And then we were on the road.

The drive wasn't far. Eiju told me which turns to take. The morning was sleepy enough that I idled alongside the bikers, and the occasional motorist scootering by, but mostly I just took my time.

The roads felt comfortable. We passed ramen stalls and convenience stores. Drove over the bridge. Idled by chicken stands and cops and some guys fixing telephone lines, and another group of dudes plugging in potholes. They worked in tandem, rocking these uniforms. Calling and responding to each other. Eiju whistled "Little Red Corvette" over and over again.

■ ■ ■ ■

When we made it to the market, our distributor was waiting by the garage. He was a stocky guy, with a too-big mustache and his hands on his hips.

Eiju, he said, extending his hand.

And company? he added, pointing at me.

Before I could answer, Eiju said, My son.

He avoided my eyes, looking straight ahead.

Oh, said the vendor. He cocked his head.

And then, without missing a beat, he said, No shit.

Must be the eyes, he laughed.

And that's why I like you, Hikaru, said Eiju. Everyone else mentions the ears.

But it wasn't long before they started talking business. Hikaru opened his building's garage, where our supplies sat in stacks. Eiju's name shined from a placard near the front. It took something like twenty minutes for me to bring all the boxes back to our truck, and another guy — skinny and scruffy — helped me while Eiju and Hikaru talked. They stepped inside the building, only to come back out with two beers, kicking their feet against the concrete.

The other guy helped me load the crates

into the car. He looked a little younger than me.

He told me he was Hikaru's son. His name was Sora.

You the new Kunihiko? he asked.

Hardly, I said. He's out sick or something.

And you're not from here.

I'm not from here.

Weird, said Sora, but he didn't say anything else.

We piled everything into Eiju's truck, grunting all the while. Every now and again, we stole glances at each other. The road mumbled behind us, along with the steady clinking of a nearby trainline, and there wasn't anything in the morning air, really, or at least no sex I could sense offhand: we were just genuinely staring.

Once we'd finished packing, we sat on the back of the pickup. Sora pulled two cans of beer from his sweater. When he waved one my way, I shook my head.

It's not even eight yet, I said.

Sora shrugged, cracking open his can.

The two of us sat, staring at our fathers.

Has yours started bugging you about the business? Sora asked.

You could say that, I said.

Mine tells me I need to start talking to

clients. But he never gives me the chance.

Your dad probably wants you to just take the initiative.

Then he needs to show me how.

And I didn't say anything to that. It felt, for the moment, like the guy just needed someone to listen.

Maybe you're right, he said, after a while. But just when I think he wants me to say something on my own, he gets the biggest attitude. Everything has to be on his terms.

Mine's the same way, I said.

And he wants me to get married before I take over everything. Make an heir. Or so he says.

How's that working out for you?

It isn't, said Sora, taking a long pull of his beer. And it won't.

You're young. It's not a race.

That's not what I'm saying.

When I glanced Sora's way, he didn't say anything else.

Does he know, I said, and I felt the kid exhale beside me, emptying all the air in his lungs.

Then he turned to his shoes, kicking at the tires.

No, he said.

I think so, he added. I don't know.

That's cool, I said. It's not your job to

know that.

We could never talk about it, said Sora. It'll never come up. I don't know what he'd do.

He'd deal with it or he wouldn't. You don't get to control that.

It's different for you, said Sora. You don't live here.

I'm from here.

But you're not *from* here. You get to leave.

Sora kept kicking at the tires. I watched him do that.

Sorry, he said.

Don't be, I said.

I shouldn't have said that.

You're not wrong.

I know. But I still shouldn't have said it.

I get where you're coming from, I said.

It's just that we only get so much time, I said. You know? And I'd hate to see you waste that.

Sora looked at me again. He scrunched up his eyes. But then he laughed.

You don't even know me, he said.

Shut up, I said. I'm your elder. I'm trying to mentor you.

Fuck, said the kid, grabbing at the other beer.

I waved for him to pass me another one, and he opened the can before he did. We watched our fathers box each other's shoulders by the garage, dodging fists.

When they'd finished bullshitting, Eiju and Hikaru walked our way. Three beers in, they laughed and laughed, burnt red in their faces.

There they are, said Hikaru. Already drunk. Looking like a couple of real men.

Eiju didn't add anything to that, just smiling. Sora took another swallow from his can, and his father squeezed his shoulder, and the kid made a face that shook me, because I knew it all too well. But I didn't say a word.

We drove back to the bar a few hours later. The traffic had picked up only slightly. The occasional car followed along behind us, before trailing off down some other lane, and Eiju sat in the passenger seat, with crumbs all over his lips, and eventually he put both hands on his knees and sighed.

You know, he said, Hikaru thinks his son's a fag, too.

I didn't say anything to that. I stopped at one light, hooking a right.

I told him not to worry about it, said Eiju.

You told him not to worry about it, I said. The man who still says fag.

Keep your eyes on the road, said Eiju.

I mean, what can he do about it? he said. The boy's not like you though. Whole different situation. Hikaru's gotta pass his place off to someone else, and that's hard to do if his kid doesn't have a kid.

What makes our situation any different?

The fact that I'm not Hikaru.

Well, I said. Sora could still have kids.

You're joking, said Eiju, looking at me. You're not in America anymore. Here we consider people beside ourselves.

I don't think any country has a monopoly on consideration for others.

You know what I'm saying.

Maybe you should be clearer, I said.

Just because you can do something doesn't mean that you should, said Eiju.

That's not Hikaru's decision to make, I said.

We sat at a stoplight. Eiju fondled a toothpick between his lips.

Maybe it isn't, said Eiju. But he's making it anyway. The property's going to someone.

So you feel sorry for him.

Is that what it sounds like?

It does.

Well, said Eiju, it's none of my goddamn business. Their family's their family. I've got my hands full with mine.

We settled in front of a light. A small troupe of schoolkids crossed in a steady jog.

If my hands weren't on the steering wheel, my fingers might've exploded from their joints.

I didn't ask what family, specifically, Eiju was referring to.

I didn't tell him that the only thing he did with his actual family was abandon us.

I don't say anything about it. I just keep on driving.

We made it back though.

Once I parked in the alley's lot, by the dumpsters and the recycling, Eiju let out the longest sigh. He asked if I'd thought at all about his proposition. About the bar.

It's okay if you haven't, he said.

No it isn't, I said.

Good. So?

I don't know yet, I said.

You don't know yet.

I have a life in Houston.

I had a life in Houston.

I've got plans.

Plans change.

Fucking stop that, I said. I've got a partner. A guy.

Eiju whistled at that. A pair of teens

298

passed by, bouncing a basketball across the concrete.

Is he like you, said Eiju, and I turned to look him in the face.

Japanese, he added.

He's Black, I said.

Oof, said my father.

He looked through the passenger window. One kid bounced his ball around the other.

May as well go all the way, said Eiju.

What the fuck is that supposed to mean, I said.

I don't even know.

But, said Eiju, it's like I told you. Your life. And I won't try to sway you. That won't work for anyone. But the bar has to go to someone.

Or you could just close it, I said, and Eiju looked at me, briefly, and there was fear in his face.

I said it to hurt him. I regretted it immediately. My father opened his mouth. He closed it. And then Eiju opened the door, letting in the cold air.

Everything looks different in context. All of it.

That's something Ben told me.

We'd just finished an argument about nothing in particular and we'd done our best to fuck it out. The sex we had when this happened was prolonged, frantic. Biting and clawing and crying. Squeezing each other until we were breathless.

Afterward, we lay on the mattress. Houston'd reached its two-week window of autumn. That brought everyone to the street, bouncing balls and standing in their driveways and vaping and talking too goddamn loud for too goddamn long by parked cars.

We'd become a tiny star inside the constellation of the neighborhood. I'd thought of popping our bubble, once or twice, but never too seriously. It was just my life now.

It wasn't the worst I'd dealt with.

It wasn't my parents.

And now Ben's legs sat on top of my belly. He massaged my hair absentmindedly.

Explain about context again, I said.

You don't get it? said Ben.

I do. But I wanna hear you say it.

There's the thing that happens, and then there's the shit that happens around it. They're as important as the actual event.

But the event is still the thing when it happens. It's its own moment.

Sure, said Ben. But then the moment passes. That reframes everything. If enough time's gone by, you aren't even the same person anymore. The event becomes history. Like, an *event*. So you just look at it a little differently on principle.

Okay, Professor, I said.

I'm serious.

I know.

I grazed a thumb across Ben's dick, and he flinched, but he didn't jump off me.

The mosquitoes still hadn't emerged from their puddles and creeks. You could still hear the crickets moaning. We'd reupped our lease with the whitegirl who managed the place a month earlier — she wore suits now — and, afterward, Ben had a look on his face.

When I'd asked him what was wrong, he asked how I was feeling. I told him I was fine. He asked if that didn't bother me.

He wore that same look now.

I started to graze him again, but this time he grabbed my thumb. Hard, at first, but then he loosened his grip.

What are we doing? he said, after a while.

I was still thinking of my answer when I felt his breathing soften.

I didn't know if he was asleep, or still waiting. But I kept still underneath him. By the time he woke up, I figured he'd have an answer for the both of us.

■ ■ ■ ■

Once, Ben told me that there was one thing the men he'd fucked had in common.

You're all hilarious, he said. Every last one of you.

But this is how quickly it can happen: one night, I was smoking a cigarette on the bar's railing, and then, out of nowhere — although I know no one ever really comes from nowhere — Tan drifted around the corner.

I watched him stroll toward me, hunched over, hands in his hoodie. I watched him stop like he was considering something, and when he looked up, I flashed him a peace sign.

Hey.

Hey.

What are you doing right now, I said. Right this second.

Tan looked at me. Some equation ricocheted across his face.

He said, Do you have anything in mind?

Tan's mother lived in Doyama, a few stops away on the local line. We sat next to each other on the train, not really looking at each other, before we drifted up the sidewalk, away from the lights, down some alleys, and toward the apartment complex. The lights dimmed behind us. Smokers loafed on the corners. Every block we walked was illuminated by some fucking love hotel or another. Eventually, we turned toward a bike shop where a dude tinkered with a faulty wheel, and a couple of kids spun the one behind it.

On the second floor of this building, past some mailboxes and a staircase, Tan knocked on his door once, and then once again.

She might be out, he said, and they were his first words since we left the bar.

But the door was opened by an older lady, and she didn't look much like Tan at all.

They spoke in their language about something while I stood behind Tan, kicking my feet.

I thought of Ben, listening to Ma and I talk in Japanese.

All of a sudden, this seemed like an entirely ridiculous idea.

That's when Tan's mother waved at me, smiling. She shook my hand.

Come in! she said, in Japanese.

Oh, I said.

I looked at Tan. He shrugged.

Hurry! said the lady, smiling impossibly wide. Come in!

She kept repeating something, and I still couldn't tell you what it was, but it made Tan blush. He covered his whole face.

She won't bother us, said Tan, shutting his bedroom door behind him.

That's fine, I said. She's your mother.

She's my mother, said Tan.

He cleared his mattress, brushing away a bunch of jackets. A stack of flash drives sat on a desk by the window, shining under the glow of a tablet, charging beside a pair of cell phones. A handful of cameras was sprawled across the floor.

Nice place, I said.

It's a shoebox.

For some pretty big fucking feet.

My place back home was three times bigger.

His room was entirely bare, except for the mattress and his desk. There was a laptop charging and a pair of headphones dangling over a messenger bag. A duffel sat on the side of the room, with its guts splayed all over the wood. I didn't know where to sit, so Tan squeezed my arm and I plopped on his bed.

You live light, I said.

No reason not to.

Still. It's different.

Did you picture anything else?

I don't know, I said, wiping my hands on my joggers.

Tell me, said Tan, did you want to have sex tonight?

I flinched, just for a second.

You're forward, I said.

You're stalling, said Tan.

I looked to see if he was serious.

He was.

I scratched at my nose.

Not really, I said.

Be honest, said Tan.

I mean we don't have to.

Sure. But do you want to?

I don't know yet, I said.

Okay, said Tan, and then he plopped backward on his bed.

The two of us sat in silence.

Then, Tan slipped a hand underneath my shirt, rubbing at my back. I let him do that.

I have somebody back in Texas, I said.

Okay, said Tan.

I just wanted to say that. I care about him.

And I never said *we* were doing anything, said Tan, but he hadn't stopped rubbing, snaking his arms around my torso.

Are you really gay, I asked.

What do you think, said Tan.

I've learned not to assume.

If we were in my country, I'd lie to you.

Okay, I said.

I leaned onto Tan's hand. He asked if that felt okay, and I told him it did.

Okay, he said. Lay on your stomach. And take off your sweater.

I gave him a look that asked why, but Tan didn't say anything. But I did what he asked. And he took off his own. And he maneuvered his legs around mine, until most of his weight sat on the center.

We were about the same size. Tan's mattress was basically wood. Just a slab of concrete underneath us. I should've felt like a pressed vegetable, but I didn't. He felt warm.

Eventually, I felt him growing on my ass.

Sorry, said Tan.

Don't be, I said.

I was hard, too. We were two horny men lying on top of each other, not having sex. But we were definitely doing *something*.

Is this okay, said Tan.

Yeah, I said. It's nice.

Good, said Tan, and that's how we stayed.

Every now and then, he'd shift on top of me. I'd adjust beneath him. He pressed the tops of my shoulders with his fingers, settling them at random intervals. We listened to the apartment's static and his mother's padding around the living room. And the occasional sirens beyond us.

But mostly we lay in silence.

I don't know who fell asleep first.

When I woke up, it was still dark. Tan wasn't on my back anymore. When I turned over, he looked groggy, eyes half-open, but he'd been staring.

Let me guess, he said, you've got to leave.

I should.

I didn't get up though. Tan just blinked at me.

I guess I'll see you later then, I said.

Maybe, Tan grinned.

But now you know where I live, he said.

Now I know where you live, I said.

Now you have something else to do in this city, said Tan.

On my way out, I passed his mother in the living room. When I cracked open the door, she jolted upward, with this wild look on her face. But then she saw it was me and she smiled.

She waved. I waved.

I walked back to the bar. A drunk woman

hobbled in front of me, giggling to herself, turning into an alley. But there was nothing else to see. The air'd gotten a little warmer.

I couldn't make out his body at first, but Kunihiko was sitting on the railing. He held his head in his hands. He had a cigarette in a fist, burning at the tip, but I didn't even know that he smoked.

When he saw me, he stood.

Where the fuck were you, he said.

Around, I said. Why?

You should've fucking been here, he said.

What?

We sent him to the fucking hospital, he said. Where the fuck were you?

Through the windows, the bar looked empty. Kunihiko must've kicked everyone out, shut everything down. I allowed myself to wonder if he'd washed the dishes before he locked up.

Then, I gave Kunihiko the most honest answer I could: I don't know.

Whenever I made it back home after my shift at the gas station, or from fucking around out in the world, Ma'd be cooking rice with miso soup or beef and potatoes or mushrooms simmered in dashi over chicken by the stove, always after a full day of her own work. I didn't have the grades for college, and of course we didn't have the money to make that happen without them. Ma'd tried reaching out to Eiju about cash, once, after I'd told her not to, after I'd thrown a mug across the kitchen in protest, but she said it wasn't my choice, Eiju owed that to me, and I didn't get to refuse, and also we probably wouldn't hear back from him anyways and even if we did, he probably wouldn't have the funds, so, knowing that, why not at least try, and Ma was absolutely right because we didn't fucking hear shit.

So that's how we lived: I fucked around. Sold cigarettes and gum and brown-bagged beer and sacks of ice. Ma sold jewelry. I fucked around some more. I didn't realize it, but Ma was biding her time. And she sat up for me after work, and we ate at the table together, not saying much of anything, kicking our feet underneath it, with our heels hardly grazing, but still. Afterward, I'd wash the dishes. We'd start over the next day.

Our constellation was, however briefly, restored.

Ma and I lived that way until I moved out, right before she took off. We talked when we could, but I just couldn't put it out of my head: she'd gone and left me and flown all the way back to fucking Japan.

One day, right before I left for Osaka, during one of our worst fights, I told Ben the world didn't owe him shit. Nothing. Not a goddamn thing.

At this point, we only touched each other to fuck: he'd set a hand on my shoulder, or I'd lean on him in the kitchen, and we'd make it happen right there, wordlessly, gruffly, and the moment we finished we'd go back to whatever other shit we'd been doing. It wasn't like I didn't know what was happening, or that I wanted us to be over, but it just felt like gravity — like I was slowly sinking into something that would eventually happen anyway and I didn't know how to stop it or turn it around or what.

We stood on opposite sides of the living room. Ben held the doorknob like he was ready to rip it off and throw it at me.

You're trash, he said.

Great, I said. That's big of you.

You came from trash, and you'll always be trash.

And what the fuck do you think that makes you?

That's my mistake, said Ben, smiling. I fucked up with you.

Right, I said. And now you'll just go back home, right? To fucking Katy? To your fucking money? Is that your plan? Do you even fucking have a plan?

You can go fuck yourself, Michael. Just fucking go away.

I should. That way someone can do it the way I want them to.

Really. Go fuck yourself.

And you're obviously the best judge of that, right, Benson? Who to fuck and who not to? Worked out really well for you.

We never talked about Ben's HIV status. It was just something he had. He took his meds over breakfast and I'd see him do that and that was it. But this was enough to end the argument. He swallowed his words right up, another first between the two of us.

Ben looked hurt, and I knew that I'd hurt him, and I wanted to hug him and apologize, but I couldn't, so I didn't.

I watched him step down the hallway, slowly. Heard him gently close the bedroom door.

That night, I slept on the sofa. Ben slept in our bed.

■ ■ ■ ■

The next morning, we didn't bring it up, and we kept on not doing that.

The next week, I left the country.
  I didn't know — don't know — how we'd talk about it if we tried.

Either way, I didn't try to find out.

I left.
  Figured he'd be there when I got back.

Later, I found out that Eiju had collapsed from exhaustion. He'd thrown up in the back of the bar. Kunihiko caught what was happening. The kid dialed 119, but before my father blacked out, he said to call Taro instead, and the doctor showed up ten minutes later, in his pajamas and an overcoat.

Eiju spent the next few nights at Taro's clinic. I stayed with him. Kunihiko visited from time to time. I told him not to worry about the bar, about keeping it open or anything, but he insisted on cleaning it, at the very least.

In the morning, I left Eiju's room for the nurses to conduct their tests. When I made it back, he was deflated and wincing.

Eventually, Taro came in to see us himself. When he asked if it was cool for me to stay in the room, Eiju only shrugged. And then the doctor told us Eiju's cancer hadn't grown more, exactly, but it hadn't shrunk either. All that had happened was time. Eiju's body was slowing down. He'd continue to lose weight. The nausea would rise. Vertigo, too. Things the treatment would've otherwise done its best to reduce. But the only thing that was happening was exactly what he'd — what we'd — known would happen. It was here. Happening. The only thing surprising about the end was how quickly it had arrived.

So I'm on borrowed time, said Eiju.
    You're on your own time, said Taro.
    I'm already dead.
    You're still here. But you need to be comfortable. Manning the bar is a bad idea.
    He's hardly ever around now, I said.
    It's time to cut it out entirely, said Taro.
    Are you telling me that I shouldn't work, said Eiju, or that I can't work?
    I'm telling you that working will kill you

faster than what already is, said Taro.

Eiju looked at Taro. He looked at his lap. Then he exhaled a noise I'd never heard from him, this whooshing thing that was somewhere between a roar and a cry and a groan.

When I started to stand to go to him, Taro set a hand on my shoulder. Eiju's chest rose and fell. He shook. Wheezed.

Eventually, he settled into himself.

Okay, he said. That's okay.

We knew this was coming, he said. Right?

We did, said Taro.

It's what we talked about? said Eiju.

It is, said Taro.

Okay, said Eiju.

Then that's fine, he said. I'll stay home.

You need the practice managing things anyways, he said, turning to me, smiling.

And I knew, viscerally, primally, that I could've just said, No.

I could've broken that man right there.

It wouldn't have taken much.

I looked Eiju in his face. I took all of it in.

I said, Okay.

One time, years back, before Ben, I was about to dick down some whiteboy I'd met at Grand Prize. Found him at the pool table, and once we made it to his place, he was tugging at my shorts, and then he'd finally gotten them off, and then he stopped moving entirely. Stopped breathing, even.

When I asked what was wrong, the white-boy said it just wasn't what he expected.

When I asked what *it* was, he smiled, because he thought I knew, although honestly, in that moment, I was thinking of everything *but* my dick.

And then he stopped smiling.

And everything clicked.

When I told that story to Ben, way later, he laughed right in my face. A rarity.

Fuck you, I said.

Be nice, said Ben.

I never laugh at your stories.

You're right. I'm sorry.

You should be.

But I wasn't laughing because it was funny, said Ben. That's not funny. It's never funny. But I have a question.

Go ahead.

Did that stop you from fucking him?

Ben had this smirk on his face. I thought about what I would say before I said it.

No, I said.

No what?

No, I said.

315

And we stared at each other.

Well, said Ben.

A few things that Eiju, even in sickness, on the literal brink of death, can't bring himself to believe in: *regular breakfasts, socks around the apartment, washing his hands with soap, a full eight hours of sleep.*

He smoked in the mornings.

I reminded him of the doctor's orders.

Eiju reminded me that he had cancer, not fucking Alzheimer's.

I told Eiju that he was exacerbating things. Making his situation worse.

He said the end result would be the same, did I think he was a fucking idiot, why was I reminding him.

I moved my futon from the living room to his bedroom. My nose brushed his shoulder at night. This was a recommendation from Taro, who thought, worst-case, if something happened, my reaction time would be quicker. Not quick enough. But quicker.

Taro told us that this moment was all about minimizing risk, that *this* was the point, and Eiju grumbled as we death-proofed his apartment.

When I wiped down the floors like Taro

suggested, Eiju asked why we didn't just take all the furniture out, to minimize the risk.

When I cooked the food Taro prescribed, Eiju asked why we didn't just skip meals altogether, to minimize the risk.

When I settled my head into the pillow beside his, smoothing my ears against the linen, Eiju asked why I didn't just sleep in the same futon, to minimize his risk to the maximum.

You think it's a game, I said. But it's not. Not even a little bit.

Eiju's head leaned against my feet. He kept his eyes closed on the wood.

You don't get it, he said. That's *exactly* what this is. All of this *is* a game. It's all a losing match.

And nobody wins, said Eiju. We all lose. That's the point.

I called Kunihiko to say we were closing the bar for the week.

Until we figure out what we're going to do, I said.

He was silent for so long that I wondered if the line had been cut.

And what are we going to do, he said.

I told him I didn't know, in as honest a

317

voice as I could.

You've said that already, said Kunihiko.

What?

That you didn't know. That you don't know. But never mind, I get it.

And then he hung up.

One morning, Natsue visited the apartment. She brought a breakfast bento sealed with plastic wrap. When I answered the door, Eiju was still sleeping, so she and I stood in his bedroom doorway, watching his chest rise and fall.

Thank you, I said, and Natsue glanced my way.

He's a dear friend, she said. One of my oldest.

Yeah, I said. But not just for that. For not freaking out about me. Being his son.

Ah, said Natsue.

She smiled, just a little bit.

I always knew, she said.

You did?

Of course. Eiju couldn't keep a secret at gunpoint.

Does anyone else, I asked, but Natsue only shrugged at that.

I think that everyone knows exactly how much they need to know, she said.

We took the food back out to the sofa. I

loafed around in sweatpants, while Natsue tugged at her blazer. Cross-legged on the sofa, she asked how I was holding up.

He's all right, I said. Considering.

Not your father, said Natsue. You.

I'm good.

Just good?

Just good. I'm not the sick one.

That doesn't mean you're good, said Natsue.

I'll be fine, I said.

Sure, said Natsue. You better be.

But check in if you aren't, she said.

One afternoon, Takeshi and Hiro visited the apartment. Sana was home with his kids, but his friends brought a six-pack from 7-Eleven. Standing in our apartment, slipping off their shoes, they acquainted themselves with Eiju's living room as he slept, gawking at the walls, and then the sofa, looking like a couple of boys.

The beers are for you, said Takeshi.

We didn't know if Eiju could drink, said Hiro, but we figured you might need it.

I asked them to stick around so we could kill the pack in the living room. And they declined, vehemently, before sitting down — until they ended up drinking three apiece, bitching and laughing and fucking around, and I hardly had to talk at all.

And then, that night, Kunihiko visited.

I expected some awkwardness between us, and it was still there when he stepped through the doorway. It was his first time in Eiju's place. Kunihiko tugged at his fingers, and I told him not to be so surprised, and he tried to make a scowl. He wandered around the living room, and then into the kitchen, taking these big-ass steps. He'd look my way, and he'd start to open his mouth, but nothing came out. And I wasn't about to help him get comfortable. And then, just as things were getting ridiculous, Eiju emerged from the bedroom.

He looked at Kunihiko. He asked what the fuck was wrong.

Nothing, said Kunihiko.

Exactly, said Eiju. Nothing. Nothing's wrong. So stop looking so scared.

Okay, said Kunihiko, and he looked at me, and I shrugged.

The three of us stood in the living room. Eiju scratched his ass.

How about you two make yourselves fucking useful and cook us some rice, he said, dropping onto the sofa.

So that's what Kunihiko and I did, standing silently beside the sink.

When we made it back to the living room, Eiju was already snoring. So Kunihiko and I sat on the floor across from each other, slipping bitefuls into our mouths.

I cooked for Eiju. I cleaned the apartment. I walked from one end of our block to the other and I wandered around Kuromon Market and I ate lunch at the curry spot behind the complex and I caught the local line to Umeda and one day I didn't ride it back, I figured I'd walk the entire way back to the apartment. Osaka isn't large. It would've only taken a few hours. But it was cold as shit. My sneakers hugged the edge of the curb. Halfway through, I gave up, and I found a local station, but the train platform I took was headed the opposite way, I realized once I was already on it, and I felt spent, just fucking done, so I knocked out in my seat after like fifteen seconds.

By the time I woke up, I was halfway across the city. A thick guy in shorts and Jordans sat across from me, looking a little spooked when I woke up. We spent the rest of the ride pretending not to check each other out, until he finally got off, throwing a final glance my way, and then I really was alone.

At the end of the week, Eiju and I chewed at some curry I'd cooked, when he suddenly started shaking. We'd both had one beer, and then I'd had a second, a third, a fourth. A rerun of a Hanshin Tigers match played on the screen, jostling across the turf through Eiju's faded, stodgy television.

But then: the trembling.

First in Eiju's shoulders, and then his knees.

His fingers.

I asked what was wrong.

The fucking face he made.

Nothing, he said.

And then he began to cry.

I sat with my beer and my curry, as Eiju shook, trembling slowly, and I did my best not to move.

When he'd finished, Eiju coughed. I passed him one of my paper towels. He took it, wiping his mouth, clearing his throat, asking if I had another beer in the fridge.

The last conversation I had with my father, before he took off from the States, was in our living room.

He walked around in his socks and his sweater. I was headed to school. When I came home that afternoon, I wouldn't see him, or that evening, or the next morning. By then, he would have effectively evaporated from my life. But that morning, I didn't know that, and he took his time with his shoes.

Before I shut the door behind me — in Nikes and this big-ass jersey, the way I used to do it — Eiju grabbed hold of my shoulder. Told me to stand right next to him. When I did that, he walked around and faced me, until he was breathing on me, and he smelled alive, and it was the closest we'd stood together in I don't know how long, and I was acutely aware of his body, and our chests nearly bumped into each other's.

Eiju didn't look down on me. He *couldn't* look down on me. By then, I'd gotten as tall as him. He met me eye to eye.

He took my hands in his.

He meshed our fingers together.

Then he smiled.

Almost there, he said.

Almost, I said.

Soon, he said, and I walked out first to catch the bus and I locked the door behind me and I wouldn't hear Eiju's voice again for over fifteen years.

Or maybe I'm lying — it wasn't the closest I'd ever been to him. That would've been when I was a kid.

One time, Eiju was out on one of his benders. One of his first in Houston. We didn't see him that night, or even the next morning, and I collapsed by the door, kicking and screaming when Ma tried to move me, and she ended up sleeping out in the hallway beside me, dragging her sheets across the carpet.

I'd kiss my father on the forehead before bed. Eiju wasn't an emotional man, but he'd do the same. Right on my ears. I couldn't fall asleep until he'd done the kiss, and he never forgot to do it. Not even once he started drinking. Before things got bad. If he wasn't around, I'd sit up with Ma, and she'd try it in his stead, but it just didn't feel the same, and we ended up waiting for him.

Whenever Eiju reappeared from out in the world, he smelled like liquor and smoke. And the first thing he did was kiss me once on the forehead. And then on my right ear. And then on my left ear. And then, just once, on the bridge of my nose.

Kunihiko and I reopened the bar a few days later. The morning beforehand, I'd asked Eiju how he felt about that, and he just made this face.

We'd sat in the living room, lounging in pajamas. Two bowls of pickled cucumbers stood on the table between us. This time, a rugby match between Australia and South Korea boomeranged across the screen. I'd rigged together a stream of the game from my laptop.

Does it even matter what I think, said Eiju.

Of course it matters, I said. It's your bar.

At that, Eiju started coughing. A gaggle of men in front of us stood locked in a scrum, bending their knees.

I waited until Eiju'd finished. Passed him a paper towel. He accepted it. Our little ritual.

Right, he said. Of course it fucking matters.

So Kunihiko and I wiped down the counters and stools, and we took stock of the liquor. He didn't say shit to me, and I did my best not to read too much into that. By then, we only communicated when we absolutely had to. I'd nod and he'd point and I'd grunt in confirmation.

This was, I thought, no different from being back home with Ben.

And then I thought about how that turned out. Or how it didn't turn out.

But this silence wasn't sustainable. I knew that. Kunihiko had to have known that.

So I waited until he'd bent over by the bar's sink and I toed him in the ass.

Kunihiko shot up, blushing.

Hey, I said, it isn't that bad.

Kunihiko gave me a long look. Then he bent over again, scrubbing at a panel below him. I stood there, and Kunihiko kept trying to ignore me, but, eventually, he looked up again.

You're still here, he said.

Still here, I said.

I know this is hard for you, I said, but none of this is a surprise.

It was a surprise to me.

Okay, I said. I'm sorry about that.

You could have told me, said Kunihiko. He could have told me. You both just left me in the dark.

He leaned against the counter, holding one wrist in the other. I scratched at my shoulder.

Look, I said. I see Eiju every day. He

knows what he's doing. And what's coming.

I couldn't help him, said Kunihiko.

That's not your job.

That's where you're wrong.

Kunihiko stood up, with his hands behind his back. Our foreheads nearly grazed each other's.

I should've been there, he said. At the hospital. When he found out he was sick. For all of it. Because *I've* been with him, this whole time. And *you* should have, too. That's the problem. The problem is that *you* were gone.

Kunihiko had beer on his breath. He was breathing on me now, leaning his forearms on the counter.

He could've died, said Kunihiko.

Bullshit, I said.

Stop. He could've. And what would you have done then?

I think that's enough, I said. Have you been drinking?

No. Maybe. But where were you, exactly? Really?

None of your fucking business, Kunihiko.

Out fucking boys, probably. While your father chokes on his deathbed.

There's this phenomenon that you'll get sometimes — but not too often, if you're lucky — where someone you think you know says something about your gayness that you weren't expecting at all. Ben called it a tiny earthquake. I don't think he was wrong. You're destabilized, is the point. How much just depends on where the quake originates, the fault lines.

Anyway. That's what I felt.

I waited to see if Kunihiko would break the silence again, but he did not.

I said, That's none of your business.

I bet you think I'm an idiot, he said.

No. But I think you're being fucking ridiculous.

Do you really think Eiju wouldn't have told me *that,* said Kunihiko. Me?

I think you're fucking pissing me off, Kunihiko.

Good. That's a good thing. You should be pissed. You should fucking care.

Kunihiko, I said, and I grabbed at his collar.

It happened pretty quickly. More like a dance than anything else. There wasn't any space for him to go anywhere, so there we were, groin to groin, and when Kunihiko tried to shift, I set my feet on either side of him.

Okay? I said. Okay?

Fine, said Kunihiko. Let me go.

No.

Listen to me, I said. I'm going to tell you a secret.

My father is going to die, I said. He's on his way out. And when he goes, who do you think's gonna decide what happens with this fucking place? And how do you think I'll feel about this particular conversation, after it happens? You think that'll help your situation?

Is that a threat?

This is a promise, Kunihiko.

So you think you're my fucking boss now, said Kunihiko.

No, I said. I *know* you work for me. Until I say otherwise.

Kunihiko's eyes bulged. But he'd stopped shifting around. It was the most upset I'd seen him.

And then the door opened behind us.

Sana stood in sweatpants and a coat, with a young woman beside him. He smiled by the door, but it slid from his face as he looked from Kunihiko to me, and the woman only blinked.

And then I saw the babies in their arms.

I could tell when Kunihiko saw them, too, because that's when he exhaled.

We both threw our hands behind our

backs, stepped away from each other.

Hope we're not interrupting anything, said Sana.

No way, I said.

Your kids! said Kunihiko.

Yeah, said Sana. And this is my wife, Erka. We were just passing through.

Maybe we're too early, said Erka.

No, I said. You're totally fine. Kunihiko was just pouring your drinks.

I wasn't doing shit, said Kunihiko.

Of course you were.

No, said Kunihiko, blinking, standing straight.

You're right, he said. If I stay here, I'd work for you. I get that. But I don't have to stay.

And just like that, Kunihiko slipped from behind the counter. He stumbled on his way out, catching himself. When Sana moved to help him, Kunihiko stopped for a moment, and then he shrugged him away, before he slipped past Erka and out the door.

That left the five of us in the bar.

Both of the twins yawned.

So, said Erka, is it like this every night?

Sana looked at me. I waved them to the stools. They both took a seat, juggling the kids, and I turned on the radio.

I asked if they were hungry. I hadn't

prepped much just yet, but I could make that happen.

Eiju never cooks this early, said Sana.

I know, I said, turning on the faucet, washing my hands.

Slowly, slowly, and then all at once.

Eiju reduced his actions to a tidy formula: he woke up, walked slowly down the road to the station. Rode the local line to a bakery he liked in the next neighborhood over. Took a coffee, bought some pastries, and, some days, he'd bring them back. Other days, he'd eat them there. But after he finished, he'd leave, find a bench, and have a smoke by the park. When he made it to the apartment, he'd lay back down again. He'd watch television, clicking through the channels. He'd cook lunch for himself, and then me, after I'd woken up. Just before I left for the bar, he'd have a final cigarette, and he'd set his head down to sleep.

When I made it back in the morning, he'd unlock the door. We'd start again the next day.

I messaged Ben.

Nothing wild. A simple hello.

What conversations do you have when you feel like there's nothing you want to say?

I set down the phone, and his response came immediately.

Ben asked me to send him a picture.

It was mid-afternoon. I sent him a photo of the sky.

He responded immediately, the quickest he'd ever replied:

I recognized the gas station by the apartment. The telephone lines by the Pizza Hut. The way the letters faded on their outer edges.

He'd sent a photo of his own sky.

After that, for no reason at all, I sent Ben photos of the things around me.

The train station. Some old folks on a bench. A sweaty beer at the bar. Some random kids shooting and missing three-pointers by the McDonald's. It didn't tell him anything about how I was doing or how I'd been. It wasn't like there was any information being disclosed. But it was a way of speaking, more or less.

And Ben sent me pictures of Ximena from work. Our front porch. Our neighbors. In one, the kids next door were throwing peace signs with their cat.

And how did everything come to such a turning point between us?

Quietly, I guess. The big moments are never big when they're actually fucking happening.

So let's play through it: We're walking around the block one night. Sometimes, we still did that. It wasn't a big production or anything, although by then Ben was throwing shit in every argument. And we argued pretty fucking often. I was generally unresponsive to that. Or I'd just call Ben spoiled. Fucking privileged. But. Still. Afterward, or more often beforehand, we'd walk from one end of the block to the other. If it wasn't too hot, we'd turn the corner and head back. And one day Ben asked me, at the edge of the road, if I wanted to keep going.

Yeah, I said, I think so. Unless you wanna go further.

When he didn't respond, I looked at his face.

We weren't talking about the same thing.

But he didn't bat my suggestion down. He saw the recognition in my eyes. All of a sudden we were on the same page. And we turned back together.

We didn't say anything else the whole walk back. We didn't fuck that night. But he held my hand until he fell asleep. I watched the way he cradled my fingers, and I tried to commit it to memory.

I'd break up with him the next evening. It would be better for us both.

When Ben flipped around, snoring, I tried to get that memory down, too.

But then, of course, Ma called to tell me about Eiju.

Questions my father has asked me since I've been in Japan: *Where do you live now in Houston? What? Why there? Couldn't find a bigger dump? You really think that's racist? Are you kidding me? You really think you've suffered? Do you live alone? Well, what's he doing? And he just let you go? To come here? To see me? And you think he really cares about you? You think anyone really cares about you? You think anyone really cares about us? Why'd you come here again? Calm down, it's not a big deal, you can't take a question but you think you've fucking been through some shit? What are we eating for dinner again?*

One night, Takeshi and Hiro goaded Sana away from his family, already six beers into a drinking game when they walked through the door. They were past piss-drunk before I asked them to simmer down.

Bullshit, said Hiro.

You aren't Eiju, said Sana.

Exactly, I said. Which means I'll throw your asses out.

At that, they all just fucking looked at me. Like I'd broken some sacred rule. But they didn't say anything about it either — they just did what I'd asked.

Later on, after all of this, they'd tell me, in that moment, I looked like him. That I sounded just like him.

On another night, Takeshi passed through the bar by himself. Usually, he was the loudest dude in his gaggle, but that evening he wasn't saying much of anything. There was a comfortable silence. He drank, chain-smoking, and I made myself busy behind the counter, and before he took off, he left too much money under his coaster. But when I called his name he waved me off, headed back into the night.

The mornings weren't exactly bright when I walked back to the apartment, and sometimes I'd pass the same huddle of kids at the station, dancing to Missy Elliott on their phones. They popped and locked by the escalator, pausing every now and again to watch one another. Whenever they saw me, they didn't stop. They let me linger, just doing their thing.

One morning, I drove the truck out to the dock for a supply run. When I handed Hikaru the list, he smoked, blowing everything just above my face. He didn't ask about Eiju. Acted like he wasn't even a factor. And once Hikaru stepped inside, he didn't come back out again. But then Sora emerged to help me load boxes, groaning the whole time about his knees. Afterward, the kid handed me two beers, and we drank them on the back of the pickup again, not saying a fucking word about anything.

I served the beer, I mixed the drinks, I cooked the rice, I washed the dishes.

It does a funny thing to your head, realizing

the moment that things begin to change.

At first, there was a pause, while the regulars acknowledged that this was their new reality. That *I* was their new reality. They were a little slower to ask for refills. A little more considerate with their conversations. They only had one person to deal with now, two feet running behind the bar instead of six.

One night, Natsue asked me how it was going, and I told her things were fine.

Really? she said.

Really, I said.

Okay, she said, and she rose her finger for another beer.

Eventually, their expectations returned. The scenery shifted.

It only happened once: one day, Hiro asked for stir-fried pork with kimchi, and it came out the way my ma made it, the way I'd been cooking it for Ben. Which was entirely unlike Eiju's. Or Kunihiko's. And Hiro opened his mouth to say the words: This doesn't taste the way Eiju would've done it.

Natsue and Hayato twitched. All I could do was nod.

But, said Hiro, it's not that bad. I can live with this.

One night, Mieko leaned across the bar and tapped my shoulder.

You didn't hear this from me, she whispered, but I have the *perfect* boy for you.

One afternoon, after a checkup, I asked Taro what to expect going forward. By then, he was visiting Eiju as a daily courtesy. We'd had the hospice conversation exactly once, and when I suggested more help, Eiju asked why the fuck I thought he'd been keeping me around.

After his check-ins, Taro and I talked outside on the railing. He'd purse his lips before he answered, considering everything.

What now, I said, and I swear to god he almost shrugged.

Nothing, said Taro.

I mean what can *I* do, I said.

I know what you meant, said Taro.

Everyone thinks there's more they can do, he said. The truth is that, sometimes, you're already doing it.

Of course Eiju didn't want to hear that shit.

He was slow to get out of bed now.

He was slow to take a dump.

He was slow to sit on the fucking sofa.

He was slow to stretch on the fucking patio.

Now, when I made it back from the bar in the mornings, I cooked breakfast for us both while he watched from the sofa. Sometimes, he'd take a single bite. Sometimes, he'd make it through his portion. Sometimes, he'd throw it all up afterward, and Eiju usually made it to the toilet, unless he accidentally, absolutely didn't.

But he always tried to eat what I made him.

When Eiju asked about the bar, and how it was going, and how his patrons were, I told him I was still adjusting. That I wasn't him.

No shit, he said. But that's not what I asked you.

It's fine. Still learning.

It's easier when you've got some help. Kunihiko's a good study.

I hadn't told him about Kunihiko, that I hadn't seen him since he left.

You'll get used to it, said Eiju.

And, despite everything, I told him I would.

■ ■ ■ ■

When things start to go, they leave all at once.

The next time Eiju falls, it's an event. He descends, spectacularly, in the kitchen, knocking over the cutting board and the ladles on the way down.

After that, his body's collapsing is a quiet, natural thing. He simply falls.

If I was around when it happened, then of course I helped him up.

Who knew what happened when I wasn't.

One morning, in the kitchen, I asked him. I'd just gotten back from the bar. We were eating on the floor, where he couldn't fall, and Eiju made this face.

Getting up gives me something to do when you're gone, he said.

Don't be stupid, I said. We should get you an emergency button.

So we can have more people fucking around in here? Get the fuck out of here.

I think you meant to say more *help*.

No, said Eiju. I'm fine. Your mother would

say I'm returning to the earth, he said. And it's entirely too early for this conversation.

In either case, said Eiju, I don't want a burial. Blow me into the ocean, all over Kansai. I don't care. Won't care. And neither will Mitsuko.

Don't say that.

It's true.

But you don't have to say it.

Now you're the one who's being unrealistic.

She won't give a shit, said Eiju. And she shouldn't.

Just promise me that you won't wait to tell her, he said. Let Mitsuko know as soon as I'm gone. Have you been talking to her?

Don't worry about that, I said.

Fine, said Eiju.

Promise me, said Eiju.

All right.

Say it.

I promise.

Good, said Eiju.

I've only got so many things to worry about now, said Eiju. Try not to give me too many more.

I'd watch Eiju to see if he'd crack. When it would happen. He never did.

I'd sit down on the wood floor beside him. I let myself lean on his legs, and when he didn't stiffen, I closed my eyes.

I waited to hear his breathing soften. When it didn't, I let myself drift to sleep.

But maybe that's the point, said Eiju, once he thought I'd dozed off.

Maybe everything comes back around, I heard him say, halfway asleep.

A memory: Eiju and me at home in Houston. We're waiting for Ma. She's flown back to Tokyo, briefly, where her parents will formally disown her. It'll be decades before she returns again.

But now, in her absence, Eiju and I make faces at each other. We're piled under a bedsheet. Our neighbors are fighting or fucking next door — doing something noisy through the apartment walls.

First, Eiju's a ghost.

Then, he's trumpeter.

Next, he's a dog.

I am six or seven.

At one point, Eiju crawls around me in a

circle, pawing at my shoulder, on his hands and knees, while I try to grab at his hair, the happiest I've ever been.

Another memory: Ma's still gone. Eiju and I are eating in the Chinese restaurant. He's brought me to work, because of course he can't afford a babysitter, or even have the first idea about where to find one. But his shift is over, and I'm sitting on the counter as he ladles noodles into my mouth. When they slip off my face, or out of my teeth, he catches them, tangling them in his fingers to eat them himself.

Slowly, he says, dangling them from his lips.

A memory: Eiju and I drive downtown, drifting through Houston in the evening. He has no one to go home to, and I'm the only person he needs to see. We've rented a car with that week's earnings, a flashy thing Ma would never approve of. I'm sitting next to my father as he names the streets, sounding them out, enunciating everything. His English is fine, but he stumbles on the Spanish and Vietnamese avenues.

When we stop at the lights, he points my fingers toward the streetlights above us.

That's where you'll live, he says, after

every glossy building we pass, with their lights shining down on the two of us.

And then one afternoon, Kunihiko showed up to Eiju's door, without preamble or explanation or rationale.

He wore sweats and a sleeveless tee. The most casual I'd ever seen him. He carried a tote full of groceries on one arm and a paper sack full of vegetables in the other.

He stepped past me, unspeaking, and set them on the counter. Eiju caught his eye, and then mine, but he didn't say anything about it.

Wordlessly, Kunihiko fished around for pans in the kitchen cupboard. He felt around for chopsticks, a spoon, and a measuring cup. I leaned on the counter beside him, watching, and every now and again he glanced my way.

Eventually I said, How do you know where everything is?

All Japanese stock their kitchens the same way, said Kunihiko.

I didn't know that.

No one expected you to. Where's the spatula?

Where the real Japanese keep theirs.

You really aren't funny, said Kunihiko.

I know. But listen, what the fuck is going on?

Kunihiko only frowned at me. He shook his head.

Nothing, he said. I'm just here to help.

Really?

Really. Same as always.

No. It's not that simple.

But it can be, said Kunihiko, sighing, looking at his feet. If you let it, then it really can be that simple. I can just be here. Helping.

That's the easy way out, I said.

You're not wrong, said Kunihiko.

He nodded. Then he extended his hand.

Truce? he asked.

He really was just like a kid.

Shouldn't I be asking you that, I said.

I was an asshole, said Kunihiko. It wasn't right.

You were.

I'm serious.

So am I.

Can you both please shut the fuck up, said Eiju. I thought you already had a goddamn boyfriend, Mike.

Kunihiko started back in on the eggs, slicing tomatoes and onions and tofu, spooning in a little potato starch, and whipping it all into something like a frittata, before we slipped it in the oven. We flopped down and

346

zoned out by the television. Eiju groaned at a shitty dub of *Rush Hour 2*. Twenty minutes later, we forgot about the casserole, burning the whole fucking thing, and we ate all of it anyways.

Another memory: Stuffing shit into the car before a drive to California, to see the coast, Eiju lifts my mother and sets her in the back seat. She screams, laughing, and a Black neighbor beside us peeps through her blinds. When she sees that it's just my parents, she waves her hand at the three of us.

Another memory: It's a long drive to San Francisco, and we only stop once, at the motel. The front desk lady is brown. She smiles with all her teeth. When my mother asks us to pull some ice from a machine down the hallway, Eiju takes me with him, half-asleep, carrying me on his shoulders, running at full speed as I carry the bucket screaming.

Another memory: Our first night in the motel room. It's so hot that I can't sleep; the air conditioning doesn't work. When I can't get comfortable in my sheets on the floor, I leave them for the carpet. When I can't get comfortable on the carpet, I take off my shirt, and then my pants. When I start crying, Eiju leaves the bed with my mother to sleep on the floor beside me. Ma finds me cradled around him in the morning. She asks why we thought this would make us any less hot.

Another memory: Eiju flips through photos on the floor, asking me if I look like his father or my mother's father. I shrug, because I don't know. He tells me that someone will tell me if I don't decide early on.

It's the ears, he says, tugging on mine.

Another memory: My mother attempts to flip a pancake on the motel room's hot plate, and it lands on the floor tile. Over the past two days, we've watched fuck knows how many roaches sprint across it. My mother's eyes never leave the pancake, and, out of nowhere, Eiju appears from the next room over, peels it off the ground, swallows it whole.

Another memory: My parents, washed from the heat and sprawled across the carpet, turn the radio to a station playing D'Angelo. Eiju leaps from the floor, where he's lying with me, and grabs Ma by the shoulders. But she isn't surprised by the suddenness: her body tenses, for half of a second, before they fall into a slow dance. Eiju croons the chorus of "Brown Sugar." Eventually, they bring their serenade to a circle around me, falling, laughing.

One day, I was lying on the sofa, dozing, and Eiju just stared. I asked what he was looking at.

My son, he said.

Stop that, I said.

Okay, he said, and I knew I'd regret saying that for the rest of my life.

One day, I found another notebook by Eiju's bed. It was full of lists, half-scribbled in English, like the one in the bathroom. I put it back where I found it. Then I changed my mind, stuffed it in my duffel.

One day, Eiju asked me to walk him to the Shinto shrine a few blocks from the apartment.

Not to be a dick, I said, but it's a little late for religion.

Shinto is for everyone, said Eiju. You dick.

Our pace was slow, but the afternoon was, too. Bikers wheeled around us. Pedestrians didn't even glance our way. Once we made it to the shrine, I walked my father up the steps, holding his elbow, toward the bell and the podium, and when I stopped just behind him, he turned my way.

What the hell are you doing, he asked. Get up here.

I started to say something, but then I didn't. I joined him.

Standing beside him, I saw how small he'd gotten. My father had shrunk. Eiju'd become feeble.

Do you know how, he asked, and I told him I didn't.

You used to know, said Eiju. You used to love coming to the shrine.

He walked me through it: we washed our hands, made our offering.

Bowed twice.

Clapped twice.

Bowed again.

Now, said Eiju, make a wish and ring the bell.

Why are we ringing it?

So the gods can hear you, said Eiju, and he wouldn't meet my face as he rang it.

He stepped to the side while I grabbed the rope.

Big guy like you, he said. They should definitely hear it.

So I rang it.

I thought about wishing, and my mind went blank.

But I rang, and I rang, and I rang.

Some nights, Kunihiko slept over on an extra tatami mat by the door, and other nights he didn't. Eiju called it Kunihiko's big wet dream. And the first time the kid heard that, he blushed furiously, intensely, but he didn't deny it.

Now, the lights were off above us. Snores floated in from Eiju's bedroom. Kunihiko and I lay head to head, arms crossed.

Mike, he said, and I looked up.

It'll be all right, said Kunihiko. Really.

Yeah, I said. You're doing a great job.

Mike.

Really. You're taking the whole thing well.

That's not what I mean, said Kunihiko.

The next morning, we ate eggs over rice. Kunihiko and I cooked side by side. And afterward, Eiju nodded as Kunihiko holed up in the bathroom.

That boy's a fool, he said.

But you really should listen to him, he said.

Then Eiju burped, explosively, monstrously, shaking the living room.

He wore the most stoic look on his face. And then I started laughing, and then he started laughing, and then Kunihiko came sprinting out of the bathroom, asking what had happened, what the hell had gone wrong.

Later, Kunihiko and I sat across from Eiju on the floor when he asked the kid if he ever thought he'd get married.

Kunihiko looked at me. I shrugged.

Before he could answer, Eiju said, I didn't.

But Mike's mother changed my mind, he added.

I'm not saying you have to, or that you should, he said.

Both of you, said Eiju. There are people out there that'll change your mind.

Eventually, Kunihiko fell asleep. Eiju and I watched his chest rise and fall beside us. The kid would shudder, every now and again, from his shoulders to his calves, but he never opened his eyes. His body settled right back into silence.

I was scared, said Eiju, a little later.

I thought he'd fallen asleep.

That's why, he said.

Why what?

You know what, said Eiju.

I was scared, he said. So I ran. That's why I came home.

I watched Eiju's toes. I stared at his thighs.

You could've told me earlier, I said.

It would've been too hard to understand, said Eiju. I didn't understand it. And you were a baby.

A teenager isn't a baby.

You were a baby.

You could've tried.

No, said Eiju. We thought it'd be better that I didn't.

We, I said.

It was Mitsuko's idea.

Both of you.

And she was right, said Eiju. As usual.

We told ourselves we'd know when to tell you, said Eiju. We'd know when the moment was right.

But you never did, I said.

I'm telling you now, said Eiju, looking my way. The moment is now.

But then there was the night that the three of us stood on the pier in San Francisco. We'd finally made it. Ma, Eiju, and I couldn't afford to do anything but walk around, so that's what we did, and Eiju cobbled together the change in his pockets for three hot dogs. When it turned out that he was short, my father told us to wait while he walked back to the car. I paced beside my mother while she smiled at the seller, a white guy. He didn't smile back.

When Eiju made it over, the white man told him that he was still short by a dime, and he tossed Eiju's loose change back across the wooden counter.

I'm told that, in Japan, my father was a fighter. Here was a man who would box over nothing, raising his fists at anyone.

But that day, Eiju only smiled. He collected the rest of his change, taking his two hot dogs from the stand.

Ma and I walked behind him. She gave me a look, and that look said to shut the fuck up. So I did that, and we reached a bench by the pier, and my mother took a bite of one hot dog, and I took a bite of the other.

When Ma offered Eiju a bite of hers, he shook his head as if he couldn't even imagine it.

When I lifted mine for my father, I expected the same result. He gave me a clear look.

But then he opened his jaws wide and took a huge chunk out of it, nearly downing the thing in one bite, and my knuckles, too.

■ ■ ■ ■

And then, and then, and then.

One night, I woke up for a piss, and I heard the silence.

Of course we knew it would happen.
  I knew it would happen.
  And he knew it would happen.

So it happened.

Kunihiko wasn't there when I found him, but he was the first person I called.

Then I called Taro.

Then I sat beside my father.

He wasn't cold, exactly. He'd gone in his sleep. I hadn't known that people actually did that, that this was something that actually happened to people.

Before Taro arrived, I called Ma. Stepped outside. The sun shone on the balcony. Some kids bounced a ball in the alley. It would've been late afternoon in Houston.

When my mother answered, almost smiling into the phone, I thought that things would be okay, they would probably work out, and I almost kept my father's death to myself, I hadn't heard hope in her voice for so long.

But I thought of Eiju.

The promise.

Ma didn't scream. Her breathing caught for a moment. And then she was speaking regularly again, talking in measured tones.

She asked if I was all right, and I told her that I was.

She asked where we were, and I told her that it'd happened in the apartment, we'd both been sleeping.

Good, she said.

Good, I said.

So it could've been worse, said Ma.

I opened my mouth, and a dry sound came out.

Listen to me, she said. You stay with him. You don't need to call anyone else. Call someone if you need help, but I'll take care of the rest. The important thing is to stay with him, while you can.

You won't get this moment again, she said. Do you hear me? This is the last time you'll get to do this, and you'll wonder why you were thinking about so many other things. I'm telling you this because I know. Do you understand?

I understand.

Are you sure? she asked, in Japanese. Michael?

I am, I said, in Japanese. I'm okay.

Good, said Ma. I'll take care of everything else.

When my mother hung up, I stared at my father.

I lay down beside him and put my hand on his chest.

His arm was loose, and I swung it over mine. I lay there, in my father's arms, for ten minutes, fifteen, until there was banging on the door, yelling for me to let them in.

Ma handled all of the arrangements that she could on her end. She contacted his family, his sister, and that sister's side of the family. Taro dealt with the authorities. But it turned out that Eiju, the prince of chaos, had laid everything else out.

There was a plan for where he wanted to be cremated and what he wanted done with his ashes afterward. A third to his family in Kyushu. A third spread out in Osaka. A third for his son, if he wanted them, and if not, those could go just about anywhere.

Everything was handled. All I had to do was deal with it.

Kunihiko manned the bar. He didn't even ask.

Just tell me when you're good again, he said. I'll be here.

Yeah, I said.

Don't rush back, he said. As much time as you need.

Yeah, I said.

Taro walked me through all the paperwork, all the administrative tasks. Natsue walked me through everything else. She said she didn't want to see the body, didn't need to. She'd known Eiju well enough.

I didn't have to sign the bar over for six months, like he'd said. The rent was paid up until then. After that, I could keep the lease going or turn it over.

You'll make money either way, said Natsue.

That doesn't matter, I said.

Natsue was polite enough not to respond immediately, but then she did.

Of course it matters, she said. He's gone. But you're still here.

Eiju didn't want a ceremony at the temple or any of that shit, so there wasn't a ceremony. He explicitly wanted everything to go on as normal.

There was a thing at the bar, and Kunihiko hosted it, but I told him I wasn't going, not to expect me, and I didn't disappoint.

That night was my first alone in the apartment. Tan showed up with a bag of convenience store food.

When I asked how he'd found me, he said Kunihiko told him.

We ate karaage and rice on the sofa, sipping beer, not talking about much. When I asked about his mother, Tan told me she was doing fine. He talked about his job. He talked about the weather. He talked and talked to fill the void, and he didn't ask what my plans were, or where I planned on going, or what I planned on doing, and when Tan stopped talking, I said, I'll be gone for a little while.

Okay, said Tan.

Before he left, he put a hand on my face

and gave it a scratch.

He said, I'll see you later.

Yeah, I said.

Yeah? said Tan.

I think so, I said. Yes.

Okay.

Okay.

I booked my flight.

I called my mother.

I texted Ben.

I sat in Eiju's apartment. I took all of him into my nose. I held him in my body, and I tried not to exhale, I tried not to push back out again. My father had left a second time. My father had tried to stay. My father hadn't tried to stay. It wasn't his fault. It was his fault. My father wasn't coming back. My father wasn't coming back.

But, a few days beforehand, I was riffling around his bedroom's cabinet. I'd been looking for loose yen or a pencil or not much of anything, sifting through the shit my father'd accumulated over years in this apartment. He hadn't stepped through that room in at least a week, stuck to the living

360

room couch at the end. I'd brought out all of his clothes to make things easier on him. Folded them up within reach. Sat outside the bath while he washed himself and shut my ears as he cried. And it was in a drawer that I found a photo of the two of us.

The hoodie I'm rocking looks entirely too big on me. My father's still got a headful of hair, and some of it sits on his shoulders. He's smiling way too wide for his face, with his hands under my arms, and I'm sitting on his lap with the ocean and the pier and the whole country behind us. I don't know if I'm smiling because I was told to or because I was happy, but my father's expression is entirely unmistakable.

Ma must've taken the photo when we were in Cali. I don't remember her doing that. But I guess that's the thing: we take our memories wherever we go, and what's left are the ones that stick around, and that's how we make a life.

So I'll take that photo with me.

I'll say that's what happened.

It'll be all that's left, as I step onto the plane.

And when I land on the tarmac, back on the ground, unbelievably, inconceivably, until the day I die, I am taking my dad

home, I am taking him back, he will follow
me wherever the fuck I end up next.

■ ■ ■ ■

BENSON

■ ■ ■ ■

1.

Mike unpacked his bags and caught a whole night's sleep, which became a whole day's sleep, which left me and Mitsuko tiptoeing around the apartment. Like we'd made some unspoken agreement to let the bear hibernate. To catch up on his rest. To ignore the problem he created, although of course he didn't create it, and now I've gone back to work barely having seen him.

The kids track mud all over the carpet. They're eager for spring break. Totally wired. Barry and I slump across the counter, watching Ethan and Xu poke each other's noses.

You heard from our girl yet? says Barry.

No, I say.

Ximena flew to Amsterdam to meet the rest of Noah's family. She'd insisted, vehemently, that it wasn't their honeymoon, which could only be in Oaxaca, with the rest of *her* family.

Sounds about right, dude, says Barry. Of course she'd leave us with the kids.

She just got married, I say. Dude.

Which is totally cool, says Barry. But when I got hitched, I showed up to work.

I don't say anything to that. Barry just smiles, satisfied with his case. Margaret joins Ethan and Xu in their roughhousing, and I look up at Ahmad, who's coloring crossword puzzles on the carpet.

Eventually, I ask him why he's doing that. The kid doesn't even look up at me. But then I get down on all fours, at eye level, and Ahmad rolls to the side.

I say, You know the boxes are for letters, right?

Not always, says Ahmad.

Well, I say, at least a significant chunk of the time.

Nah, says Ahmad, sighing and rolling toward his stomach, bringing our chat to a close.

They just need to be filled, he adds, already scribbling again.

Back at the apartment, I catch Mike in the living room.

He's sitting with his mother. Mitsuko's fucking around on her tablet. An urn stands between them, and it hasn't moved for the

366

past two days, and I haven't asked what's in it because I already know.

They're making arrangements. Mitsuko's hair is precisely all over the place. But her poise is postured, perfect. She and her son couldn't be any more different, and yet they look exactly alike. A few hours earlier, Mitsuko booked her flight back to Tokyo, and she chose a seat by the emergency exit. She'd decided that it was time to go, and Mike hadn't disagreed.

I figure there won't ever be a better time to tell him.

Hey, I say, do you have a minute?

When Mike looks up, there's something new on his face, underneath this grin. He's been cheesing since he landed. It's fake, and I wonder if I'm the only one who notices. We've spent too much time together for me to miss it — and in reality, underneath the smile, he looks entirely exhausted. But if Mitsuko sees that, she doesn't show it.

Ma? says Mike.

Mitsuko doesn't even blink. If anything, she licks a finger for her tablet.

No, she says, we're busy.

It'll only take a second, I say.

Ma, says Mike.

Really? says Mitsuko. Right now? With everything that's going on?

She follows that with something in Japanese to Mike, but now she's looking at me, and all I can do is smile.

What's up, Ben? says Mike.

You know what, I say, it can actually wait.

It'll have to, says Mitsuko, slipping off her glasses, shifting her body toward mine.

Ma, says Mike, and when his mother groans, he adds, Just let him talk. We're all family now. You two have gotten to know each other.

Whatever kernel of loss Mike's feeling is in his voice. Right there.

Mitsuko puts her tablet facedown. She looks from me to Mike.

Boys, she says, I haven't asked any questions. I've gone along with everything. Michael left, and I said nothing. I stayed with a young man I'd never met, for an undetermined amount of time, and I said nothing. But now, of all moments, you're telling me to wait. No.

You can wait, says Mitsuko. Just this once. It won't hurt you. Michael is back. Soon, you'll have him all to yourself again, and you can tell him whatever you want to, for however long you want to tell him. But right now, we have things to do. Right now, we're busy.

And with that, Mitsuko turns back to her tablet.

I look at Mike. He purses his lips.

So I say, All right.

And I shut the door behind me.

But not before Mitsuko groans an audible, breathy, *Jesus.*

Under any other circumstance, I'd have texted Ximena immediately, but she never bought an international phone plan, and I won't be fucked with a trillion-dollar bill.

I'd text Mike, but he's sitting in the center of the sun.

I'd text Omar, but he's on the other end of the solar system.

So I reach out to my sister.

Spring in Houston is scalding sidewalks and sun-drunk lovebugs. It's dead grass and midday thunderstorms. It isn't the beginning or the end of anything, just a prolonged in-between through dead-end traffic on I-45.

Mike may be back, but I still take his car. I drive to the park a few blocks away, and then I just sit in the quiet, where I can hear myself think. Everyone's bracing themselves for the sun. The Third Ward's residents lounge on their front steps, fanning themselves, halfway watching their kids. The daughter next door to us throws grass at a kitten, enticing the stray with Spanish. The humidity's negligible for once, which only happens a few times a year, but once everyone's outside, and the weather finally turns civil, the block looks less like a gentrification exhibition than a living, shitting neighborhood.

Eventually, Lydia's car ambles toward mine. She steps out of it in shorts and a sweater, fondling a vape pen. We make our way to a swing set, dragging our feet below us, smoking as the chains clink beside us.

You better be going through it, she says. Making me drive all the way out here.

It's not that far, I say.

You could've came to me.

I could've. Mike's back.

That's enough for Lydia to whistle. She leans against her swing, passing me the pen.

Is that a good thing, she asks.

It's a thing, I say.

Sorry, bubba.

Nothing to be sorry about.

I know. But I'm still sorry.

I ask how Lydia's been doing, and she responds with a shrug. She's been living with our father three days out of the week. In the photos she sends me, sometimes, he looks absolutely miserable. But the thing is that he's present, and she's right there beside him.

I tell her that it's cute, and Lydia scoffs.

Nothing cute about living with an old fucking man, she says.

I wouldn't mind that, I say. If I could find one to put me up.

You've already got a nice little mister.

Maybe not, I say. That might be about to change.

Lydia looks at me. She turns my way, crossing her legs.

Everything changes, she says. Change isn't good or bad. It's just change.

Is that supposed to cheer me up?

It's not supposed to do anything. Just throwing it out there.

Moving on isn't a bad thing, says Lydia, yeah? It's just a thing. And it happens to everyone. Whether you want it to or not. So do you want it to?

I don't know, I say.

Of course not, says Lydia. If it helps, I like Mike. But I like you more.

Thanks, big sister.

You're welcome, baby brother.

Lydia squeezes my shoulder, massaging the edge of it. A cloud drifts just above us, shielding us from the glare. I tell my sister that, worst-case, I might need to stay at the house for a while, and she turns my way, frowning, and then she exhales a mouthful of smoke, falling into a laugh.

That's fine, she says, grinning. But I'm already sleeping in your room.

When I make it back to the apartment, Mitsuko's asleep on the sofa. There are dishes in the sink, and Mike's washing them, slowly. But before I speak up, he puts a finger to his lips, wiping down his hands, waving me toward the bedroom.

We've hardly shut the door before he wraps his arms around me.

The first thing I do is flinch.

And then I realize it's just a hug.

All Mike's doing is hugging me.

I open my mouth, and he shushes me.

We'll deal with it, he says. We'll figure it out.

But, says Mike, let's just do this for a minute, please, and I can't remember the last time I heard him use the word.

So I sink my head into his shoulder. Mike closes his eyes. I tremble.

When I wake up, it's way past midnight. The living room's silent. I figure Mitsuko's sound asleep, and Mike's tapping on his phone, and I can't tell if he sees me or what.

So I ask him to pass me a pillow. I tell him I'll sleep on the floor.

Now you're just being fucking ridiculous, says Mike, pulling me onto his stomach.

We lie there for a moment, just breathing on each other.

So, I say, you went to Osaka.

Yeah, says Mike. Now I'm back.

And your father, I say, and I regret it the moment the words leave my mouth, but all Mike does is scratch the bridge of his nose.

I slip my fingers in his hair. Mike's shoulders relax.

I've been seeing someone, I say.

I don't know what I expect to happen, but I brace myself.

Mike blinks once, and then once again.

Seeing seeing? says Mike. Or are you two just fucking?

I don't know, I say.

Okay, says Mike, and his body relaxes even further.

In that case, he says, I met someone, too.

He looks me in the eyes when he says it.

Despite everything, I don't feel anything.

It isn't serious, he says.

Right, I say.

We just met.

But it's serious enough for you to bring it up.

Mike licks his lips at that. He weighs whatever he's about to say next on his teeth.

His name's Tan, says Mike. And what's your guy's name?

He's not my guy.

Fine. Your person.

This conversation is insane, I say.

Maybe, says Mike. But tell me about him.

I'd rather not.

You were ready to dish earlier.

Stop it.

His name's Omar, I say.

Omar, says Mike. That's a nice name.

Don't be a dick.

I meant it, says Mike. It's a nice name.

Fine, I say.

Do you like him?

No.

And then I say, I might like him.

But I don't know, I say. I don't know what we're doing.

I lie with my hands in Mike's hair. He keeps letting me do that.

I guess we left our situation up in the air, says Mike.

No, I say. *You* left.

I left, says Mike.

Our heater strains above us, and we can

hear its muscles flexing. A sneeze slips in from the living room. Neither of us brings it up.

I might be leaving again, says Mike.

You're joking, I say.

No, says Mike. A surprise for a surprise. Now we're even.

That's not even remotely the same thing.

Ben, says Mike, my dad is dead.

He's gone, says Mike. And that is what it is. But he left me something. And I think I should take it, at least for a little while.

Something, I say.

A business. It's a little complicated.

A business, I say.

Yeah, says Mike.

The two of us flex our toes. They accidentally brush.

So it's something you don't even know if you'll like, I say.

No, says Mike. I don't. And, honestly, I could hate it. I might already hate it. But I think I'd like to find out.

Our neighbors slam the screen door, but neither of us jumps. A scattering of Spanish slips through the window, followed by laughter and clinking bottles.

Well, I say, I can't possibly pay for this place on my own.

If you were making that kind of money,

says Mike, this would be a very different conversation.

Stop fucking around, I say, and Mike settles his chin on my shoulder.

We're silent for another five minutes.

It turns into ten.

So you're not even gonna ask to come, says Mike.

I look at him.

To Japan? I say.

You know where, says Mike.

I look him in the face. He isn't smiling anymore. I don't see the joke.

I say, Are you asking me to come?

Mike says, Would that change your answer?

I say, What the fuck would I do in Japan?

You'd figure it out, says Mike. Same as people figure anything out. Other people have done it.

Not people like me.

Because you're Black?

Because I have a life here, Michael.

You say that like I don't. Like all my people aren't here. Everyone I fucking care about. Like that isn't my life, too.

You do, I say. But it's different.

It's the same fucking thing, says Mike.

No, I say. You'll have your mother, this business thing. I wouldn't have anyone.

I won't have shit, says Mike. You've spent more time with her in the past few weeks than I have in the past few years.

If anything, he says, I'm losing two people. The two people that actually give a fuck about me and my fucking life. That's my fucking situation.

It's the tensest I've ever seen Mike. But he delivers everything in an even tone. He cracks his knuckles over his stomach, so I set my palms on his belly to stop him.

You won't lose me, I say. Even if you leave. Either way.

Everyone says that, says Mike.

I'm not everyone, I say. You won't lose me. Okay?

Right.

Do you believe me?

Okay, says Mike.

Okay then, I say.

I say, So.

I say, You think I just go with you? And then it's happily ever after?

Mike rubs his palms on top of mine. He kneads them, slowly, like he's smoothing out the wrinkles.

Eventually he says, There's no such thing.

It could be, I say.

It could be, says Mike.

I squeeze his knuckles for him. They

crackle like tiny fireworks.

But no, says Mike. I really don't think so.

And just like that, the air whooshes right out of my body.

And I tell Mike I don't think so either.

And once the words leave my mouth, they actually feel true.

So what are we doing, I say. You know. Until?

Until?

Until you're gone.

I'm moving, says Mike. Not dying.

You know what I'm saying.

Mike waves his hands at the apartment. I watch them glow, taking everything in.

I think we ride it out, he says.

Yeah?

Yeah.

And then Mike and I don't say anything else.

The air from the heater is aggressively warm. We're sweating, both of us, on his bed, and our bodies aren't touching. Then I reach for Mike's hand, again, and it takes him a minute to squeeze. But eventually he does. We don't wrap our fingers around each other's. We just fucking hold on.

And then.

And then.

And then slowly, suddenly, I'm asleep and when I wake up, it's six in the morning.

Mike is snoring. The sound mingles with his mother's murmurs, wafting in from the living room. She's speaking on the phone in Japanese, warmly, decisively. She pauses every now and again, and I can practically hear her nodding. If you really squeeze your ears, the two noises suction in harmony, with Mitsuko and her son rising and falling in tandem, conducting their own tiny orchestra.

2.

I can count the times we've said we love each other on two hands. I wouldn't even have to use all my fingers.

The second time, we were out driving. The traffic around us mellowed. We were lodged between SUVs, and I don't remember where we were going, just that we weren't headed anywhere in particular. Then the car started blowing hot air, and then hotter air, and then no air at all.

When I started to roll down the window, the button wouldn't budge.

Mike tried from his end, and that button was stuck, too.

Is this just how it's gonna be now, I said.

Guess so, said Mike.

Hope it's not a sign or anything.

Hopefully, said Mike.

And then he said it.

We rode on in silence. Soaked in sweat. The traffic getting worse and worse.

That thing happened where you hear the words leave someone's mouth, and they rebound through your ears, again and again, coming and going.

The truck in front of us wouldn't move. Mike's windows wouldn't open. He put the car in park, reclined his seat, and closed his eyes.

The next time was over a nothing dinner in the middle of the night. I'd gotten hungry, and Mike was snoring in bed, and I stumbled over his thigh to make something in the kitchen. Our fridge was always loaded, but that means nothing when you don't know what to do with what's in there. I slapped a pan on the stove, cracked an egg on the counter, and it wasn't five minutes before the fire alarm popped off.

I didn't notice Mike until he'd started fanning the smoke behind me. Then he wordlessly, silently, set a wok on the stove. He fried me two eggs, and another pair for himself and we ate them on the counter, swinging our legs against the wood.

It came out under his breath, between chews, under the alarm.

It was entirely too loud, but he enunciated everything.

■ ■ ■ ■

The fourth time, he was fucking me. Said it right before he came.

3.

A few hours later, it's the knocking that wakes me up. Or I'm up, and Mike isn't beside me. Doesn't answer when I call out.

Suddenly, totally, I get this fucking chill.

There's a text on my phone from Omar. It's only a smiley face.

There's another text from Mike: he and Mitsuko have gone for a walk. They'll be back soon.

And then there's a phone call from my sister, and then another phone call, and then a third.

The text message below that says: Heads up, otw.

Right after Lydia moved out of the house, and I was still living with my father, I spent the night at her place on Sul Ross. We walked to the Shell for beer and got fucked up in the parking lot, stumbling back toward her apartment. We passed some teens kick-

383

ing a soccer ball by the park, calling after one another in Spanish, so we sat in the grass to watch them, and, at some point, the most confident one skipped over to Lydia.

He asked for her number, just like that.

She asked to join their game.

I told my sister that wasn't wise. Lydia told me it wasn't a problem. And the boys were hands-off with her, at first, but after she'd scored two goals, they made a point to rough her up. The one who'd been hitting on my sister kicked at her ankles. When she made him fall on his hands, he spat in the dirt. And then she scored again.

Afterward Lydia still gave him her number. He held it up like a trophy, jigging between his friends. And at the end of that match, my sister's shorts were filthy with mud, and her sneakers, too, and she was still a little groggy, and she couldn't have smiled any wider.

I guess what I'm saying is: She really does try her best.

And then they're at the door.

My sister, my father, my mother.

My family.

Lydia scrunches her nose, and my mother

purses her lips. She asks if my guests are around.

It doesn't *matter,* says my father. It's too fucking *humid,* let us *in.*

The last time we'd all sat in the same room, we were still together in the old house, picking at a meal my mother cooked. A few days earlier, she'd told us she was leaving. Dinner felt like a consolation prize. She'd made beef patties and ackee. So we all took a bite, and we did our best not to enjoy it, but we found ourselves filing back to the kitchen for thirds and fourths.

At one point, the three of us stood with a patty in each hand. For a beat, we waited for someone else to snatch the last one. But the palm that finally swooped in belonged to my mother, sweeping her fingers over the entire bowl.

We watched her chew through the flakiness, slowly, and then she stood up and she left us.

Now my family sits on the sofa. Crammed like donuts in a basket.

Your father has something he wants to share with everyone, says my mother.

It's not a big fucking deal, says my father.

I'm in therapy, he says. Surprise.

My mother wipes her face. My father sneezes. In the dim light of the apartment, we all look filtered. Sickly.

I squint at my parents, and it doesn't look like they're joking.

What, says my father to me.

When I don't respond, my mother says, It *is* a surprise.

Dad's making an effort, says Lydia. That's good.

Right, Benson? says my mother.

It's great, I say. Lovely. Wonderful. Fine.

But, I say, what the fuck does that have to do with me? Why the fuck did you have to come here to tell me this?

Everyone shifts in their seats. My father flexes his toes.

Are you going to say it? says my mother, nudging my father.

He obviously doesn't want to hear it, says my father.

That's a part of the process, says my mother. Remember?

When I make a face, my father says, Guillermo thinks it's important to share.

Guillermo, I say.

The therapist, says my father. He says that *my* successes are my *family's* successes. *Your* successes are *my* successes.

And Guillermo is *correct,* says my mother.

386

Albeit nine or ten years too late, says Lydia.

Guillermo sounds like a fucking grifter, I say.

The three of them look at me. But, really, they're taking in the apartment. They're looking for something to explain me, clues to my life, I think — except there's nothing to find.

I still don't understand why this couldn't have been a text message, I say.

Really, says Lydia.

For fucking real. You could've called.

We *did* call, says my mother.

And anyways, she adds, you wouldn't have answered.

The light in the room shifts from a dingy blue to a muddy red. We all turn a shade darker. My mother crosses her legs.

We came here to see your world, says my father.

You just wanted to take the pressure off yourself, I say.

Benson, says Lydia.

It's the truth, I say. *He* knows it's true. Things get hot on your end for once, and you're trying to deflect.

You aren't being fair, says my father.

It's all you fucking do. Has Guillermo told you that yet?

And you're no better, I say to my mother. Why do you even care? Don't you have somewhere to be? Isn't there a whole other family out there you should be taking care of?

Ben, says Lydia, don't be a dick.

How about you don't be fucking complicit, I say. I'm here taking all of this heat, and what are you doing? Chilling? Going with the flow?

The air behind my eyes feels warmer and warmer. It's a little like gravity — I know I should decelerate, but the words just keep coming.

Do you know how it felt when you didn't say shit once I came up positive? I say. When you guys left me? When you fucking shit me out on the street? And I had to deal with that fucking shit on my own? It felt like the worst thing. I can't even fucking tell you. And now you really drive up here looking for some sympathy heart-to-heart bullshit? From me?

All Lydia and my mother do is stare. They don't look upset. Or even exhausted, really. But my father's got this look on his face, like he's got some big secret in his chest. It slips a bit, and a grin cracks his face.

Say it! I yell. Fucking speak up!

Son, says my father, that's the most I've

heard you talk in who knows how long.

This Mike must really be doing a number on you, he says.

You sound like a little boy in love, he says.

Lydia bites down a laugh. My mother chews her cheeks. It feels like the four of us are caught in a loop, like we've already lived through this moment before. And before I can curse my father, before I can really unload, the door unlocks behind me, and it's Mike and his mother standing in the doorway.

Mitsuko speaks first.

She says, Not again.

My mother says, Hello.

Lydia says, Hey, Mike.

My father just sits there with this blank look on his face. He makes a noise with his throat.

Mitsuko stands with her arms crossed and a satchel on her shoulder. She's dressed in Mike's clothes, a too-big SUPREME sweater and basketball shorts. They both smell like cigarettes, and Mike's in a tank top, and he's got a sack of groceries in his arms, and his face is entirely unreadable, and I don't know if it's on me to speak up or what.

But I don't know what I could possibly say.

So I don't say anything at all.

And then I open my mouth.

And what comes out is, Well.

That's when Mitsuko steps across the room. She sits on the sofa across from my parents. My father's eyes widen, and Mitsuko doesn't flinch, and my father says, I've heard a lot about you from my daughter.

You're pretty infamous, too, says Mitsuko.

I hear Mike migrate toward the kitchen with the bags, and it's clear that he's left me afloat. But a few seconds later, he's back in the living room. He's right beside me.

He squeezes my mother's hand and says, Ma'am, it's nice to finally meet you.

He leans over to hug Lydia, whispering something in her ear.

He stands in front of my father, a little wider, a little shorter.

And my father, for no reason in particular, stands up to face him, nearly towering over him.

Mitsuko sighs. Lydia laughs. My mother elbows her ribs.

Then, inexplicably, my father extends his hand.

I'm Ben's father.

I know, says Mike.

Good.

And I'm your son's boyfriend.

So I've heard, says my father.

My father says, It's nice to meet you, and Mike lets go of his hand.

Mike looks at the whole of us. He looks at me.

Mike asks if anyone's hungry. He says, I was just about to start dinner.

4.

The fifth *I love you* came in the middle of the night. I'd started living at Mike's place. There was a banging at the door, a frantic sort of slamming, almost like a pleading, and it woke me up first. So I nudged Mike's shoulder until he finally moaned, swatting at my hand, and then I squeezed the bridge of his nose.

What the fuck, he said.

And then he heard the door, too.

Mike rolled out of bed. Didn't even bother with a shirt. As he stumbled down the hallway, I called out after him to leave it alone, but of course he didn't listen, flipping on the hall lights and all three front door locks with his elbow.

The knockers were a pair of college kids from up the road. Brown, and sweaty, and stoned out of their minds.

When they saw Mike, they started giggling. One told him that they were cooking.

They needed some butter, and paprika, and the words came out between spurts of laughter, with the two guys leaning all over each other.

But Mike gave them two sticks and a vial of spice anyway. He told the boys to get home safe.

Rolling over me on his way back to bed, he palmed my stomach, whispered the words into my ear.

The seventh time came at a party. Mike had rescued me from a conversation with a half-drunk mother. I'd been drinking, but I was lucid, and it slipped out of his mouth the way words sometimes do. And this was the first time I said it back.

5.

In the kitchen, with my family in the living room, Mike tells me that he wants to meet Omar. I don't respond, juggling a trio of eggs, pacing around the stove. Mike has already assembled some kind of rice casserole with chicken, tofu, and carrots, simmering three slabs of cod with white onions splayed across them, prepping dashi in the pot beside them. As many times as I've seen him cook, I've never really just *watched* him, but his rhythms mirror his mother's, right down to the shuffling of his feet.

I'm peeling potatoes beside him, and then I'm boiling them, sautéing onions and pork in a pan on the other end. Mike glances my way, once, and then once again. When I start folding the potatoes into the sauté, he asks what I'm making, and I tell him: potato korokke.

He blinks, once.

Korokke? he asks.

Yeah, I say.

Really? Potato croquettes?

That's what I said, I say, stirring.

Then Mike opens his mouth a third time, but nothing comes out. He turns right back around.

At first, Mike watches me move around the kitchen, grabbing and shifting and slicing. Eventually, he joins me, taking care with his body, negotiating it around mine. We've never cooked together, but we move through the room like we've been doing it for years. There are moments when I know he could say something about how I've cut one thing, or stirred another, but he doesn't. Mike just watches, doing his own thing, complementing mine.

He asks about Omar a second time, and then a third, before I tell him that it's inappropriate, it'll never fucking happen, and that's when the first egg falls on the floor, followed by another pair behind it.

And now, maybe an hour later, our families sit down to eat. We chew at the casserole, sip the soup. Mike and Lydia and I laze on the floor, and my parents sit beside Mitsuko on the sofa, juggling their chopsticks and spoons. I eye Mike's mother nibbling a croquette, and when she looks my way, she winks.

Overall, the meal is simple and filling, but I still didn't think it would take. I'd never even seen my father so much as sip from a bowl of tomato soup, let alone anything entirely unfamiliar.

But now he chews silently.

The six of us chew silently.

The only ones who speak are Mike and Lydia. They ask each other questions, laughing at shitty jokes. Mike doesn't bring up his absence, or his father, but he'll address something to *my* father, and Lydia will answer, and Lydia will direct something to Mitsuko, and her son'll answer in her stead, and, at one point, Mike asks how my mother's family is doing — her other family — and before I can kick him in the balls, she says that everyone's fine.

Healthy and happy, says my mother.

Great, says Mike.

Comfortable.

I'm glad.

Tyler and Teju are growing out of everything.

Kids do that, says Mike. Ben talks about that all the time.

They'll stop soon, I say. Everyone grows up eventually.

You never did, says Mitsuko, to Mike.

Except that's the thing, says my mother. You don't want it to stop.

You know it will, she says. Eventually. No matter what. So you try to prolong it. Every parent's their own magician. And we just try to stall that distance for as long as we can. And the trick is to do it without messing up your kid.

As my mother says this, her voice is bright. But her face is not.

I glance at Lydia, and then at my father. My sister keeps her eyes on our mother. My father just tugs at the hair on his forearm.

It's futile, says Mitsuko, sighing. That's just the way it goes.

But we still have to try, says my mother.

I can't imagine doing it again, says Mitsuko.

I couldn't either, says my mother, laughing. And I really don't know how I ever did it at all.

I'm sure you're doing the best you can.

Everyone's doing the best they can, says my mother. It's what we have to tell ourselves.

Well, says Mitsuko, pointing at me, you did all right with this one.

He took care of me, she says.

I made it hard for Benson, Mitsuko says,

but he didn't complain.

My father looks up. My mother makes a face I haven't seen in a very long time. For once, everyone in the room is looking at *me*.

Except for Mike.

He's got that look of consideration again.

Or at least he didn't complain too much, says Mitsuko. Only a reasonable amount.

It's the least Benson could do, says my mother. Trust me.

I wish he could say the same for me, says my father.

But what are the odds, he says. Two good boys finding each other.

My father nods at Mike, and, for the first time, my partner, who I've never seen flustered, looks a full crimson sheen.

Who would've thought, says my father.

Wait, says Lydia, I'm the one who fucking told you about him.

And everyone groans.

The sky gels into a hazy amber. I walk my family to their cars.

My mother squeezes my hand before she slips into her van.

My father says, I'll see you whenever, slamming Lydia's car door.

Beside me, Lydia lingers over our patio.

She says, We should make this a regular thing.

I smile.

I say, I hope you enjoyed this, because it'll never happen again.

And Lydia starts to laugh, until she sees my face, and that laugh disappears. But her teeth resurface, slowly, with a grin. She puts her palm on my cheek.

Lydia says, Little brother, you really never learn.

And now: Mike and I stand in the kitchen. He's washing dishes, and I'm kicking at the counter. Mitsuko's in the living room, flipping through channels. Eventually, her snores settle over the television's drone.

Just ask him, says Mike. Don't be scared.

Scared has nothing to do with it, I say. It's fucking awkward.

Nah, says Mike.

Is this something you really want to argue about?

No, says Mike. So ask him. Come on.

I tell Mike that I'll do no such thing, and he just grunts.

Sorry, I say.

Stop being so fucking sorry, says Mike, scrubbing intently, racking the plates.

■ ■ ■ ■

Twenty minutes later, I text Omar. On a whim. That morning, he'd reached out and I'd left his message unread.

Honestly, we weren't anything yet. Nothing had been decided. But we'd fucked, again, at his place, and then another time after that, and afterward, once we both came a second time, I'd asked Omar what he wanted, and Omar told me he wasn't sure.

My fingers drummed on the flat of his back. We were in Omar's bed. I couldn't see his face, just his hands as he played with a pillow.

You tell me, he said.

I asked you.

I know, said Omar. But I also know you've got certain, uh, restrictions that I don't have.

That's one thing to call my boyfriend, I said.

Sorry, said Omar, and I squeezed a chunk of his ass.

Don't be, I said. I'm the one that's here. I'm the one complicating things.

Well, said Omar. You said it. Not me.

Hey!

You said it!

400

But look, said Omar.

He shifted on the mattress, looking me in the face. We were both naked, both soft against the sheets.

This can be as serious as you want it to be, he said. Or not. I'm not saying we'll adopt a puppy or anything.

I know, I said.

Good, said Omar. It's low pressure. This'll go however you want this to go.

But I like you, said Omar. And I think I could keep liking you. So I guess I just want you to know that.

And things had been low pressure since then.

I stare at my phone, despite myself, willing a text to emerge.

When Mike steps into the bedroom, he says, Young love, and I tell him to fuck off.

Shouldn't you be packing? I say.

Don't look so excited to see me go, he says, grinning, but not really.

Mike sits on the floor, rearranging his clothes. It's been months since we sat in the same room without speaking. And I know I should follow that up with an apology, some declaration of affection and appreciation.

But I don't.

I don't know why.

So the moment passes.

And a few hours later, Omar replies. The text is littered with emojis.

It says: Should be fun!!!!☺☺☺☺

6.

The eighth *I love you* came after a fight, our last big one before Mike left.

I'd thrown a candle at the wall. Mike picked it up and threw it right back at me. He shoved my shoulder, and then I grabbed his arm, which brought us to the floor, where he latched on to me as I slapped at his face. Eventually, I stopped squirming, and Mike stopped squeezing, and I tugged at his shirt, and he pulled at my shorts. He slid down my body, grabbing at my hair, and afterward, we stayed on the wood, sweaty and stinking, not talking, falling asleep.

I woke up to Mike sweeping at the candle's cracked remains. He was bare except for boxers, hunched over the broom. I watched him sweep in silence, with the moon against his back, and I knew, right then, I think, clear as day, that eventually our moment would end.

I also realized I didn't want it to.

And it was okay for me not to want it to.

And maybe okay for it not to end right now.

But it had to.

Probably.

And that's when Mike stepped on broken glass. He yelped, hopping around.

Stop, I said, you're only gonna make it worse.

You can't be fucking serious, said Mike.

So I told him to sit. We kept some gauze in the bathroom. I wiped the area around his instep with alcohol and grabbed a knife from the kitchen. It was the sharpest one I saw, and Mike's eyes glowed when I fondled it, so I told him to relax, and Mike said he wouldn't blame me if I cut him.

I'd blame myself, I said.

When my palms shook, I took breaks. I moved the blade slowly, incrementally. It took ten minutes, but the shards came out.

Afterward, I wiped down Mike's foot with antiseptic, wrapping it with the gauze, and when I looked up, my partner had literally, totally, fallen asleep.

I don't know if he heard me say it, but his body tensed, loosened, settled.

7.

Two mornings before Mitsuko leaves America, I find her washing rice in the kitchen. She nods my way, sifting her hands through the pot, and I sit down on a stool across from her, and she's looking down at her hands again.

Mike's out making arrangements with his coworkers. He hasn't told me what he's going to tell them, but I know it's not going to go well.

When Mitsuko's finished washing the grains, she sets her pot on the stove. She crosses her arms, keeping her eyes on the ceiling.

So Mike's going home, I say, and Mitsuko looks my way.

You could also say he's leaving it, she says.

You'll be happy to have him closer though?

I'm always happy to see the child that I made.

For fifteen minutes, neither of us moves. I

watch Mitsuko transfer her rice from the pot to the eggs in the frying pan. She's crowded it around sweet potatoes, cheddar, a radish, and garlic, and Mitsuko folds the omelette until it encases everything. The omurice simmers gently, until we're staring at what looks like the beginnings of a meal.

She asks, Were you waiting for something else?

No, I say, I'm leaving.

But you haven't eaten, says Mitsuko, grabbing a bowl.

She sets one across the table for me.

I couldn't, I say.

You could, says Mitsuko. You don't have many of these left to look forward to.

I could always cook one myself.

If you say so, Benson.

I sit across from Mitsuko, and she settles across from me.

I'm sorry, I say.

About?

You know, I say, and that's when it starts — and the crying floods my cheeks. I don't know where the tears are falling from until they finally leave my face. I'm shaking, a little bit, and then a lot. The chair dances underneath me. Sounds leave my mouth, animal noises I don't recognize, and as I try to choke them down, they turn into something else. My hands sit on the table. Ten fingers form two fists. My thumb digs into the pit of my palm, rooting for blood, and then Mitsuko's hand is on top of mine, slowly pulling it out.

Benson, says Mitsuko. Look at me.

Look at me, she says, a second time, and I cover my face.

I know, says Mitsuko.

You don't, I say.

I do. You did nothing wrong. Nothing.

That's what Mike says his dad told him, I say, wiping my face.

I'm sure he did, says Mitsuko. That is a thing that my husband would have said.

At some point, the shaking stops. My breathing settles. I am looking at Mitsuko, again, and now she's watching me watch her.

She picks up her spoon, smearing ketchup over my omelette.

Eventually, I pick up my spoon.

We eat.

You should talk to my son, says Mitsuko, chewing.

We talked about it, I say.

He's always been a little funny, says Mitsuko. Since he was a boy. He'd tell me one thing, start in on it, and decide on another. Or he'd get tunnel vision.

Mitsuko stares into her bowl, stirring the eggs with her spoon. She scoops the ketchup again, gradually, piling it on one end of the plate, before she picks it back up, redistributing everything.

How old were you when you started tying your shoes, says Mitsuko.

What, I say, wiping my eyes.

You asked me to tell you a story. How old were you?

I don't know, I say. Shit. Six?

It took Michael eleven years, says Mitsuko. It took that long for my son to get it through his head. He just didn't believe he could do it. The laces fell right out of his hands. I would show him, and his father would show him, and he'd try to do it on his own, but then he'd just give up. Nearly four thousand days of life. He had to wear Velcro sneakers until middle school.

I watched Mitsuko play with her food. She kept not watching me.

So what happened, I say.

What always happens with my son, says Mitsuko, smiling a little. He figured it out. He made the decision to do it at one point, and then he did it. The same way my son figures that he needs to run this bar, or whatever it is, in Osaka. The same way he figured that he needed to see his father

408

through the end.

But you didn't even want him to leave, I say.

Correct, says Mitsuko. I didn't. That was not the decision I wanted my son to make.

But he needed to, she says. And he knew that he needed to. So, from time to time, Michael can see past the front of his nose. He's gotten better about that, apparently. And even if I never tell him this — and you will never tell him that I told you — I'm proud of him for it. Seeing him make decisions, big decisions, makes me proud. But I don't think that this is one of those times.

Mitsuko crosses her arms, leaning onto the table. Finally looks up at me.

Do you see what I'm getting at, she says.

I'm not sure, I say.

I'm saying that if you leave Michael to his own devices, he'll come around eventually. He will. But that might be too late for you. My son likes you.

I love him, too.

Exactly, says Mitsuko. So tell him that. Those exact words.

And then he'll change his mind? I say.

I don't know about that. It could look like a lot of things. But that's when he'll make the decision he wants to make, as opposed to the one that he thinks he should. Or the one that's actually the easiest path forward.

You'll be all right, says Mitsuko. It'll be all right. I promise.

If you say so.

I say so.

You came from good stock, says Mitsuko, and before she leaves the kitchen, she sets a palm on my neck.

When I spot Ximena at the daycare, I don't know what I'm expecting her first day back, but she's flipping through a magazine before we've opened for business.

Ximena winks my way once she sees me.

Noah left the place a fucking mess this morning, she says.

Happy wife, happy life, I say.

Shut up, says Ximena. He's a slob. Cups on the table and everything. He said he'd do better, but here he goes, fucking making problems.

It's the little things.

My ass. I'm no fucking maid.

So much for the honeymoon period, I say. Welcome back.

That's got nothing to do with anything, says Ximena. The wedding's been over.

But look, she says, and Ximena shows me her tan, and her skin is a pulsing bronze from her shoulders to her fingertips.

I'm literally fucking *glowing,* says Ximena.

That's the difference, she says. That's what matters.

You could've done that without him, I say.

No shit, Kierkegaard. You think I don't know that?

But here's the thing, says Ximena, winking, I wanted to put him on, too.

The kids are restless today. When I ask Marcos and Lorraine to cool it with the running, they just puff up their cheeks, sprinting even faster. When I ask Silvia to stop with the colored pencils, she snaps a pair in half. I ask Xu and Ethan, for the fifteenth time, to do me the biggest of favors and keep their hands off each other, and the brothers blink simultaneously before doing exactly that, opting for head-butts instead.

Shit, says Barry. It really is the end of the world.

Go figure, says Ximena.

The kids just shrug. They do their thing.

But honestly, truly, we can't blame them. It's not their fault. We did the same thing at their age — would do it again if we could.

At the end of the day, once Barry and Ximena start vacuuming and mopping and wiping, I sit with Ahmad by the door. He's the last kid to get picked up, and quiet, with his fingers in his lap. He spent his morning coloring in a sketchbook — the one he told me his parents bought him — and his afternoon shooting basketball on the court. First, with Barry. Then with Ethan and Xu. Then with Thomas, and Margaret, and Silvia, until Ahmad was the only one left.

Now, he's still coloring. The pastels blend into one another, forming tiny, lucid solar systems.

I ask if he's still on strike.

Strike's over, says Ahmad. You're late.

Well, I say, at least you finally got a haircut.

It looks good on me, says Ahmad.

One hundred percent, I say.

Daliah recommended it.

Daliah.

She's this girl at my school.

Well. Five points for Daliah.

She's the smartest person I know, says Ahmad. Mostly.

Mostly? I say.

Yeah, says Ahmad, biting his lip, really thinking about it.

He adds, Ximena's pretty smart, too.

Look, he says, and then Ahmad shows me what he's been drawing, folding the sketchbook across my knee.

There's a green planet on the page, strung together by a loose assortment of stars. Two men are drawn in the center of it. One of them is very obviously his brother. The other one desperately needs a haircut.

Can I ask what it is, I say.

You don't see it?

It's generally polite to ask.

The universe, says Ahmad, matter-of-factly.

And also, he says, waving at the two men. You know.

Omar finally comes to pick up his brother, and he's changed out of his scrubs, into a hoodie and shorts.

We still getting dinner? he says.

Ahmad lets his brother run his hand over his head. The two of them don't look anything alike, but they look like they fit with each other.

People said the same thing about me and my father, and my father and my sister.

The same is true for Mitsuko and Mike.

The same was true for Mike and me, too.

Yeah, I say, unless you've changed your mind.

Nah, says Omar, tapping my shoulder, I can take it.

■ ■ ■ ■

On our way out, I catch sight of Ximena and Barry watching us — they're grinding on each other, tongues out and laughing at me. I start to wave them off, but Ahmad catches my gaze, so I don't.

The kid doesn't say anything though. He just rolls his eyes.

Omar drives the three of us down Montrose, catapulting toward the Burger Shack's parking lot. A slurring Beyoncé booms over the speakers, until Ahmad snatches his brother's phone and switches the track to some sort of K-pop, something entirely too synth-heavy. He turns around to ask if I know it. I tell him that I don't.

The lyrics are easy, says Ahmad. You'll learn.

I start to say something, but Omar catches my eye in the rearview mirror — and I, again, keep my words to myself.

When we spot him, Mike's already sipping on a water bottle. He's got on shades and shorts. It's fucking hot, the beginning of the Southwest's hellish season, and the patio's fans strain toward the cluster of bodies beneath them. Omar tiptoes toward the table, and when he stutters a greeting, I touch the small of his back, which, somehow, inadvertently, turns into something like a caress. Ahmad doesn't even blink at us, thumbing the cash Omar handed him for our burgers.

Mike pats the bench beside him. When I start to sit, he waves me away.

This one's for our new friend, says Mike.

You don't even know each other, I say.

Hence this little meeting, says Mike. Come on.

Omar takes the bait. I slide beside Ahmad, who's returned with a tray holding four cuts of beef.

Facing these two men, they could be the A- and B-sides of my life.

What I say to Mike is, No beer?

No beer, he says, shaking his head.

So, says Omar, how'd your day go?

You know, says Mike. Making moves. Settling accounts.

Benson told me you're leaving town soon.

Go figure. Ben's doing his best to get rid of me.

I'm not, I say.

Okay, he's not, says Mike.

I ask Mike how work went, and he gives a quick nod. There's a shadow on his face. It passes just that quickly.

All's well that ends well, says Mike.

I start to say something, but then Ahmad tugs my sleeve. He shows me something on his phone. A note that he's typed out.

It says: r u ok

I give the kid a look. Take his phone.

I type: yes ☺

When I look up again, Omar and Mike are talking at each other.

I watch them do that.

I turn back to Ahmad.

So, I say, how are you?

Without even turning from his fries, Ahmad flashes his teeth at me.

Eventually, we settle into something like a comfortable silence. The white folks around us chat into the air, and an old Astros game drones across the screens behind us. If you really strain your ears, the traffic on Montrose dies down, but the surroundings all blend into one thing, a vacuum that swallows us whole.

Ahmad looks at his brother and asks how much longer they're going to stay. When Omar tells him not to be rude, the kid makes a face.

But we're not *doing* anything, says Ahmad.

416

Everything doesn't have to be an action movie, says Omar.

We're enjoying each other's company, says Mike, with his hands on his stomach. It's nice outside. I'm getting a little fatter.

You're not fat, I say.

You're beautiful, says Omar, and we all turn to him, and he looks completely earnest.

For the second time in two days, Mike looks genuinely baffled.

Omar says that about *everyone,* says Ahmad, tapping at his brother's phone.

Honestly, it was exhilarating to hear, says Mike.

He's just trying to get on your good side, I say.

No, says Omar, sternly, looking at me. It's true.

He leans back into the bench, crossing his arms.

I mean look at us, says Omar, spreading his arms. Isn't this amazing? How we ended up here?

And, a little delirious from the words, the three of us look up at the wooden awning above us.

I mean it, says Ahmad, he tells *everyone.*

Not one of us finishes our food. We're

stranded with stray ounces of burger. Ahmad packs his to go, along with Omar's leftover fries. Everyone stands, not really knowing where to put our hands, until Omar finally opens his arms, and Mike finally embraces him.

Then I hug Omar.

Then Mike hugs me.

In between, each of us squeezes Ahmad's hand, and he shakes his head at all of us.

To Omar, he says, Can we *please go*?

I tell Omar I'll see him soon, and he nods, grinning. Despite myself, a smile rips across my face. And I realize I'm still wearing it in the car when Mike points it out.

It's nothing, I say.

Nothing's nothing, says Mike. You look happy. I'm happy for you.

And he likes you, says Mike.

Shut up.

No. That matters. And you like him, yes?

I look at the road in front of us. We're only just entering March, but the concrete's starting to shimmer. One day, we'll look up, and it'll be summer again. None of us will see it coming.

I don't know yet, I say.

That's fair, says Mike.

But you *could* like him, he says.

Well, I say.

Yes, I say. Yes. I think I could.

Then that's the most you can ask for, says Mike, turning left, and I don't look at his face, and I don't want to think about what's probably there.

On our way inside the apartment, we're ambushed: a skateboard, from across the street, makes its way over to Mike, nearly colliding with his ankle. He isn't paying attention, isn't even on this planet, it seems like. But he catches it with his heel nonetheless, smirking at the kids who kicked it.

There's a slight delay, and then they appear all at once. They're our neighbors. They are sorry. They ask Mike if he's all right, and in the same breath implore us not to say anything to their dad.

He'll break the skateboard, says the oldest one, matter-of-factly.

Please please please please por favor por favor please please, says the youngest.

Mike purses his lips like he's considering it. Then he hops onto the board, gently, tenderly. He leans on one end, and then the other, before he pops a little wheelie. As the kids realize what's happening, they start smiling, and then laughing, and then they're

clapping and whooping alongside him, and
I am crying, and clapping, too.

8.

My father says, Isn't that what they say?
You lose them the way you get them?

I ask him who *they* are, and he asks me to
pass the syrup. We're eating at a diner just
outside the loop. There are cops at every
other table, and all of them ignore us. I've
left Mike and his mother to each other for
the rest of the afternoon. She flies out
tomorrow, and her son will follow a few
weeks later, and we still haven't figured out
what that looks like yet, but Mike's told me,
more than once, that his dad left some
money for that, too.

My father's therapist told him to try new
places, to put himself back in the world,
and my dad grumbles about that in between
bites of pancake, but I know it's the news
he's been waiting to hear. He's started
tutoring again, in a limited capacity. He'll
do a little more in the fall, once school starts
up again.

Now he sits in our booth, with his legs crossed and a mug of orange juice in his hand. A stack of student papers stands stilted beside him. They're riddled with green ink and a scattering of blue.

I ask my father about Lydia, and he grunts.

Your sister thinks I'm a drag.

She just likes to do her own thing.

Everyone likes to do their own thing, says my father. Doesn't mean you can't share your time.

She moved in with you, Dad, I say, and from the way he sips his juice I know he appreciates it, and he wants me to know that he appreciates it.

He and my mother have pledged to meet for coffee every once in a while. When I tell him that Once in a While is pretty vague, my father says my mother told him that was the point.

She's convinced it puts the pressure on me to plan something, he says.

It does.

You're your mother's child.

I am, I say. But I'm yours, too.

The pancakes aren't bad. We ask our waitress, an older Black lady, for another jug of syrup. My father's convinced that he'll take his therapist up on trying every last diner surrounding 610.

He's a nice guy, says my father. Young. Mexican, I think. The flag's on his desk. I was worried he'd be full of shit at first, because, you know, they don't teach you about old niggas in any school I've ever heard of.

I actually don't know.

Yeah, you do.

You're being a bigot.

You're the most optimistic pessimist I know.

I worry about your students, I say.

They'll be fine, says my father. You turned out fine.

But my doctor, says my father, he might be, you know. Like you.

Like me.

You know.

Say it.

Gay, says my dad.

I blink at my father. He only shrugs.

When he stands from our booth, slapping a twenty on the table, what he's saying clicks between my ears like a car alarm.

I don't need you setting me up with anyone, I say.

You never know, says my father.

Don't.

I told him you'd be perfect for him.

423

I'm good at the moment.

Sure. But sometimes the moment passes.

We step outside with our hands in our pockets. My father nods, dipping toward his truck without a word. The highway stands behind us, catapulting toward an assembly of bridges, and the air smells a little like oil, and a little like biscuits, and a little like Houston.

My father adjusts his mirror, clips his seat belt, and I watch as he pulls through the parking lot. Before he slips onto the feeder, he turns to me and waves.

On my way back to the apartment, I get a haircut. Nothing too wild. Just enough to make me feel like something about me has changed, concretely. I just cut off the usual shit.

And then I'm on my porch.

And then I'm in the doorway.

And Mike is hunched over his mother's suitcase, really leaning into it, working to get the zipper down.

I tell him he looks like a cartoon.

How about you shut the fuck up and help me, he says, grunting.

I ask where Mitsuko is, and Mike nods toward our bedroom.

424

The door's locked, and the sink's running in the bathroom, but muffled sobbing overlays it. I look at Mike, but he's focused on the suitcase. Sweating, willing himself away from his mother's tears.

So I get down on my knees. I lean next to him, pushing at the bag. It really won't budge, and I'm just about to quit when I feel Mike shift, hunching over me, wrapping his arms around my belly. I keep my palms on the suitcase — because it'll burst if I don't — and Mike doesn't say anything about that. All he gives me is a squeeze.

There's still something there. It's not hot enough to scald. But it could be, if I wanted it to, and I am surprised that I have to wonder.

In my ear, he says, You could still change your mind.

I kneel there for a moment.

And then I say, I could.

Okay, says Mike. That's all. As long as you know. And as long as I know that you know.

I do, I say.

And at that, the bathroom door unlocks, and Mike folds across my body to seal the rest of the bag, and it shuts.

Mitsuko's face is flushed. Her hair is all over the place. She's wearing a sweat suit, wiping at her cheeks, and I can't help but think that, even in despair, she looks entirely too beautiful.

She says that if we're done fucking around, she's ready to go.

I ask Mike what she means, but all he does is shrug. He says they've got to run an errand. If I really insist, I can tag along.

It's possible to drive from one hub of Houston to another, only to end up feeling like you're in a whole different country. Bellaire to Sugar Land to Katy to midtown to downtown to River Oaks to Montrose to the Heights to East End to the Third Ward to the Warehouse District and back.

But, sometimes, you don't have to go very far at all, and that's where we drive, over a bridge and onto Wheeler. We take that until it turns into Elgin, which turns into Studemont, which bends into Memorial. Mike stops his car in front of the park, just over the bayou, and he and his mother emerge simultaneously, as if this whole thing's been rehearsed.

We walk along the path leading into the park. It's the middle of the workweek, so there aren't too many people out. A couple of homeless guys lie with their legs crossed in the grass. A young white couple suns beside them on a blanket, with a baby and a bottle of wine.

We stop in front of an overpass by the bayou. Mitsuko slips on some shades. Mike glances at me, and then he pulls something from his backpack: the urn. He looks at the top for a moment, and I flinch when he kisses it, because it's the kiss you give something you know you won't be seeing again, something you've been conflicted about for decades, your whole fucking life, and then Mike passes the urn to Mitsuko, and she doesn't even think about it, she takes the urn and she opens it and the ashes fly right out of there.

We watch them dissolve in the air. They move through the sky, all at once. And bits of them sift, until they melt away so small that the eye can't see, caught in the bridge's wooden slats or in the river or into nothingness altogether, until we're the only ones who'll take the fact of their ever existing at all on with us, until we end up losing those memories, too, although even then they'll still probably be around somewhere. It isn't very beautiful.

Mitsuko takes off her shades. I turn to Mike, and he shuts his eyes. His mother grasps the bridge's railing, standing on her toes, and then she says, with her entire body, *FUCK*.

Mitsuko tells us she isn't cooking on her last night in the country, so we drive to a profoundly nondescript Tex-Mex restaurant around the block.

The atmosphere is entirely too festive for our mood. Salsa plays over the din of white folks cashing in on happy hour. A young guy in a tuxedo shepherds us toward our table, giving us a once-over, and then a twice-over. After that, he hands us off to a waitress who can't be older than fifteen.

But she doesn't miss a beat. She notes everyone's orders, and all of Mike's addendums, and asks questions, and makes suggestions, and after repeating it all back to us she disappears.

Mike ends up with a water to start. I finagle a beer. Mitsuko sits across from a margarita the size of her head, and none of us says anything while dining party after dining party screams around us.

In the booth across from ours, I catch a kid peeking over his mother's shoulder. When I try squinting him away, the little boy doesn't even blink.

After two long pulls, Mitsuko reduces her margarita by half.

So, she says, what are our plans?

Your flight's at six, says Mike. We'll have you there by five.

No, says Mitsuko, waving him away, and turning to me.

What do you plan to do about each other? she says.

Benson, says Mitsuko, has my son told you what he wants?

I turn to Mike. He's looking at his mother, with yet another face I can't read.

We aren't talking about this right now, he says.

Of course we are, says Mitsuko. Benson?

Mike's leaving, I say. To Osaka. And I'm gonna stay here.

And that's it? says Mitsuko.

I think so, I say.

Mm, says Mitsuko, and she downs the rest of her margarita.

When our waitress flies by the table for refills, Mitsuko asks her for another round.

Ma, says Mike.

Beloved, says Mitsuko.

Look, she says, once the drink is across from her. Did I ever tell you about my first date with Eiju?

I was living in Osaka for a bit, says Mitsuko. He suggested a bar. Which is entirely original. No one's ever done that before.

And in my head, I'm not thinking, I'm better than this. I'm not thinking that he's just out here for a good time. I'm not even thinking about what he's really after, because I had a boyfriend at the time, a good one. Stable. He was Eiju's cousin, actually. And I didn't know shit then, but Eiju told me where to meet him, and I told him that was okay. And when I made it to our spot a little early, I scoped out the place. It seemed perfectly normal. I got my little drink and I waited.

Three hours passed before I left. One hundred and eighty minutes. He never came. Never showed. I was mad and I was relieved because this was exactly the sort of thing I should've expected to happen, but it eliminated any choice I would've had to make. I saw my boyfriend the next afternoon, and I didn't even tell him about it, and I thought to myself that this was just an act of God. This was Him course-correcting my life.

Our waitress returns with another guy in tow. They set three platters of fried fish and stewed pinto beans and yellow rice on the table. The new guy ladles tortillas into a bowl, and he lingers a moment to stare at Mike, but Mitsuko's son doesn't even look up, he's just watching his mother.

Mitsuko picks up a fork, slicing at her food, not really eating any of it.

I don't see Eiju again until the next week, she says. He knocks on my door until I open it. And when I do, he's all beat up. He's got bandages on his knuckles. Bruises all over his face. He's so tarnished that I have to ask what happened, and do you know what he tells me? None of your business. And just like that, I'm only *someone* to him. Or no one. Just this girl who's dating his cousin. I shut the door in his face.

He and I don't speak again for months, even though he's always at my boyfriend's house, smoking on the sofa. But a few weeks later, one of my boyfriend's friends told me it was my boyfriend who'd beaten Eiju. Either the morning of our date, or the evening before. He'd gone to his apartment and sat on the sofa and then beat the life out of his cousin. I didn't believe that at first, and when I asked my boyfriend, he denied it. But he was lying, and I could tell. The truth came out. He told me he was too ashamed to tell me. He was afraid of losing me, he loved me so much, and I told him that whatever we'd had was over.

I stopped going to my boyfriend's apartment, so Eiju had to come back to me. And eventually he did. In the middle of the

431

night. Fully dressed in a suit and a jacket, looking like a clown. I asked if he'd been drinking, and of course he had, but he said he wanted to take me out. By then, I knew better, but I figured it was the least I could do. I told him we weren't going anywhere too far. So I changed into some slippers, and I threw on a jacket, and we ate at the curry place across the road.

The whole meal, all Eiju talked about was how good the curry was. But I'd grown up with it. I'd been eating there for years whenever I was in Osaka. He ordered one bowl, and then another, and I asked him why he hadn't told me it was my boyfriend who'd done it. And, Michael, your father looked at me with food in his mouth, and he said, For one thing, you wouldn't have believed me. You would've thought I was bullshitting. But the thing about guys like that is they eventually show their asses, and you liked him too much. It would've fucked you up if I'd said anything, if you hadn't found out on your own.

Mitsuko stops cutting at her food. She looks at the space between us in the booth.

I told Eiju that it hurt more to find out that way, and he said it wasn't the same thing. Not even a little bit. He said there are some things that it's better for us to find

432

out on our own. He didn't want to be the one to tell me that. It wasn't how he wanted me to think of him.

And that was it, says Mitsuko. Eiju walked me back home. He didn't even pay for my meal. Barely had enough money to pay for his own.

By now, Mitsuko's finished slicing up her meal. She's also tanked her third margarita, fondling the lime beside it. Behind us, a quartet of teens has assembled in mariachi gear, settling into their stances to start in on a birthday tune. The woman they're serenading beams beneath a hijab. Her friends sit alongside her, clapping as the teens strum along.

So, says Mike, what was the point of all that?

Point, says Mitsuko.

The point of your story, says Mike.

What are you talking about, says Mitsuko.

The point is that this is how you came to be, she says. One thing happened, and then another thing happened. We didn't think about whether it would work or not. We just did it.

You're not making any sense.

You just don't want it to.

No, says Mike, laying down his silverware.

433

Dad told me, says Mike. A few days before he died, he told me about how he waited for you. I didn't even ask him. He just told me.

Dad flew to Japan, said Mike, and we were supposed to follow him. You made sure that we didn't.

I look at Mitsuko. I look at the saltshaker on the table. The noise in the booths surrounding us seems to decrease all at once.

Of course that's what Eiju told you, says Mitsuko.

Because it's true, says Mike, isn't it?

Dad told me how we were supposed to follow him to Japan, says Mike, wiping at his eyes. That's why he left. He went ahead, and we were supposed to follow. But we didn't, because you didn't want to. You didn't want to put us back together.

Mike's looking at his mother now, staring her straight in the eyes. Only, now, he's tearing up. When the tears start, they roll down his cheeks. I start to pass him the napkin in my lap, but he lets it fall, and Mitsuko's right there beside him, but honestly, she's already looking past him. She takes another sip of her margarita.

Look, says Mitsuko.

Let's say, hypothetically, that you're onto something, says Mitsuko.

434

If you were right, says Mitsuko, it would change a few things. It would mean that Eiju really isn't a monster like I've been telling you for the past sixteen years. Hypothetically, it would mean that I was at fault. That I broke up the family. For all his flaws, that would make me worse than him.

Mitsuko runs a finger over her earring. She taps at the side of her margarita glass.

But, she says, imagine what it would've taken to *make* that decision. To pull you away from your father. Think about how I would've thought that through. How it would've eaten me up. That would mean that I'd taken stock of the situation, and I'd decided that you growing up without him was better than growing up with whatever man your father could potentially become, whatever he had become when he left. That would mean that I believed in *us* — in you and me — more than I did in whoever your father might, just maybe, someday, become. And I would have to live with the consequences of knowing that I might be wrong. And that, if I was wrong, I could never take it back. If I was wrong, I would bring that decision to my deathbed.

Mitsuko turns to watch the teens play their song until they've finished, cheering entirely too loudly. They look our way. One of them raises a fist.

When our waitress reappears, she asks Mitsuko if she wants another margarita. She nods, and Mike shakes his head. He tells his mother that she's finished.

Bullshit, says Mitsuko.

Ma, says Mike, still crying.

Don't Ma me. I made you.

You haven't taken a bite of your food.

Benson. Tell him.

I don't really think it's my place, I say.

That's your problem, says Mitsuko, crossing her arms. Both of you. That's your issue right there.

I'll have one more, says Mitsuko, turning to our waitress. And I think that I'll take all of this food to go. I think I'll finish all of this later.

Mike takes the short way home, but there's still a little time to look up at the sky. Once we're in the neighborhood, he parks fast and unevenly, gets out of the car without looking at either of us, walks even faster toward the door, past the neighbors calling his name. I wait for Mitsuko, who steps out of the car, gingerly, before she ambles to the porch and plops down on our steps.

Mitsuko opens her to-go box, unpacking the fork and knife. As she starts to eat, she looks at me. I sit down beside her.

Fireflies buzz under the lone light above us. Everything is shrouded in gold. The Venezuelan mother next door is sitting on their porch, too, and she waves at Mitsuko, who raises her plate in return.

We sit there, sweating, saying nothing. Fanning herself with her free hand, Mitsuko squints into the neighborhood, kicking her shoes off.

And then, Mitsuko says, All I'm saying is, you two are fine.

Okay, I say.

You'll *be* fine, says Mitsuko. You'll figure this out. It's not a waste, is what I'm saying. There are no wastes. Either nothing is a waste, or everything is a waste. But you two could do worse than each other, than being in each other's lives. Do you understand?

I do.

So don't be upset.

I won't.

You have to promise, says Mitsuko.

I promise.

Good, says Mitsuko, lifting another forkful.

We sit outside, watching the traffic, until all we can see is each other, but we don't have to see everything around us to know that it's there. And, eventually, Mike opens the screen door to say that Mitsuko really should get to bed, before she tells him that of course she knows that, does he think she's never flown before?

9.

The first time is a memory that I've thinned down to the basics: We are, I think, walking through the neighborhood. I tell Mike that I love it, or that I could learn to love it here. He looks up entirely too quickly, but it's too late, I've already seen his grin. But right there, at the height of a potential catastrophe, Mike points to a house and tells me that he loves the way it leans. I point to a cat sunning under a streetlight and tell Mike I love how it's navigating the world. Mike points to the wildflowers growing next to the road. I point at the lamps above us. We both point behind us, below us, in the corners, through the windows of the houses we're passing, at everywhere but each other, although of course I've since realized that this was an acknowledgment, too.

10.

The next morning, I wake up and look at my phone, and there's a message from Omar: an assortment of hearts.

There's a message from Ximena: a selfie where she's smiling, on a plane, with the kid in her lap and Noah cradling her elbow.

There's a message from my mother: she's asking how I'm doing.

There's a message from Lydia: wondering when I'll be free for lunch.

And there's a message from Mike: a series of photos.

He must've taken them when I wasn't looking. The first one is of me and his mother. And then there's another one of just me. And then there's one of our front porch.

And then there's one of my butt, filtered and expanded. And then there's one of Mike, smiling into the camera.

But it's a real smile. And that's the one I

know I'll remember. Regardless of how this goes. That's the one that I save.

Mike's already up, lying next to me and staring at the ceiling.

When we're finished dressing, Mitsuko's sitting in the living room. She's wearing the same clothes we picked her up in, the very same jacket and the very same shades.

The drive to IAH is short. Mike's crabby at the traffic, even this early. Mitsuko glances at me once, and then once again in the rearview mirror, and it's early enough to count whatever ugly stars are still in the sky. The moon is an ugly purple, a shade I've only ever seen in this city, but one I'm pretty sure you won't find anywhere else, and I know that I'll look for it wherever I go.

When we stop at Departures, Mike and I help Mitsuko with her luggage. Her son opens his mouth once, and then he closes it. Then he tells her that he'll see her soon. Mitsuko asks if he means soon, or sooner, and before Mike can answer, his mother leans over to whisper something in his ear — and that's when Mike's face cracks, and he is bawling, again, with his mouth hanging open just a little bit.

Then Mitsuko leans over to whisper

something in mine.

But instead of words, what I get is a kiss.

So I watch Mitsuko take her luggage. She doesn't look back as she steps into the airport. She turns the corner for her ticket, and she swivels up the escalator, and she ascends slowly, gracefully, beatifically, until she's gone home.

ACKNOWLEDGMENTS

Arlena and Gary.
Alison and Patrick.
Adam and Rachel and Sanda and Isaac.
Thu.
Alex.
Joanna.
Rhonda.
Paul.
Allegra.
Nicole.
Kuniaki and Yuji.
Ryosei.
Hiroyuki and Shinji.
Aja.
Szilvia.
Na.
Lou.
The Riverhead crew.
Lavina.
Ashley and Min Jung and Raven.

Laura.
Danielle.

ABOUT THE AUTHOR

Bryan Washington is a National Book Award 5 Under 35 honoree, and the author of the collection *Lot.* He has written for *The New Yorker, The New York Times, The New York Times Magazine, BuzzFeed, Vulture, The Paris Review, Tin House, One Story, Bon Appétit, GQ, The Awl,* and *Catapult.* He lives in Houston.

The employees of Thorndike Press hope you have enjoyed this Large Print book. All our Thorndike, Wheeler, and Kennebec Large Print titles are designed for easy reading, and all our books are made to last. Other Thorndike Press Large Print books are available at your library, through selected bookstores, or directly from us.

For information about titles, please call:
(800) 223-1244

or visit our website at:
gale.com/thorndike

To share your comments, please write:
Publisher
Thorndike Press
10 Water St., Suite 310
Waterville, ME 04901